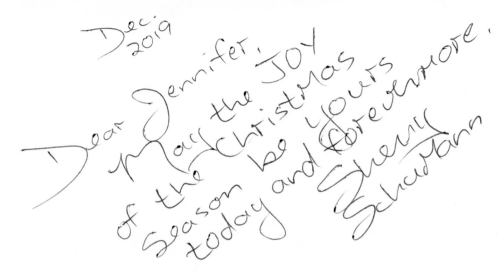

Dec. 2019

Dear Jennifer,

May the JOY of the Christmas season be yours today and forevermore.

Sherry Schumann

THE CHRISTMAS
Bracelet

Lots of love at Christmas!

Lynn

SHERRY SCHUMANN

WestBow
PRESS
A DIVISION OF THOMAS NELSON

WestBow Press books may be ordered through booksellers or by contacting:

WestBow Press
A Division of Thomas Nelson
1663 Liberty Drive
Bloomington, IN 47403
www.westbowpress.com
1-(866) 928-1240

ISBN: 978-1-4497-8425-6 (sc)
ISBN: 978-1-4497-8427-0 (hc)
ISBN: 978-1-4497-8426-3 (e)

Library of Congress Control Number: 2013902282

Printed in the United States of America

WestBow Press rev. date: 2/22/2013

DEDICATION

To the Glory of God:
Seven years ago, You planted a seed in the soil of my heart. Having
protected it during the winter months, You nurtured the seed with water
and sunshine in the spring. It took root and began to grow. This fruit,
which it now bears, is given to Your Glory.

To my beloved husband:
You are my traveling partner in this journey called life. Our lives are
intertwined and tied with the love of Christ.

ACKNOWLEDGEMENTS

This has been an incredible seven-year journey. Along the way, God sprinkled my path with love and encouragement.

To the staff at WestBow Press
God plopped you directly in my path. Your patience and professionalism have been unprecedented.

To Dorothy D., Fran J., Susan W., Elizabeth W., and my friends at Word Weavers
You've always encouraged me to tackle the next stretch, to round the next bend. Thank you, dear friends.

To Sarah C.
The most profound change in this novel occurred after your insightful and honest critique of the original draft. I am eternally grateful to you (and so is Kathryn).

To Marianne N.
You are my editing angel. Thank you for walking me through the maze of hyphens, comma splices, and run-on sentences.

To Martha H.
Bless you for sharing your story of healing with the women at our church.

, mother-in-law
pirit and loving heart inspire me daily.

A daughter is blessed when her mother is her best friend.

To Skip, Brandon, Jairus, and Lauren:
I treasured your cheers each time this manuscript reached a new milestone.

To my husband:
From Lowcountry oyster roasts to Christmas at Biltmore Village, you traveled every step of this journey with me. Thank you for insisting that I remain true to the characters and to myself.

To the Daughters of the King
God bless you.

CHAPTER ONE

John was life's smile but now he was gone...

THE FRENZIED SOUNDS OF THE Christmas season pressed down upon her making it difficult to breathe. At the front of the store, a toy freight train emitting clouds of black smoke clattered its way around an artificial tree. Its piercing whistle split the air. A shopping cart screeched for oil as it turned down another aisle. A young couple standing in line aired their financial woes. Above the din, a faceless voice boomed over the store's intercom system, enthusiastically reminding the customers that they had only one more shopping day left before Christmas.

Kathryn Sullivan exited through the automatic doors. Her gnarled fingers afflicted with arthritis offered the only clue that she was seventy-four years old. She carried her five-foot-nine stature with the elegance and dignity of a true Southern woman, one raised in a privileged world. Her lovely Charleston accent had only been slightly diluted by forty-seven years spent living with her husband, John, in the mountains of Western North Carolina.

A strong wind cut across the parking lot. Clutching the ten-pound bag of rock salt with one hand and a small bag of essential groceries with the other, Kathryn grimaced in pain. Another gust of wind whipped around her and forced her to put down the packages. She fumbled with the top button on her navy blue trench coat.

"Gracious, this button-hole is stiff," she said. The coat was relatively new, purchased last spring from an end-of-the-season sale. Frustrated,

1

she picked up both bags and continued the short but arduous hike toward her car. If only she had thought to bring a scarf.

Whipping in the wind, an inflatable twelve-foot Santa Claus caught Kathryn's eye as she unlocked the door of her green Buick. The thick vinyl Santa was dressed in red from his head to his feet, except for two enormous black boots anchored by cables to the store's roof. His outstretched arm held a sack that bulged with toys while his other arm waved to shoppers scurrying like ants across the parking lot.

She watched in amazement as a strong gust of wind pitched the inflatable Santa precariously close to the roof's edge. The anchoring cables quickly snapped him back into place, and the unflustered Santa resumed his holiday greetings. The same ridiculous smile remained plastered across his face.

"Times certainly have changed," Kathryn thought as she tugged the heavy car door closed and buckled her seatbelt. She was not fond of the inflatable decorations which had become popular even among her upscale neighbors.

Yuletide festivities woven into the fabric of American culture, especially those customs rooted in Victorian Britain and steeped in tradition, enchanted Kathryn as a girl growing up along the Carolina coast. The rich textures and aromas of Christmas--cornucopia of orange kumquat and gilded pears; boughs of dark green holly interwoven between banisters on the staircase; and steaming cups of wassail, heavy with cinnamon and clove--exhilarated her.

An Episcopalian by birth, she insisted upon attending the candlelight service at the Cathedral of All Souls on Christmas Eve. All Souls offered a unique blend of elegance, tradition, and warmth. The notes of "Joy to the World" on the chancel organ with three-thousand pipes resonating in perfect harmony made her heart soar as she looked with pride upon her handsome family. Unfortunately, life grew complicated after the early years of her marriage, and attending church on Christmas Eve became a lost tradition for everyone in her family except John.

Her last stop of the day was to buy birdseed from Sandra's feed store.

Mixed right there in the warehouse, the birdseed had a high percentage of hulled sunflower seeds to attract woodpeckers plus safflower to discourage grackles. As a special favor to Kathryn, the men in the warehouse usually added extra thistle seed to draw in goldfinches. She also wanted to pick up a fruit and suet ball for the migratory Yellow-bellied Sapsuckers. They were always ravenous after their long journey south.

Her heart sank as she pulled into the gravel parking lot. Here it was the twenty-third of December, and the feed store looked closed for the holidays. Knowing that she had a five-pound bag of birdseed on one of the shelves in the garage, a bag thrown into the grocery cart months ago as a spur-of-the-minute decision, she reluctantly put the car in reverse.

"Generic birdseed is better than no birdseed at all," she sighed.

As she shifted out of reverse, she noticed the store's owner dressed in denim coveralls and white hip boots frantically waving to her from the porch step.

Kathryn rolled down the window. "Are you open for business, Sandra?"

"For my best customer, of course."

She gathered her purse and stepped from the car. "I'm sorry that I'm such a nuisance."

"We closed early today for the holidays." Sandra tucked a pencil behind her ear. "You're not a nuisance. I was just finishing some year-end paperwork."

Kathryn held onto the wooden rail and cautiously climbed the rickety steps leading up to the front porch. According to local folklore, construction of the building occurred before the turn of the 20th century. The front third served customers while the back two-thirds functioned as the warehouse. An old-fashioned sled with a huge red satin bow stood on end, leaning against the porch.

"The sled adds a nice touch," she said.

"That ole thing? I literally stumbled across it yesterday in the shed, so I dragged it out here on the porch. If the weatherman is right, I might need it by morning."

The two women hugged like old friends and hurried inside to escape the wind.

Sandra walked to the other side of the counter, pulled the pencil from behind her ear, and picked up a memo pad, the kind with carbon used by waitresses at a local hamburger joint. She peered over her reading glasses as if to say, "What do you want?"

Kathryn set down her purse. "May I have two ten-pound bags of seed, plus a fruit and suet ball?"

"Extra thistle seed?"

"Of course."

"Just one fruit and suet ball?"

"No, make that two."

As Sandra measured out the seed, Kathryn wandered around the store. She picked up a metal trowel with a lime-green handle and turned it over in her hands before hanging it back on a rack. She smiled at the doggie bandanas touting North Carolina's major college competitors. Her husband had been a devout Tar Heels fan. He particularly loved UNC basketball. Lost in her memories of John, she nearly stumbled over a galvanized pail that had fallen off a lower shelf.

Her joints ached as she stooped down to retrieve the pail. Having watched her maternal grandmother suffer with crippling arthritis the last twenty years of her life, Kathryn was determined that she would not to submit to this terrible affliction. She intentionally pushed herself to stay active by gardening and walking. After returning the pail to its rightful place on the lower shelf, she stood up and stretched her back. It wasn't surprising that her arthritis seemed particularly annoying in today's cold, wet weather.

Sandra hoisted two ten-pound bags of birdseed on top of the counter. "Do you have big plans for the holiday?"

"It will be quiet. Just the birds and I."

"Is this your first or second Christmas without your husband?"

"Christmas marks the first anniversary of his death." The heartache that had become Kathryn's constant companion since John died felt like indigestion.

"Are you okay?"

"Me? Oh, I'm fine," she lied. "My arthritis just has me a bit down."

She was hesitant to share that while she had received holiday invitations from all three children, she graciously declined their offers. Her children were grown, scattered hither and yon, with families of their own. She simply did not have the fortitude to travel cross-country this holiday nor did she want to choose between their homes. To be perfectly honest, without her beloved husband, the festivities of Christmas held little or no meaning.

She thanked Sandra profusely for throwing in a fruit and suet ball free of charge and for making two trips to load the bags into the trunk of the Buick. After a quick hug, Kathryn was on her way.

Her fingers ached as she gripped the steering wheel in the holiday traffic. Despite the pain, she was glad that she had braved the wind and the Christmas rush. With the weather report promising six inches of wet snow for Asheville by morning, her dear cardinals and wrens, even those irritating Blue Jays, were sure to have trouble finding food.

A wave of melancholy swept over her as she pulled into the winding driveway leading up to her magnificent Tudor home. The house looked dismal and dreary this Christmas, almost barren, except for one evergreen wreath haphazardly hung on the front door in the hope that her neighbors would not consider her a total Scrooge.

"My life," said Kathryn to herself as she closed the garage door, "has become as empty as that inflatable Santa whipping around today at the mercy of the wind."

CHAPTER TWO

BEFORE THE GRANDFATHER CLOCK CHIMED eight, Kathryn slid out of bed and wrapped her body and soul in the comfort and security of her old terrycloth bathrobe. The pale pink robe was a treasured gift from her mother. Once plush and luxurious, it was now almost threadbare, worn completely thin with age. Her initials, embroidered in white thread more than forty years ago, were barely visible.

She groaned as she stretched upward, reaching for the drapes which concealed the glass sliding doors that led to the back deck. Kathryn was very conservative in her dress; however, when it came to interior decorating, she had a flair for the dramatic. The drapes, custom made from an exquisite black-and-white floral pattern of silk brocade, spanned the side wall. Eight feet in length, each panel provided a protective barrier to the sun.

She discovered the beauty of autumn's splendor after being swept away as a young bride to the mountains of Western North Carolina. In a single burst of brilliance before their long winter's nap, the maple trees and laurel oaks outside the sliding doors painted the landscape in vibrant shades of crimson and gold. For the past two months, she tried to push beyond her grief by taking pleasure in the colored leaves. There was no doubt that it had been a season, for the record, breathtaking and bold, more vibrant in color than she had ever seen. She secretly wondered if nature intentionally displayed its finest textures and colors in the hope of cheering her. Unfortunately, autumn was now gone, and winter's darkness loomed ahead.

With a panel in each hand, Kathryn drew the draperies apart. A dazzling world, beautifully adorned in a blanket of white, awaited her.

It was the second day of winter and all remnants of color were gone, buried beneath inches and inches of snow. The snowdrifts, Kathryn had to admit, held a certain magical, almost theatrical, quality. The sagging aluminum shed, which held their garden tools and John's riding lawn mower, was no longer an eye sore. Sometime during the night, it faded into a background of white. She made a mental note to hire someone to cart the shed away at the first sign of spring.

The grief that greeted her each morning suddenly seemed more oppressive than usual. Maybe it was the snow, or maybe it was her husband's shed. She had armed herself with as much knowledge about grief as possible before John died. She had accepted that it was a necessary journey with definite stages, and she had anticipated that this holiday would be a difficult one. No book, however, could have prepared her for the physical pain of feeling one's heart shatter into a million pieces. John was her life, and now he was gone.

She sighed deeply and drew the robe tightly around her waist. Somehow she needed to chase the pain away before it consumed her. "Let's start the coffee." Her words, spoken to no one, sounded unnaturally loud.

While the coffee brewed, she slipped her trench coat over her robe, tugged her snow boots over her slippers, and pushed through the door leading from the mud-room to the garage. She was determined that the snow would not deter her from her morning routine. It was a ritual, which they had shared for forty-seven years of marriage, a habit that included the morning newspaper and two cups of piping-hot coffee, rich with half and half. Kathryn always grabbed the front page; John claimed the comics and sports section.

Their home was built away from the road on the edge of a steep hillside. She usually enjoyed her walk down the driveway to fetch the newspaper from the mailbox; however, the snow that accumulated during the night, coupled with the driveway's sharp incline, would make this morning's walk a strenuous hike. She drew in a breath before beginning the slippery journey downward. Her coffee might be scalded before she returned.

CHAPTER THREE

"Mrs. Sullivan, look at my snowman."

Kathryn looked up to see two pigtails flapping from under the hood of a bright pink snowsuit as her seven-year-old neighbor, Abigail Hansen, scampered up the hill toward her. Sniffing, the young girl wiped her nose on the back of a knitted mitten already matted by tiny ice pellets. She pointed across the yard toward four unassembled balls of snow lying on the ground. Blades of grass and mangled leaves stuck out from sides of the largest one.

Celebrating two vastly different seasons of life, Kathryn and Abigail were a contrast of sorts. One was knocking on the door of winter while the other had barely entered into spring. Shivering in her threadbare robe and trench coat, Kathryn towered over the young girl. Layered in multiple shirts and sweaters, stuffed and zipped inside a heavy snowsuit, Abigail sweated profusely.

A disparity existed in their conversation as well. Naturally reserved, Kathryn used words economically, almost sparingly. On the other hand, Abigail chattered incessantly. Hers was a steady stream of consciousness, randomly skipping from one subject to the next, like a dragonfly darting to and fro across a pond, lighting upon a single lily pad, lingering but a moment before moving on again. Despite their differences, the two shared a special relationship.

Abigail's parents, Brian and Sarah Hansen, moved next door six years ago when Abigail was still in diapers. Kathryn remembered the day that they moved in like it was yesterday. It was a cold and dreary day in mid-April. The movers argued among themselves as they wrestled an antique dining room table to the top of the steep driveway. A flimsy piece of plastic, covering the table, flapped in the wind.

Huddled under a golf umbrella as they walked across the yard, trying to protect an apple pie from being pelted by the hard rain, Kathryn and John exchanged knowing glances. The neighbors' move was not going well. One look inside the moving van, which was still filled with furniture, suggested that this move was not going at all.

The front door was awkwardly propped open by a broom handle. Inside, a man was crawling on the floor, frantically sweeping his hand back and forth across the living-room carpet. The man's wife bounced a sobbing toddler on her hip. Neither John nor Kathryn could tell who was more exhausted--their new neighbors, the infant, or the hired moving company.

John stuck his head through the open doorway. "Hello. We're the Sullivan's, John and Kathryn, from next door."

Surprised, the man picked himself up from the floor and began brushing off the front of his khakis. "Welcome. Please come in. We're the Hansen's. I'm Brian, and this is my wife Sarah. Our little screamer is Abigail. She doesn't do this all the time; I promise."

John shook out the umbrella and leaned it against the brick. He and Kathryn stepped into the foyer. "Is there anything that we can do to help?"

"Can you recommend a pediatrician?" The young mother looked exhausted. "I am afraid that Abigail has an ear infection. This is her second one in a month."

John's voice was reassuring. "I'm a pediatrician. May I take a look at her ear?"

"Are you sure that you don't mind?"

"I don't mind in the least. Let me get my medical bag," he said. "Is there anything else that you need?"

"By any chance, do you have four screws that would fit this crib?" Brian asked. "They've mysteriously disappeared in the last twenty-four hours."

"Let me check. I'm sure that I have something on my workbench that you can use."

After nearly forty years of marriage, Kathryn was still impressed by her husband's ability to put others at ease. He oozed a quiet but gentle confidence. It was a trait that he inherited from his father.

John grabbed the umbrella and made a mad dash down the front steps and across the driveway. The rain was coming down in torrents now.

Standing at the front door, she offered the young couple a reassuring smile. "I hope that you like apple pie. It's still warm from the oven."

"It's one of our favorites. Thank you," Brian said. "Why don't you ladies get acquainted?"

As Kathryn followed her new neighbor to the kitchen, the baby's wails escalated. It was obvious that the young mother was at her breaking point.

Kathryn set the apple pie on the kitchen counter. "You will have to forgive me. I am bad with names."

"I'm Sarah, and this is Abigail."

"Do you think that Abigail will let me rock her?"

Sarah ran her fingers through her hair. "The rocking chair may still be on the truck.

"I had the movers put it in baby's bedroom," Brian answered from the living room. "Go up the stairs, first door on the right."

Kathryn gathered the exhausted infant into her arms and wandered upstairs. It was fortuitous that the movers had haphazardly, or maybe not so carelessly, flung an afghan in the seat of the chair. She bundled Abigail in the blanket and began to rock back and forth, the motion perfectly timed to the repertoire of lullabies which she once sang to her own children. Within minutes, Abigail's cries turned into whimpers, and the whimpers turned into sighs. The sighs dissipated into the sweet sound of sleep, but not before special bonds of love were forged between the two.

Abigail transformed from an active toddler to an inquisitive and imaginative little girl. She clung to John and Kathryn like a leaf on a vine, embellishing their lives in ways that they could not have previously imagined. One Saturday morning when she was about five, Kathryn jokingly referred to the three of them as the "Three Musketeers," and the name stuck.

Abigail accepted John's illness better than any of the adults around her. She crafted homemade cards for him nearly every day. The fronts of the cards were decorated with crayon illustrations, scenes drawn from her memories of the three of them spending time together. Some pictures depicted them working in the garden, planting carrot seeds, or digging up potatoes. Others showed them looking at birds through the binoculars or making snow angels on the hillside. While the scenes on the front varied, the insides of the cards always read the same: "To Dr. John, I love you, From Abigail."

John's favorite card from her sat on his nightstand until Kathryn removed it, one month after his funeral. On the front of the card was a series of detailed pictures. The first scene showed them, armed with paper sacks, standing at the split-rail fence, collecting long cones from the loblolly pine. The second scene showed Kathryn lathering the cones with peanut butter. The third one was a delightful depiction of Abigail with a dab of peanut butter stuck to her nose, rolling the buttered pinecones in bird seed. The fourth and last illustration was accented with four yellow stars, because it was a special picture of John hanging their homemade bird feeder from a tree.

Abigail broke into Kathryn's memories. "Mama gave me this carrot for the snowman's nose."

The carrot, bumpy and overgrown, was definitely not made for human consumption. "It should make a fine nose."

"Mrs. Sullivan, you know what?"

"What?"

"I drew a picture of a snowman, but I threw it away."

"You didn't like your picture?"

"Nope."

"Why not?"

"Because my teacher made me draw three circles."

"Three circles for three snowballs. That sounds reasonable."

"Why?"

"I've never really thought about it," she answered. "I guess because there's the head, the chest, and the stomach."

"Well, my real snowman will have four snowballs. The last one is for his bottom."

Kathryn chuckled. The child's candor and vivid imagination never failed to amuse her.

"Santa is coming really late tonight. Don't tell my mama but I'm gonna stay awake. My friend, Jill, she sits right next to me at school, well um, she says that you can hear Rudolph's nose buzz when he's on the roof." Abigail wiped her nose on the back of her mitten. "I'm going to leave hot chocolate for Santa. Do you think he likes marshmallows?"

"I suspect."

"How many carrots should I leave the reindeer?"

A distinctive loud drumming, like the sound of a hammer, resonated from the woods and interrupted Abigail's chatter.

"What's that?"

"A pileated woodpecker."

"What's he doing?"

"He's stripping the bark in search of ants or beetles."

"Yuck. How's come?"

"He eats insects."

"Double yuck. Where is he?"

"Look at the dead maple tree, the one that was struck by lightning last summer." She guided Abigail's head toward a huge stump at the edge of the woods. "See the big bird with the bright-red crest? That's a pileated woodpecker."

"The bird with the zebra face?"

Nodding, Kathryn soaked in the scenic beauty. The black-and-white striped male with its bright-red crest blazing against the freshly fallen snow created the perfect scene for a Christmas card. Known to be shy and retiring, the woodpecker uncharacteristically delighted his audience with an encore of *kuk-kuk-kuk*s before entering into flight.

They watched as the woodpecker escaped from sight deep in the woods behind their two houses.

"Where's he going?" Abigail asked.

"He's looking for his mate."

"What's a mate?"

"A mate is his wife."

"Do woodpeckers get married?"

"In a manner of speaking," she replied. "The male and female pileated woodpeckers are very devoted to each other, just like your mama and daddy."

"And you and Dr. John, before God took him to heaven."

Kathryn winced. Why was grief always lurking in the shadows, just waiting to raise its ugly head?

The sound of a woodpecker drilling for bugs could be heard, in the distance.

"We need to make bird feeders," Abigail said. "Mama bought peanut butter."

Kathryn rubbed her brow; the thought of making feeders without John, the third Musketeer, was unbearable.

Abigail persisted. "When are we going to make the bird feeders?"

"Another day, dear. When I'm not so tired." Her words had barely been spoken before she felt convicted of speaking out of turn. It was a commitment that she never planned to keep.

She was thankful when Abigail diverted the conversation back to Santa Claus.

"Mrs. Sullivan, do you think Santa gets tired?"

"I'm sure he does."

"What if he gets too tired to come to my house?"

"I don't think you have to worry about that."

"How do you know?"

"Because I know Santa Claus."

The Hansen's front door opened, and Abigail's mother stepped onto the porch dragging their Boston terrier, Hezekiah, by the leash. In spite of the snow covering his hindquarters, Sarah was determined to coerce the obstinate terrier down the steps in order to tend to his business. She hollered across the yards. "Good morning, Kathryn. It is freezing. What brings you outside so early this morning?"

"Routine. I need the morning newspaper."

"My daughter can do that for you. Abigail, run down to the bottom of the driveway and pick up Mrs. Sullivan's paper for her."

"Yes, ma'am. Mrs. Sullivan, can you hold the snowman's nose for me?"

"It's the least I can do." Kathryn jammed the overgrown carrot in the side pocket of her trench coat.

As Abigail's fluorescent-pink snowsuit disappeared from view down the hill and around the curve, Sarah yelled again. "Does five o'clock still suit for dinner?"

"It's perfect."

"I hate to eat so early, but the church service begins at seven."

"Five o'clock is just fine."

"You know that you are welcome to attend church with us tonight."

"I know. I need to see how I feel."

"Do you still feel up to making benne seed cookies?"

"Of course."

All the neighbors adored Kathryn's benne seed wafers. The recipe, which belonged to her great-grandmother, was originally brought to Charleston by West African slaves in the 17th century.

The women continued to holler pleasantries back and forth across their yards while Abigail trudged up the driveway with the newspaper securely zipped inside the front of her snowsuit. Whoever said light travels faster than sound did not know Abigail's flair for the dramatic.

An exaggerated huffing and puffing could be heard long before her pink snowsuit appeared in sight.

"I need to get Hezekiah inside." She scooped the Boston terrier into her arms. "Abigail, give Mrs. Hansen the newspaper. You have fifteen minutes to finish your snowman. Then it's time to come in the house and help me in the kitchen."

"Yes, ma'am. Bye, Mrs. Sullivan." The child wrapped snow-covered arms around Kathryn's waist and gave a tight squeeze before bouncing off in the snow with her carrot in hand. Her pigtails bobbed up and down as she retraced her steps across the yard, leaping from one footprint to the next.

Reaching the split-rail fence which divided their yards, Abigail turned around and yelled. "Daddy says that I'll be a princess if I believe."

Kathryn simply smiled, recalling time eons ago when her own daughter had twirled down the hall in a pink taffeta dress-up and a silver tiara, enchanted with fairy tales and dreams of being a princess. Such dreams dissipated when the trunk of princess dresses was carted off to the Salvation Army in exchange for womanhood and a strong dose of reality.

Abigail wriggled her way between the rails of the fence. "Daddy says you can be a princess, too, Mrs. Sullivan."

"I once was a queen," Kathryn thought wryly as she walked toward the garage. "However, my kingdom crumbled the morning John died."

CHAPTER FOUR

K NOWING THAT THE SNOW PACKED between the treads of her soles would quickly melt in the warm mud-room, Kathryn placed both boots in a metal washtub before padding her way through the kitchen and down the front hallway. As she hung her coat up in the hall closet, the grandfather clock began to chime. She peered around the closet door and stared in disbelief at the grandfather clock's gold face. Nearly thirty minutes had passed since she had ventured outdoors for the morning newspaper.

Enticed back to the kitchen by the rich aroma of coffee, she grabbed a cup and saucer from the China cabinet, poured her first cup of morning pick-me-up, and plopped a whole bran bagel into the toaster. Waiting for the bagel to finish toasting, she sat at the kitchen table and folded half and half into her coffee. She scanned the newspaper for a human interest story that would bolster her sagging spirits.

The title to an article on the front page of the newspaper caught her attention: Eight-Year-Old Boy Battling Leukemia Receives a Nintendo from Anonymous Santa. There was the photograph of a frail boy, his body gaunt from multiple rounds of chemotherapy, his eyes encased in dark circles as if they had been silhouetted with a thick black marker. He reclined on a hospital bed surrounded by his family and a devoted nursing staff, proudly displaying a new Nintendo. Kathryn smiled as the camera's focus drew her eyes to the beam of joy spreading across the boy's face.

In years past, she saw similar smiles on the faces of children hospitalized during the Christmas holidays. John and the other pediatricians in his practice once organized fabulous celebrations for the patients, families, and staff confined to the children's ward on Christmas Day. The parties included surprise visits from Santa, mounds of beautifully wrapped gifts, and impressive amounts of food. Because of the parties, the children's ward never had a shortage of nurses on Christmas Day.

Kathryn remembered one shopping trip to the local dime store with particular fondness. The weather was unseasonably cold and rainy for mid-December. Their children were bundled in the back seat of the family station wagon, laughing hysterically as John mimicked Bing Crosby's rendition of "White Christmas."

Having received instructions to pick out a puzzle, the latest board game, or a book appropriate for a boy or girl, his or her own age, the children raced into the dime store. They deliberated for nearly an hour. She remembered her children's faces, bright with excitement, as they scurried toward the front of the store with their selections tucked securely under their arms. They fidgeted among themselves, trying to peak over the counter as the teller rang up the gifts on an old-fashioned register. Before exiting the dime store, they begged, "Daddy, could we please have peppermint sticks?"

John, who was always a tease, pretended to ponder the question. "Mama," he asked with a twinkle in his eye, "do you think that it would be okay with Santa if I bought our children some peppermint?"

Kathryn nodded, her eyes smiling at the man she loved.

Ruddy cheeks made rough by the winter cold...reflections of wonder in her children's eyes...John's laughter ringing throughout the dime store...the smell of peppermint candy filling the car. . . As memories of Christmas-past came rushing back to her, Kathryn's grin faded into sadness.

"Time has a way of changing things" she sighed. "Including traditions." The hospital was forced to adopt strict rules, making it virtually impossible to host the Christmas celebration. It was about the same time that their three children outgrew shopping trips to the dime store, peppermint sticks, and even John's imitation of Bing Crosby. No one, except maybe the nursing staff on the children's ward, was more disappointed with these changes than John.

She skimmed over the front page and then flipped through the rest of the newspaper until she found the classifieds. She needed to check this section to verify that the newspaper had run her advertisement for the family farm. Initially, she had decided not to sell the farm, which was located on the outskirts of Asheville. It was not just another piece of property with a house and a barn; it was a part of her children's legacy left to them by John's father. The farm offered her children life experiences that growing up in the city could not offer. Birthing a foal, catching fireflies in glass jars, and hauling watermelon to market were only a few of the snapshots from their childhood memories.

Unfortunately, she was forced to face the fact that her adult children were settled in different parts of the country, successful in their own careers, and the chances of their return to the mountains of North Carolina were slim to none. The brutal reality in this fickle economy was that the family farm had become monetarily, physically, and emotionally draining.

After finding the ad for the farm in the classified section, she gently laid the newspaper down and picked up a napkin to dab away the tears which pooled in her eyes. Her world was blanketed in snow, and she had no place to go until dinner with Abigail's family. Maybe she could afford herself the luxury of reminiscing about John and the children and a time when loneliness did not consume her soul. After all, it was Christmas Eve.

CHAPTER FIVE

ATHRYN'S THOUGHTS WERE INTERRUPTED BY a gentle rat-tat-tat at the front door. "Abigail," she exclaimed, "what brings you out in this cold again? Come in quickly before you freeze."

Abigail handed her a dinner plate covered in aluminum foil. "They're my mama's cinnamon rolls, the ones that she bakes every Christmas."

The scrumptious aroma of cinnamon and sugar permeating the hall caused Kathryn's stomach to rumble.

Abigail giggled. "What was that noise?"

"My stomach. Can you tell that I haven't had my breakfast?"

"You haven't had breakfast?"

"No. I was so busy reading the newspaper that I forgot to get my bagel out of the toaster."

Like a puppy at the heels of its master, Abigail followed Kathryn to the kitchen.

"Please tell your mother that I am beholden to her."

"Be... what?"

"Beholden."

"What's that mean?"

"I have an idea. I could use some help eating these cinnamon buns. Why don't you take off your jacket and mittens while I make us some hot cocoa? Then we can look up the word in the dictionary."

Thrilled for an invitation to stay, Abigail wiggled out of her jacket and mittens while Kathryn dialed the Hansen's phone number.

Sarah answered the phone. "Are you sure you want her to stay?"

"Quite sure. It will be good for me. I'm in a bit of a slump this morning."

After hanging up the phone, she moved the kitchen stool beside the gas range and patted the seat for the youngster to climb aboard. Then she grabbed the quart of half and half from the refrigerator and the sugar canister from the kitchen counter.

She began shuffling through the antique baking cabinet. Glancing over her shoulder, she explained, "I'm looking for my tin of powdered cocoa. It's somewhere here in the back."

"I thought that we were having hot chocolate," Abigail said.

"We are. I make it from scratch."

"What's scratch?"

"It means that I start with the basic ingredients like cocoa and sugar and milk."

"Mama buys Swiss Miss, the box with the little marshmallows. I don't like hot chocolate without marshmallows."

She pulled a silver tin from the back of the cabinet. "I'm afraid that I don't have any marshmallows."

"That's okay. I'll bet scratch hot chocolate doesn't need marshmallows."

Kathryn smiled. Enjoying life through a child's eyes offered a temporary respite from her pain.

Abigail fidgeted on the stool. "When can I help?"

"In just a moment. Let me get things started."

After bringing the half and half to a slow boil and folding in carefully measured amounts of chocolate and sugar, she demonstrated how to stir the cocoa without slopping it over the sides of the saucepan. "Now it's your turn to stir."

A look of delight spread across the child's face. Abigail carefully moved the spoon around the edges of the saucepan, just as Kathryn had demonstrated. Steam began to rise from the pan. Together, they ladled the hot cocoa into two sturdy mugs and topped it off with a pinch of cinnamon, a teaspoon of finely grated dark chocolate, and a dollop of whipped crème.

While the cocoa cooled, they ventured through the French doors of John's office in search of a dictionary. It was a daunting task. John's built-in bookcases stretched the full length of the room, ten feet from floor to ceiling, and were primarily filled with his journals dating all the way back to medical school. John was not one to throw away a single text.

"Here it is." Kathryn withdrew the New World College Dictionary from a bottom shelf. The dictionary belonged to her eldest son. Extremely intelligent and academically unchallenged, Jack spent more time in a college fraternity house than a college library; therefore, it came as no surprise to her that the dictionary, received as a high-school graduation gift from a distant aunt and uncle, was still new.

"Beholden... obliged, to feel grateful, owing thanks, indebted." Overcome with emotion, she struggled to read the words.

Despite their prominent position within the community of Asheville, both John and Kathryn maintained very private lives. They never disclosed their needs, not even after John was diagnosed with pancreatic cancer. Although it was in their natures to give generously, both were ill-at-ease receiving acts of kindness. Friends and acquaintances would have gladly helped if only given the opportunity.

Beholden, however, was the perfect word to describe her feelings toward Abigail's parents. Similar to their daughter's gentle raps on the door, Brian and Sarah's acts of kindness were subtle yet perfectly timed. The behind-the-scene things which they did without being asked, such as baking warm cinnamon buns on a cold winter day, made life bearable during John's illness and the year following his death.

Abigail looked from the office into the living room. "Excuse me, Mrs. Sullivan. Where is your Christmas tree?"

"I decided not to put up a tree this year."

"But you have to put up a tree. Where will Santa put your presents?"

Kathryn winced. How could she tell her young neighbor that without John, decorations and gifts and all that goes along with Christmas seemed like an empty production? Instead of admitting the truth, she surprised herself by suggesting, "Why don't you help me drag the Christmas boxes out of the closet in the guest bedroom?"

With the cinnamon buns and hot chocolate long forgotten, the two of them mounted the front staircase leading to the upstairs bedrooms. Kathryn opened the closet door to the guest bedroom and turned on the overhead light. Stacks and stacks of boxes marked in red marker with the word *Christmas* filled nearly every inch of usable space in the walk-in closet. Even more amazing was the fact that the contents of each box were catalogued by a large white packaging label neatly secured on the flap.

They worked up a healthy sweat, dragging the heaviest boxes from the closet floor and removing the lighter ones from the top shelf. Only half of the boxes fit on the room's king-sized bed.

Abigail didn't need an engraved invitation. She plopped down on the bed amidst the mound of boxes and began reading labels. She pronounced the words phonetically. "Or-na-ments." After counting six boxes of Christmas ornaments, she asked, "How many ornaments do you have?"

"I probably have enough ornaments for this entire neighborhood."

"Where did you get so many?"

"Here and there."

Satisfied with the vague answer, Abigail continued reading. "Christmas pil-lows and throws. What is a throw?"

"A blanket."

"Oh." She was obviously unimpressed.

Kathryn tried not to laugh.

"Manger. Can we open this box?"

Kathryn nodded and picked up the box, which was relatively light in weight. She ran her thumb fingernail along the box lid's center seam, splitting the clear packing tape straight down the middle, wincing at the tongue lashing her mother would have given her had she not been dead in her grave for nearly ten years. According to her mother's extensive list of etiquette rules, a true Southern lady never disgraced herself with broken nails or calloused palms. In her mother's opinion, these were signs of the working class.

She removed a wooden crèche from the box. It had been carved by John's father from a choice piece of cherry grown on the farm. Its grain was sanded smooth as silk. Running a fingertip along the grain, she could almost feel the sweat and toil that went in such a gorgeous piece of woodwork. It was more than a commitment to excellence; it was a labor of love.

The accompanying pieces, Mary and Joseph, the manger, the barn animals, all were carved with the same quality of craftsmanship. Each piece was magnificent in both simplicity and perfection. Each piece, that is except for the cow.

Abigail giggled. "What happened to this cow? His ear is broken clean off."

"We had a lab puppy who liked to chew."

"Did he get his bottom swatted with the newspaper? That's what Mama has to do sometimes with Hezekiah."

Kathryn didn't stifle her laughter this time. "No, I didn't swat his bottom."

"What happened to him?"

"He was happier on the farm where he had plenty of room to run."

The child flitted to another box label before she had a chance to uncover the three carved shepherds.

"Village s--" Despite being an avid reader at the age of seven, Abigail stumbled on the word *scene*.

Kathryn pointed to the writing on the box. "It is a difficult word to read, because the letter *c* is silent. Try it again."

"Scene."

"Well done. You are becoming an excellent reader."

"Is it Santa's village? Are there elves?"

"No. It's the Biltmore Village, built by the combined geniuses of Richard Morris Hunt and Frederick Law, right here in Asheville." She treasured her miniature Christmas replica of the village, picked up years ago on a shopping whim from one of the village artisans.

Together, they began carefully removing the bubble wrap from each piece. Abigail became animated when she recognized the array of buildings from her own excursions to the Biltmore Village. There were historic homes, specialty shops, and gourmet restaurants. The last piece to be unwrapped was All Soul's Cathedral.

"Mama said that you may go to church with us tonight after dinner."

"It depends how I feel."

"Please say that you'll go."

Kathryn did her best not to look exasperated, but she was beginning to be weary of the child's incessant chatter. Cinnamon buns and a dictionary word search had developed into much, much more than she had intended. She never meant to drag the Christmas boxes from storage this holiday season. The thought of having to dress for a church service seemed overwhelming.

The telephone rang, interrupting any further discussion. There was a familiar voice on the other end of the line.

"Good morning again," Sarah said. "Has my daughter worn out her welcome yet?"

"If I were a rug, I would be threadbare."

"Then give her a gentle shove homeward. You know that she would stay with you all day if I let her."

"Abigail, it's time to go home."

The seven-year-old hurried from the bedroom, but not before wrapping her arms around Kathryn's waist for one final hug. Good and tight.

Kathryn reached for the switch to turn off the light illuminating the bedroom closet, and her fingers froze as she glimpsed a forgotten box, stuffed like a small coffin in the far corner of the top shelf. Even before she stretched on tiptoes to coax the box from the closet's shadows, before she caressed the smooth silk of the beautifully finished wood or inhaled the sweet aroma of hewn cherry, she knew. It was her beloved Christmas bracelet box.

CHAPTER SIX

K ATHRYN PRESSED HER FINGERS TO her temples and rubbed slowly, desperately trying to ease the tension which threatened to explode into a full-scale migraine. Why, today of all days, did she stumble upon the magnificent jewelry box, a time capsule of sorts, which housed the story of their love affair? And who took the liberty, either as an act of kindness or possibly a burdened sense of responsibility, to return the splendid jewelry box to its rightful place on the closet shelf?

She buoyed her nerves by pouring another cup of coffee and adding a generous portion of half and half. Thank goodness she was thin and could afford the calories; she couldn't imagine her morning coffee being dark like the java beans from which it was brewed.

With a quick glance across the room, she beheld the box sitting majestically on her kitchen table. It was a small chest constructed from cherry, slightly larger than a shoe box but smaller than a milk crate, masterfully crafted by her father-in-law as a gift for John's mother.

Kathryn sat down at the table, skeptical about the wisdom in choosing to open the chest on Christmas Eve. Her mind saw beneath its handcrafted lid. There was a large stack of Christmas cards meticulously organized and beautifully tied together with a red satin bow, forty-eight cards in all, each one housed in its original envelope. The oldest card was on the top with its envelope faded yellow. The most-recent card was on the bottom, still bright white.

The hinges on the jewelry box squeaked with age as she lifted its lid. When she looked inside, her heart leaped at the sight of her Christmas bracelet neatly displayed across the stack of envelopes. It had gone missing not long after John's death, and for months upon months she had frantically searched the house. The obvious thought of looking in the Christmas bracelet box had simply never occurred to her. Trembling, she removed the gorgeous piece of jewelry and draped it across her wrist.

Her arthritic fingers groaned, struggling to secure the bracelet's minute clasp. Like her wedding ring, she had always worn it around her left wrist, the side closest to her heart. With a small click, the clasp closed. The silver bracelet, laden with memories of Christmas-past, offered Kathryn a surprising sense of comfort and joy.

She rested for a moment, taking a sip of coffee. Then, she removed the stack of Christmas cards from the box. Untying the bow, she gently laid the two strands of red ribbon to the side and slipped the first Christmas card from its envelope. She opened the card. Her fingertip traced John's elegant penmanship, and her lips moved silently as she read his note. The words, which she committed to memory nearly a half century ago, swept her away to the fall of 1960 . . .

The Lowcountry of South Carolina is a geographical and cultural region. In the more liberal definition, it stretches along the coast from Myrtle Beach to Hilton Head Island and includes Charleston. Outsiders considered the area to be backward and slow; however, local residents preferred their relaxed pace of life. They still do. Genteel, they call it.

Nestled in the heart of the Lowcountry is the lovely city of Summerville, a bedroom community of Charleston developed as a summer sanctuary from disease-carrying mosquitoes and swamp fever. At the start of the twentieth century, it gained fame as a primary site of healing for tuberculosis and other diseases of the lung.

Residents of Summerville anticipated the arrival of oyster season like New York Yankee fans anticipate baseball's opening day. Avoided during the summer months when the animals spawn, oysters are harvested from the middle of September until the last day of April. The season is conveniently remembered as those months containing the letter *r*. It was a longstanding tradition that Kathryn's parents hosted a community oyster roast the first weekend in October.

The air felt chilled. Kathryn walked the grounds of her childhood home, overlooking final preparations for the evening's oyster roast. With only an hour before the guests were scheduled to arrive, everything seemed in order. The oyster tables, which were nothing more than naked planks of plywood mounted on tall sawhorses in the backyard, were already in place. A nearby fire pit was dressed with dry logs and tinder from the old pine tree blown down during last year's tropical storm. Two garden hoses were stretched from the garage beneath the house. The oysters had been washed and were piled in a trailer, ready to be covered in wet burlap and steamed on a sheet of metal.

Her father carried one last armload of wood out to the fire pit. He was a burly man. Clad in blue jeans and a flannel shirt stretched over a sizable paunch, he looked more like Paul Bunyan than a revered circuit court judge. It was rumored among the locals of Summerville that he checked his fabulous sense of humor at the door before entering the judge's chambers.

"Hey, Daddy." Kathryn looked at the cloudless skies and setting sun. "It's going to be a great night for an oyster roast."

"None better."

"Is there anything that I can do to help? We're done inside."

"Just sit quiet and look pretty."

"It will cost you a half bushel of oysters to keep me quiet," she teased.

"Do you want singles or clusters, my dear?"

"Singles, of course."

Judge Clarke laughed uproariously. Then, he changed tones with his only daughter.

"You run along and get prettied up for the party. I hear that your brother has invited a friend from medical school. He is from the other Carolina, but we won't hold that against him."

She uttered an exasperated groan as she headed toward the house to change clothes. The fact that she was twenty-five and did not have a steady boyfriend was a constant source of worry and disappointment to her parents. She hoped that Kevin, her twin brother and closest confidante, had not bought into their latest match-making schemes.

Raised by her mother to be conscious of the latest fashion trends, she chose black pencil thin stirrup pants, which complemented her lanky frame, plus a pink sweater with a cowl neck. She defied the fashionable beehive modeled by Jackie Kennedy, choosing instead to tie her long brunette mane into a ponytail pulled taut at the back. A quick glance in the mirror told her all that she needed to know: she looked absolutely sensational.

She was checking her lipstick one last time when she heard car doors slam in the horseshoe driveway at the front of the house. The drive quickly filled, and the remaining cars had to be rerouted to the side yard and along the street.

Kathryn entered the kitchen just as her mother was lifting a tray from the top shelf of the pantry. "What can I do to help?"

Her mother cast a glance in her direction. "Don't you look lovely. Be a dear and take these knives outside."

Nancy Clarke was a Southern debutante, raised on the peninsula of Charleston, who prided herself on being the consummate hostess. She meticulously and efficiently ran their home like a well-oiled machine, beautifully wearing the latest fashions, and demanding no less from her husband or children. In her daughter's eyes, she demanded perfection to a fault. There never seemed to be a margin for error, especially when they were entertaining.

Kathryn dutifully carried the tray of oyster knives down the steps and to the backyard where the guests were assembled. Designed as levers for prying, the knife blades had one basic style, blunt and rounded at the tip. Some of the handles were made from wood; others were made of steel. One unique oyster knife had a handle made from a deer's antler.

As she rounded one of the plywood tables, she heard her father introducing himself to Kevin's friend from medical school.

"So you're John Sullivan from North Carolina."

"Yes, sir."

"Have you heard of the Battle of Sullivan's Island?"

"A battle in the Revolutionary War." John happened to be fascinated by history. Strategic battles of World War II, especially those battles which occurred in the Pacific, were his forte.

"Precisely. But have you heard of General Charles Lee?"

"No sir, I haven't."

"On June 8th, 1776, a British fleet anchored off the coast of Charleston at Five Fathom Hole; they were three hundred guns strong. Their intent was to capture Charleston and drive a wedge between the Southern colonies. General Charles Lee, a Patriot, arrived with two thousand men from your state of North Carolina. He had orders to take charge of the fort on Sullivan's Island, which was being constructed under the command of our own Colonel Moultrie."

"Lookout, everybody. Here's the first batch," Kevin hollered as he dumped a shovelful of oysters in the center of a plywood table. A loud cheer went up from the crowd gathered around the tables.

The judge guided John to the other side of the table. "Let's move out of the way. Now where was I?"

"The fort was under the command of Colonel Moultrie," John said.

"That's right. The fort was made of palmetto trees rafted in from the mainland and the other islands. It was only constructed on the seaward side. Do you know what General Lee called it?"

"No sir, I don't"

"He called it a slaughtering pen of trees and sand."

Kevin yelled from his post beside the fire. "John, I tried to warn you about my father. Just wave a white rag when you get tired, and I'll come running."

The judge placed a protective arm around John's shoulder. "Your friend and I are having a friendly chat."

John grinned. "Please continue, sir. I am truly fascinated."

"At nine o'clock, on the morning of the twenty-eighth, only six days before the Americans officially declared their independence, the British

29

Admiral Parker fired a single shot on the harbor. By eleven-thirty, the British had launched a full-scale attack, firing mortar bombs into the walls of the fort."

Excited that he actually remembered the story from his seventh-grade history class, John interrupted the judge. "But the spongy palmettos and sand absorbed the shock of the bombs and smothered them before they could explode."

"Bravo, you're correct. Lee's only regret, which he admitted to later, was that he ever doubted Colonel Moultrie and his men."

Kathryn's mother called from the porch. "Kevin, the oysters can wait. Your friend needs to be rescued, or he'll never come back to visit us."

"Yes, ma'am." Kevin walked over to the oyster table. "Dad, I'm sorry to spoil your fun."

The judge turned to John and winked. "We'll talk later."

"I'll look forward to it, sir."

The judge patted John on the back before turning away in search of a new candidate, someone else to regale with stories of the Carolina coast, someone who was not in his wife's direct line of vision.

Kevin saw his twin across the table. "Kathryn, give this mountain boy an oyster knife."

Dazzled by her striking appearance, John watched Kathryn walk around the table. Unlike her brother who had a fair complexion, she resembled her father. She had his olive complexion, lush brown hair, and dark eyes exaggerated by thick lashes. She did not have her father's size and swagger; nor did she have her mother's short and petite figure. Instead, she was tall and thin. To John, she resembled a runway model.

Kathryn moved alongside the two men.

"John Sullivan, I want you to meet my younger sister."

"Younger by a whole eight minutes," she corrected. "My brother has been using that line ever since our first-grade teacher taught us how to tell time."

"That old battle ax still thinks that I am incorrigible," he bragged.

"You are incorrigible. And insufferable."

John laughed, clearly amused by their good-natured teasing.

"Speaking of time, I need to see if the next bushels of oysters are ready to come off the fire," Kevin said. "Kathryn, will you look after John for me?"

John protested. "I don't want to be a bother. I can manage here by myself."

Her smile was genuine. "It's no bother. I am ready to eat a few oysters myself."

Along with twenty other people bellied up to the plywood, the two of them began to shuck the oysters, succulent singles claimed from the Carolina coast. Kathryn was reticent by nature; however, she felt at ease in John's unassuming presence. Their conversation which began at the oyster table continued on the screened-in porch long after the oysters were eaten and the other guests, including the biting mosquitoes, had gone home for the night.

CHAPTER SEVEN

LIVING WITH A LARGER-THAN-LIFE FATHER, an overly critical mother, and an incorrigible twin brother was not easy for Kathryn. As a young child, she built a stoic, impenetrable fortress around her heart. While its stone drawbridge relaxed on occasion, it never fully opened. Members of the opposite sex were initially enchanted by her beauty but quickly became disconcerted when conversations with Kathryn remained superficial, seldom dipping below the day's forecast or her week's lesson plans. However, for some untold reason, the drawbridge to her heart opened for John Sullivan.

"What made you want to be a teacher?" he asked as they shared a pizza the week after the oyster roast. It was their third date of the week.

"Our first-grade teacher, Miss Harper, the one who thinks that Kevin is incorrigible, profoundly changed my life."

"How?"

She giggled as a thin strand of mozzarella cheese stretched from the slice of pizza in her hand to the bite in her mouth.

"Being a twin can be difficult," she explained. "Kevin delighted adults with his adorable grin and quick wit, while I was a shrinking violet in his midst."

John was shocked. "I can't imagine you ever being a wall flower."

"Actually, I was more like a giant sunflower needing sunshine," She took a sip of sweet tea. "By the time that I entered preschool, I was gangly and awkward, six inches taller than any other child in the class. I wore black horned rimmed glasses and had big buck teeth."

"My guess is that Kevin looked like a movie star."

"Exactly. Appearances are a huge deal to my mother. I remember being paraded for the relatives at every family function. We were dressed in identical outfits, but all eyes were on Kevin. It was almost like I didn't exist."

John reached across the table and covered her hand. Kathryn knew that he understood. It was inconsequential that she had grown into a beauty; the scars from her childhood were still there.

"Tell me more about your first-grade teacher."

"Miss Harper was the first person in my life who treated me as someone special, an individual, not as Kevin's twin. She encouraged me to be my own person. I adored her and would literally ask to stay in at recess, to staple papers, to sharpen pencils, to wash desks, anything that allowed me to bask in her kindness. At the age of six, I decided that I wanted to be Miss Harper when I grew up."

"Do you still keep in touch with her?"

Kathryn wiped some pizza sauce from the corner of her mouth. "At every family function. She married our uncle the summer after we turned eight. Kevin was the ring bearer, and I was the flower girl."

"Someday, I hope to meet your Aunt--"

"Harper. That's what I call her, Aunt Harper."

On their initial dates, Kathryn did most of the talking; however, over the course of the next eight weeks, she began to uncover a great deal about John Sullivan, and she liked what she found. She learned that his father was a blue-collar worker, working in the textile mills outside of Greenville. Their lives were simple but loving. In order to save money for college, he joined the army at age seventeen and served a two-year stint. He dreamed of being a doctor after watching his mother waste away from cancer when he was a young boy. His eyes danced whenever he laughed, and when he listened, he rested his elbows against his knees with his hands folded.

Three days before Christmas, she wandered up and down the aisles of the department store in a terrible quandary. She was swirling in a sea of indecision. Although she had been groomed in the art of shopping by her mother, who had a keen eye for sales and an incredible knack of selecting presents, Kathryn could not find a suitable gift for John. But then of course, she had never been in love.

From wallets to pajamas, briefcases to cologne, everything seemed either too impersonal or too intimate. Nothing struck a balance between the two extremes. Deciding to err on the side of caution, she chose a lovely pale blue cardigan, one that would highlight his blond hair, big blue eyes, and ruddy complexion. She only hoped that the sleeves would be long enough for his tall frame.

They decided to exchange gifts that evening after taking a stroll along the Battery where the magnificent antebellum homes, once fired upon from Fort Sumter, were adorned with evergreen wreaths and multicolored Christmas lights. John's arm around her waist was reassuring and comfortable as they passed dark alleys on the way back to his car. Before returning to Summerville, where she still lived with her parents, they stopped at a Krispy Kreme doughnut shop. Their orders were nearly identical: a large cup of coffee with extra cream and one chocolate glazed doughnut. Unlike her, he preferred his doughnut with sprinkles.

She tucked her skirt under her and hopped onto a stool at the doughnut shop. John slid onto the stool beside her. Except for a teenager dutifully stationed behind the doughnut counter, they had the place to themselves.

"Did anyone ever give you a nickname, like Kathy or Katie?" He took a bite of the doughnut.

"Never," she said. "My father forbade me to use anything but my given name."

"Remind me not to make that mistake." The multicolored sprinkles crunched between his teeth.

"Besides, nicknames don't fit someone like me. Just look at my size-ten feet."

"Your feet?"

She impulsively kicked her legs from under the table, proudly displaying her bright-red stilettos. Utterly carefree, she wiggled her feet merrily, swooshing them back and forth like wipers across the windshield of a car. The teenager behind the counter untied his apron and peered anxiously at his watch.

Returning her feet to their rightful position beneath the table and smoothing down her skirt, she grew serious. "Think about it. Kathy and Katie are names for cute, petite high school cheerleaders, not schoolmarms in their twenties with gargantuan feet. My given name definitely suits me better."

John washed the last bite of his doughnut down with a swig of coffee and said, "Then, Kathryn it is."

They toasted their Styrofoam coffee cups and laughed like old friends. Kathryn felt incredibly happy. Draining the last drop of coffee from her cup, she hopped off the stool and slipped on her coat. "Let's go to my house and open Christmas presents."

Lighthearted laughter accompanied them as they exited the Krispy Kreme. Somewhere between the parking lot and the road to Summerville, John became noticeably quiet. His sudden shift in moods troubled Kathryn. She had the sinking feeling that her childish behavior in the doughnut shop had embarrassed him.

Her parents were shuffling upstairs, preparing for bed, when she quietly unlocked the front door. John followed her down the wide hall, and into the parlor lit by a single tiffany lamp. Less impressive than the formal living room with its twelve-foot ceilings and crystal chandelier, this room was comfortably furnished with a love seat and matching recliner. Wrapped in a shirt box and sitting on the end table in the shadow of the lamp was the pale blue cardigan purchased earlier that day.

Removing her coat, she sat down on the love seat and motioned for him to join her.

"I need to apologize for my behavior--" she began hesitantly.

John interrupted her before she could finish her thought.

"I'm sorry for being so quiet on the way home. It's just that I'm a bit nervous." He stood up and reached inside his overcoat. "Would you mind reading the card first?"

She noticed that he was trembling as he withdrew a white envelope and a slender jewelry box from his coat pocket. The gift, which was wrapped in silver foil and tied with a red satin bow, had been purchased from her favorite jewelry store, Nora's on King Street.

Kathryn slid her fingernail along the seam of the envelope and withdrew a beautiful Christmas card from Hallmark. She swallowed hard as she read John's words, beautifully scripted on the inside of the card.

Christmas 1960

Dear Kathryn,

My mother's prized possession was a gold charm bracelet given to her as a wedding gift by my father. Every Christmas, my dad took my little brother and me to the local jeweler to select a new charm for our mother's bracelet. We spent the entire morning at the jewelry store trying to select just the right charm. I will always remember her look of delight on Christmas morning when she opened our gift. The last charm we ever picked was a heart. I was only ten.

I hope that this gift is not too presumptuous. Is it too forward of me to say that you are gracefully dancing your way into my heart?

Fondly,

John

A sideways glance in his direction told her that he was intently watching her, and even though her reaction was carefully being scrutinized, Kathryn's eyes filled with tears when she lifted the gift from its box. In her hands was a gorgeous silver charm bracelet with a single charm, a delicate silver heart.

Without saying a word, she kissed him on the lips, and regardless of what her mother might say, she didn't feel the least bit silly.

KATHRYN'S ARTRITITIC HANDS ACHED AS she picked up her cup of coffee and took another sip. She returned the cup to its saucer. Wincing in pain, she rotated her wrist from side to side, sifting through the charms which John had given her. It took her two or three minutes to locate the silver heart, and by the time she found it, she was angry.

She fussed at John as if he was sitting directly across the table from her. "You didn't flutter your way into my heart, John Sullivan. It was an incredible, heart throbbing stampede, and now I don't know how to live without you."

She put the Christmas card into its envelope, wiped a tear from the corner of her eye, and removed the next envelope from the stack. As she removed the card from its envelope, memories from their forty-seven years of marriage came rushing back.

CHAPTER EIGHT

KATHRYN BREATHED A SIGH OF relief as she loaded the last of her fifteen kindergarten students onto a school bus headed for home. Shielding her eyes from the afternoon sun, she waved at the little faces peering through the glass. The bus drove around the circle driveway of the elementary school before turning onto the main road.

The day had been chaotic, beginning with the morning's eight o'clock bell. Her students filed into the classroom, carting adult-sized shoe boxes and paper sacks filled with Valentine's Day cards. She was forewarned by the seasoned teachers on her hall that any instructive work, such as calling out the alphabet or counting to twenty, needed to take place by nine o'clock. And they were correct. Most of the morning was spent making Valentine's Day mailboxes out of the shoeboxes and pre-cut squares of brightly colored paper and white paste that smelled like bubble gum.

While the kindergarteners ate lunch and fidgeted through afternoon naps, their Valentine boxes dried on the window sill. Chaos ensued at one-thirty with the arrival of two trays of iced cupcakes, four cartons of Neapolitan ice cream, and more gallons of red punch than she cared to count; plus, two out-of-control room mothers who couldn't have been much older than Kathryn.

Watching the exhaust of the school bus dissipate into the air, she waved one last time before walking into the school building. Her long strides quickly caught up with Mr. Jeb, the school's one and only janitor, pushing the dust mop down the kindergarten hall. She believed him when he bragged that he was as old as the salt marsh and as feisty as the fiddler crabs that live there.

As Kathryn turned into her classroom, she heard a voice from across the hall bellow her name. Pat Baldwin, a state recognized kindergarten teacher and superb mentor, motioned for her to visit. Three of the other kindergarten teachers from their hall were assembled around Pat's desk. Lori Martin, a five-year veteran whose bright smile and inherent enthusiasm had been squelched by recent bouts of morning sickness, sat at Pat's desk slowly sipping ginger-ale. Hunched over a wooden chair was a shriveled old woman, ashen in color, who looked to be at least eighty even though she was only in her mid-sixties. It was Joan Archer. Her long gray braid, normally wound in a taut bun, hung freely down the middle of her back.

Pat turned to Kathryn. "Did you survive the afternoon's festivities?"

"I survived, but my room didn't."

"Take a peek at my room." Joan's hacking cough from years of smoking interrupted her sentence. "Then you'll feel better."

Lori complained. "I just wish that we had a few days to recover. My back is killing me."

Pat directed the attention back toward Kathryn. "How did Terence handle today's heightened activities?"

"Amazing, as always."

Terence, a precious six-year-old, battled the crippling effect of muscular dystrophy and a severe stuttering problem. The sight of him eagerly handing out homemade Valentines was heartwarming for Kathryn. Just as compelling was the knowledge that the students were no longer aware of his heavy leg braces and metal crutches, his jarring movements, and the repetition of his consonants.

Lori took a sip of ginger-ale. "He was stuffing candy hearts in his pants pocket as he hobbled toward the bus. I couldn't help but laugh."

"He loves candy, that's for sure."

Pat began erasing her board. "You have worked miracles in that boy's life. He arrived on the first day of school, painfully shy, like a withered old man. Ever since October or November, he has come alive."

"I truly haven't done anything," Kathryn protested. "It's all been Terence and his grandmother."

"You tilled the soil, so to speak, providing a safe and nurturing environment, a place where he could bloom," Pat insisted. "You have a rare and special gift, and you are unwilling to recognize it."

"I guess that I've always rooted for the underdog," she replied.

Without warning, Joan Archer stood up from the chair and shuffled her Nikes toward the door. "Have a good afternoon, ladies," she hacked. "I've got to go home and take a load off my feet."

Everyone knew the real reason for Joan's sudden exit; she needed a cigarette.

Lori hauled herself from the chair. "Wait. I'm leaving with you."

The two teachers walked out the door side by side, one doddering because of marked age and poor health, the other waddling with child.

Once they were alone, Pat inquired, "What does your handsome Doctor Kildare have planned for Valentine's Day?"

Kathryn deftly tried to avoid anything too personal by saying, "You know that he won't be a doctor until he graduates in May."

"Then, what does your handsome medical student have planned for today?"

"Nothing special."

"No roses or diamonds?"

Kathryn blushed.

"Love is wasted on the young," Pat bemoaned.

"What about you and Marvin? Are you doing something special for Valentine's Day?"

"Oh, you know Marvin. A romantic evening to him is reheating a can of pork and beans and watching reruns of the six o'clock news."

"He can't be that bad."

"Actually, he's worse. He works incredibly long hours on the loading docks. That's why I have to live vicariously through the young teachers on this hall." Pat pointed her index finger at Kathryn. "I expect a full report tomorrow morning about Doctor Kildare."

Fast becoming friends, they lingered in the hall, sharing ideas for next month's lesson plans, chatting about Lori's surprise baby shower, and discussing Joan Archer's rapidly declining health. Unlike many of the other teachers on their hall, Kathryn felt incredibly at ease with Pat and was disappointed when the late bell rang at four o'clock.

"Time for me to go before the traffic becomes unbearable," Pat said. "Are you leaving soon?"

"In about an hour."

"Don't stay too long."

Kathryn's hopes of leaving by five o'clock faded when she walked across the hall. Her classroom was ransacked. There were hunks of vanilla cupcakes with white icing and multi-colored sprinkles smashed on the tile floor. Pieces of torn tissue paper and globs of paste were stuck to the students' desks. Red and pink streamers hung down, partially unattached, from the front bulletin board. To think that fifteen delightful, well-behaved kindergarten students had created such a mess was incomprehensible.

She noticed that a plate of cookies and sweatshirt were left at one of her student's desk, and her heart swelled with love and affection. The desk belonged to Terence.

In order to clean up her classroom, Kathryn was going to need a large garbage can, one which easily moved on its wheels. She kicked off her red stilettos and marched down the hall toward Mr. Jeb's janitorial closet. She couldn't help but notice that all the other classrooms were dark, their doors closed and locked tight for the afternoon.

"They must be coming back early in the morning to clean their rooms," she marveled.

The other kindergarten teachers considered her too disciplined and regimented for her own good. "If you don't learn to pace yourself, you will burn out quickly at this job," she heard time and again from various seasoned teachers on her hall, especially Joan Archer.

Still, procrastination always left her feeling anxious.

Jeb's closet contained only one garbage can on wheels. She pulled the can into the hallway. The wheels rebelled, sporadically reversing directions as she coerced it down the empty hallway. She missed smashing her knuckles against the classroom's doorframe by a narrow margin.

Still walking in her stocking feet, she began stripping red and pink streamers from the bulletin board in order to make room for tomorrow's Presidents' Day display. She was thankful that the silhouettes of George Washington and Abe Lincoln, made during her year of student teaching, were still in good condition and waiting on the shelf.

She bent and removed the streamers from the tile floor. As she straightened, she noticed an oversized envelope propped against the lamp on her desk. Letters clipped and glued from a magazine spelled out the words TO MY VALENTINE on the front of the envelope. Her heart sank. Had one of her students returned home, tearful and rejected because his or her card had been overlooked during their party? Or had one of her students shyly left this card for her at the end of the day?

Kathryn jumped at the sound of a man's voice.

"Open it." John was standing in the doorway.

Inside the envelope was an adorable homemade card, a heart cut from pink construction paper and glued to a white doily. Tiny cinnamon candies at the center spelled out the words: BE MY VALENTINE.

Sweeping into the room like a modern-day knight dressed in khaki pants and penny loafers, John knelt directly on the floor in front of her. His eyes flooded with tears, and his voice quivered. "Kathryn Clarke, I love you."

The well-rehearsed proposal practiced numerous times throughout the day went unfinished as he fumbled with the diamond ring hidden in his shirt pocket. Before he ever popped the question, Kathryn sealed her answer with a kiss

She couldn't wait to tell Pat.

CHAPTER NINE

THE RESIDENTS OF CHARLESTON WERE surprised that year by winter's quick transition into spring. Balmy breezes boldly chased away the winter's chill and rejuvenated the townsfolk's souls, filling the air with the faint smell of wisteria. Pink and white petals floated down from dogwood trees. Azaleas bursting into bloom cloaked the Carolina Lowcountry in a bouquet of vivid color.

Unfortunately, summer was viciously biting at the heels of spring. John's graduation from medical school took place the second Friday of May in ninety-five degree heat. The skies were clear and the air still. Dressed in flowing dark robes, members from the university's prestigious faculty and board of visitors mopped perspiration from their brows while the graduates processed across the outdoor stage.

The dreadful heat wave persisted into June as the school doors closed for the summer. With temperatures climbing into the triple digits, Kathryn bid tearful adieus to John. With his pediatric internship at Duke beginning the first of July, he had only a few short weeks to move to Raleigh and locate a suitable apartment within walking distance of the hospital.

As residents along the Carolina coast cautioned each other about the extreme heat and contemplated the occurrence of a late-summer hurricane, Kathryn contended with a vortex of her own, namely her mother.

When it came to planning a wedding, the two women agreed upon very little. Kathryn dreamed of a Christmas wedding; however, her mother insisted upon having the wedding the Saturday after Thanksgiving. Kathryn adored a tea-length wedding dress made of organza, which she found in a magazine for Southern brides. However, her mother was relentless about the full length, chenille lace gown displayed on the floor model at one of Charleston's high-society boutiques.

To make matters worse, the men in their lives were noncommittal. Kathryn's father was determined not to get drawn into the crossfire between his wife and his daughter. Each time the wedding was discussed, he disappeared into his study under the guise of having legal journals to read. Working ninety hours a week as an intern, the groom was too fatigued to care if his wedding tuxedo had tails or not.

The biggest tussle between Kathryn and her mother occurred when it came time to choose a location. Naturally, Nancy Clarke assumed that the wedding would be held at their home church in Summerville; however, her daughter was not so inclined.

Ever since Kathryn's fifth-grade class went on a field trip to Charleston, she had dreamed about being married at St. Michael's Episcopal Church on Meeting Street. Awestruck by the beauty of St. Michael's, she squeezed to the front of the group and listened attentively as the tour guide gave life to the church's rich history. He explained that the white steeple, which towered over the city, was an easy mark for British naval ships positioned in the harbor during the Revolutionary War. In a desperate attempt to disguise the steeple, members of the congregation painted it black. Unfortunately, Charleston's brilliant blue sky made the black steeple an even easier target.

The tour guide's description of the eight church bells left her spellbound. Pilfered by the retreating British as a prize at the end of the War of Independence, the bells were harbored in England until a British merchant discovered them and arranged for their safe return to South Carolina. Hostilities between the States forced the bells to travel up the road to Columbia, where they were stored in a shed for protection from the invading Northern troops. Cracked when the shed was torched during the burning of Columbia, the bells were cast at a foundry in London, transported back to St. Michael's, and hung in 1868. The new frame was improperly installed, and the bells remained stationary. Instead of being rung, they were chimed with clappers.

Enchanted by the sojourns of the bells, Kathryn harbored a secret dream. She dreamed that a miracle would occur on her wedding day and that the bells would ring.

Her mother's response, upon hearing the news that Kathryn wanted to be married at St. Michael's, was less than favorable. "Don't be ridiculous. Why would we ask our friends and relatives to drive thirty minutes to Charleston when our church in Summerville is perfect?"

Kathryn argued. "St. Paul's is too small."

"Your father and I were married at St. Paul's, and it was beautiful."

"But I want to be married downtown at St. Michael's."

Her mother was unbending. "It's too late. I have already contacted the altar guild. Should we have white ribbon or silver ribbon on the sconces? I can't decide."

Aghast, Kathryn threw her hands up into the air. Her mother was a virtual tornado running roughshod over her. "And your plans for the reception?"

"We will have it here at the house, of course." Nancy Clarke smoothed her hair away from her face and puffed it at the back. "Do you think that we should hire valet parking?"

"Whose wedding is it, yours or mine?" Kathryn was desperate to ask. Instead, she poured her iced tea down the drain and slammed the glass into the sink before storming from the room.

She found her father whistling as he sorted through a stack of journals in his office.

He removed his glasses. "Come in, baby girl."

"Daddy," she stammered. As her fury escaped in the form of tears, her father rose from his chair, moved around the massive oak desk, and enfolded her in his arms.

"It's Mother. She is just so--"

"Demanding, controlling, and manipulative," he said. "You forget. I've lived with your mama for more than thirty years."

"How do you tolerate her? She has planned my entire wedding without even asking me."

Her father chuckled. "Do you remember the day that I referred to your mother as a little bulldozer?"

She recalled the conversation. "I asked you what you meant, and you told me that someday I would understand."

"I learned long ago that while she is demanding and controlling, not to mention fiercely determined to have her own way, your mother has a heart that is bigger than the state of South Carolina. She only wants the best for those she loves," he said. "Here is the hard part. While she is a bulldozer, pushing away the opinions of anyone who crosses her path, your mother has an incredible knack of being right. Years ago, I learned to trust her judgment, especially if it involves guests."

"But it's my wedding."

"You don't want to hear this, baby girl, but I think you should reconsider your mother's suggestions."

"Nothing with Mother is a suggestion; everything is her decision."

"Take the next twenty-four hours and give serious thought to your mother's ideas. If it is not what you and John want, then let us know. If the need arises, I will run interference between you and the little bulldozer. Don't ever forget that, by controlling the checkbook, I have the key to your mother's motor."

Kathryn spent a sleepless night wrestling under the weight of indecision, ruminating like a cow chewing its cud, hashing and rehashing wedding plans until there was nothing left to reconsider. Having barely slept, she wiggled from beneath the down comforter, slid out of bed, and padded silently to the comfort of her bedroom window. The view that awaited her was nothing short of spectacular. It was an artist's canvass smudged in brilliant shades of pink as a new day dawned. Mesmerized, she watched the morning sun climb above the horizon, its individual rays coalescing into a single beam of yellow light, which sparkled like diamonds through the long chains of Spanish moss hanging outside her window.

Her decision was made. The wedding ceremony would be held on November twenty-fifth, the Saturday after Thanksgiving, at St. Paul's Episcopal Church in Summerville. A reception at her parents' home would follow.

There was one point of contention, however, upon which she refused to bend.

"I am wearing the tea-length wedding dress of crisp white organza, not a floor-length gown of Chantilly lace," she adamantly told her father that morning at breakfast, "no matter what Mother says."

CHAPTER TEN

URING THE MONTHS PRIOR TO their wedding, the couple lived not only in two different states; they lived in two separate worlds. Clad in pale blue scrubs and a long white coat, tongue depressors stuffed in one pocket and a stethoscope crammed in the other, John blended into the hospital surroundings. Day and night, he worked. Vital signs on premature babies needed to be monitored; antibiotics for toddlers with ear infections needed to be ordered; broken bones in adolescents needed to be set; and grieving parents, no matter the age of the child, needed to be comforted. A metaphorical sponge, naturally absorbing both knowledge and experience, John was quickly gaining the reputation for being one of Duke's top pediatric interns. In the meantime, summer melted into autumn, and Kathryn flitted from one bridal shower to the next in her A-line chiffon dresses and matching heels.

The morning of their wedding was crisp, clear, and cool. She sat at her grandmother's antique secretary and finished writing thank-you notes. Her foot tapped in perfect rhythm to the music of Bobby Darin. The small clock on the top shelf of the secretary reminded her that she had less than an hour to go before her bridal luncheon. She heard a gentle knock and looked up to find John's father standing at the door with a package in his hands.

Kathryn made her future father-in-law's acquaintance not long after her engagement to John was announced. Together, John and she had driven to Asheville where she met both his father and his only brother. She had taken an instant liking to both, as they did her.

William Sullivan was a hardworking mill worker who became a widower in his early thirties. He devoted his life to raising his sons and managing their forty-acre farm on the outskirts of Asheville. Kathryn recognized many of the qualities that she adored about John in her future father-in-law. While John's father was much more reserved than his son, both men had a generous and good heart.

William carried the package into the room. "I have a wedding gift for you."

"Should I wait for John to open it?"

"No. This gift is only for you." He pulled up a chair next to her. "As you know, I try my hand at woodworking now and then."

Kathryn smiled. She observed his gorgeous woodwork during their first visit to the farm. To say that he tried his hand at woodworking was a monumental understatement. William Sullivan was a master craftsman.

"I made this for Rose, John's mother, as a gift on our wedding day, and now it seems only appropriate that I give it to you. I'm afraid that I don't wrap too well," he said shyly.

She jerked off a piece of scotch tape and then another piece and another. She gasped when the last of the wrapping paper fell to the floor. Sitting on her lap was an exquisite jewelry box, carved from solid cherry. "William, this has been a part of your family for years. I can't possibly accept it."

"In a few short hours, my dear, you will be a part of my family, too." The penetrating blue eyes, which were so much like John's eyes, flooded with tears. "I'm asking you to accept it. Rose would want you to have it, and so do I."

She reached over and kissed him on the cheek. "Thank you."

A poignant and magical ten seconds, it was a moment that forever cemented their love, friendship, and mutual respect.

His new dress shoes squeaking, he returned the chair to its original position and walked across the living room.

"William, thank you."

"The gift is yours to cherish."

"This time I wasn't referring to the jewelry box," she said. "I'm thanking you for John. You've raised a wonderful son."

Choked with emotion, her future father-in-law tapped the doorframe, twice, before exiting the room.

John and Kathryn's wedding was nothing short of spectacular. On the front page of Sunday's society section, it was described as *impressive, dazzling,* and even *flawless.*

As the evening festivities drew to a close, Kathryn descended the front staircase in her beige going-away suit, pausing on the landing long enough to locate her groom. The sight of the ring bearer, an impish six-year-old balancing on metal crutches and stuffing the pockets of his tuxedo with pink sugar mints, made her laugh. "Terence and his candy," she thought. "Some things never change."

Her mother approached, carrying a large white bakery box tied by string. "Do not open this package until you cross the state line into North Carolina."

The sound of her father's voice boomed from the living room where he was holding court, dazzling some guests with embellished fishing stories from his childhood along the Edisto River. Like most of his stories, they were stretched just within the limit of plausibility.

Suddenly, he bellowed. "Where is my baby girl?"

"Here I am, Daddy. It's almost time for us to leave."

"Hold on little girl. I've got something for you."

Within a matter of seconds, he was striding down the hallway; in his hand was a large plastic bag.

"No daughter of mine is moving to that God forsaken state of North Carolina without a decent bag of her daddy's boiled peanuts."

The wedding party and their guests roared with laughter. Throughout the evening, he had been complaining to anyone who would listen that his wife and daughter vetoed the idea of serving boiled peanuts at the reception.

He theatrically bowed to John. "Boiled peanuts are another Southern delicacy, not unlike slurping oysters from a shell."

After placing the bag in John's hand, Kathryn's father turned his attention on his only daughter. Gently, he cupped her chin in his huge hands and looked directly in her eyes. Tears spilled unabashedly down his cheeks. "You will always be my baby girl."

The crowd went wild with applause. Rice was thrown as the bride and groom made a mad dash down the front steps. Kathryn cradled the white bakery box, and John clutched her daddy's bag of boiled peanuts. The sound of a car door slamming and tin cans jingling against the pavement announced their departure.

As requested, the box from her mother remained untouched on the front seat of their Chevy until they crossed the border. However, as soon as they passed the sign which read "Welcome to North Carolina," Kathryn peaked under the lid. Everything in the box reminded her of Charleston. There were benne seed wafers from Aunt Harper; pralines from her favorite candy store at the Market; and ten sand dollars. All ten were perfectly shaped and bleached white by the sun. She instinctively knew that the sand dollars were from the family beach house on Edisto Island.

Her mother's note was simple:

Take our love and a bit of the Lowcountry with you, wherever you go.

AFTER A BRIEF THREE-DAY HONEYMOON in the mountains, John and Kathryn settled into their new roles as husband and wife. He returned to the pediatric floor the following Wednesday, leaving her to spend the majority of her days and nights alone.

Challenged for the first time in her life to live within the limits of an extremely strict budget, she scoured yard sales for a small dinette set that could be refurbished with an inexpensive coat of white paint. In a few short weeks, a newly painted table and chairs sat in the center room. Pictures of their families on the walls and curtains sewn from a set of paisley sheets found at the Salvation Army transformed their drab garage apartment into a home.

Decorating for the holidays presented problems that required creative solutions on her part. The apartment included one bedroom, one bathroom, and a kitchen-living room combination. The only available space for a

Christmas tree was on top of the washer in the farthest corner from the front door. A perfect solution presented itself one afternoon when she was out walking. Lying in the curb beneath a massive pine tree was a broken branch. Giddy with excitement, she carried it home and propped it on top of the washer in an oversized coffee can that she filled with water.

They had no extra money for ornaments, so she created them with scraps and items on hand. She used remnants of silver ribbon left over from the wedding to hang ten miniature pinecones and ten sun-bleached sand dollars. The pinecones were from the mountains, and the sand dollars were from the sea. The irony that their first Christmas tree represented a true blending of their lives was lost on neither Kathryn nor John.

John possessed little if any control over his hospital call schedule, especially during the holidays. He shaved and dressed early Christmas morning, careful not to disturb Kathryn's predawn slumber. After pausing beside the washing machine, just long enough to nestle his gift for her against their tiny Christmas tree, he stuffed his stethoscope in the pocket of his winter coat and slipped silently out the front door.

Kathryn awakened three hours later. Her heart skipped a beat when she wandered into the main room and spied the gift. It was wrapped in silver foil and tied with a red ribbon. Tears sprang to her eyes as she read the card, which John drafted multiple times before being fully satisfied that its message captured the true feelings of his heart.

Christmas 1961

My Dearest Wife,

Merry Christmas and Happy One-Month Anniversary! A marriage isn't created by the ringing of wedding bells. A marriage is established when two lives and two hearts (like ours) are melded into one.

I am already missing you today, and the sun has yet to rise.

Your husband,

John

Upon opening the gift, she discovered another silver charm to add to her bracelet. It consisted of two wedding bells, tied by a single bow, ringing in festive celebration.

"How many years has it been since I thought about my first year of teaching?" Kathryn wondered as she poured herself another cup of coffee. She reached into the refrigerator for a smidgeon more cream.

After moving to North Carolina, she kept abreast of school news by exchanging Christmas cards with Pat. She was saddened to learn that Joan smoked until the day that she died from lung cancer. Lori quit teaching after the baby was born. It was rumored, but never confirmed, that her husband was transferred to Oklahoma. Marrying his college sweetheart, Terence graduated with a master's degree in education and worked for the Greenville school district until losing his battle to muscular dystrophy. He was only thirty-nine. Pat became a widow at the age of sixty-five, retired from teaching ten years later, and as far as Kathryn knew, was living in a nursing home near her daughter in Atlanta.

Aware but not caring that the steady drip of an icicle outside her kitchen window signaled the passage of time, Kathryn sat down at the kitchen table with a fresh cup of coffee. Her thoughts lingered on those earlier years, and she gazed at the charm bracelet dangling from her wrist. With fingers badly crippled by arthritis, she gripped the silver bells.

She spoke to John again, this time almost sheepishly. "There is something that I never told you."

She took a sip of coffee before continuing.

"I thought that I heard bells of St. Michael's ring on our wedding day."

"Those were the bells of our hearts," he answered.

It made her glad to hear his voice, even if it was only in her imagination.

CHAPTER ELEVEN

JOHN CURLED UP BY HER feet and watched in fascination as Kathryn folded an 8x11 sheet of white paper in half. Then she folded each side toward the center at a sixty degree angle. Holding the corner between the thumb and forefinger of her left hand, she cut the edges in a wide ark and proceeded to cut away a large portion of the paper that remained.

Placing the scissors on the floor, carefully unfolding the paper, she displayed a giant snowflake. Its six-sided radial symmetry was cut to perfection. She punched a hole through her creation and threaded a piece of a fishing line through the hole. After tying a knot in the line, she laid the snowflake in a basket, picked up another piece of paper, and repeated the process.

"What do you think about when you see a snowflake?" she asked.

"Work."

"I'm being serious."

"So am I."

"How is that being serious?"

"Simple. Snowflakes cause accumulation, and accumulation causes sled riding. Sled riding causes accidents, and accidents cause casts and stitches."

She grimaced. "Casts and stitches mean that you go to the office."

"Or to the hospital."

John completed his pediatric internship at Duke in May, 1962, and was offered a position in Asheville with his childhood pediatrician, Doc Lawrence, who at sixty-nine was counting the days until his retirement. The opportunity to practice medicine in his hometown, to fill his lungs with crisp mountain air, and reside in close proximity to William and the farm, was a dream come true for John. After only eighteen months, his practice in the Blue Ridge Mountains was booming.

Kathryn was thrilled that the opportunity to leave Raleigh presented itself. With precious little to occupy the hours of the day, time crept at a snail's pace the last six months of John's internship. Sitting in their tidy garage apartment, waiting for John to return home from fourteen-hour shifts at the hospital and every third night call, depressed her.

Moving to Asheville removed the self-imposed hold button on her life. She poured her creative energies into the three-bedroom ranch, which they purchased at a steal, scrubbing it from top to bottom with Lysol, sewing gingham curtains for the windows, and crafting those finishing touches that turn a house into a home.

Not long after their move, she began to dream about teaching again. She yearned for the smell of crayons, the sight of an opened lesson plan book, and a classroom to call her own. Most of all, she pined for the children. She was a natural-born teacher, and she belonged in a classroom filled with students. John encouraged her to make herself known at the local board of education. A return phone call offering her a position teaching kindergarten made Kathryn's fairy- tale world complete.

Now it was Valentines' Day. Having treated themselves to steaks on the grill, the two nestled on overstuffed pillows by the fireplace in their tiny living room, chatting easily while she cut snowflakes for her class unit on weather.

Kathryn dangled two paper snowflakes in the air. "Look at these. What do you see?"

"A Valentine's Day spent cutting paper."

"Hush. Guess what I see."

"You've got my rapt attention."

"The snowflakes are different."

"And that's important because--"

"Because different conditions in the clouds, like temperature and humidity, make them develop differently."

"Aha. There are no two snowflakes exactly alike." He was aware that she still wrestled with her need to be recognized and appreciated as an individual instead of a twin.

"Correct. Watching my students being transformed by the world around them is amazing." Kathryn spoke with an unusual display of animation. "They absorb information, like little sponges soaking in water, processing and assimilating, changing and growing in response to that assimilation, but growing differently, depending upon their personalities and experiences. They are like snowflakes passing through different parts of a cloud."

John watched Kathryn with fascination, savoring her excitement, treasuring the rare times she relinquished her guard and openly shared her soul.

Self-conscious by her sudden outburst, she resumed working. She handed him a hole-punch and ten inch pieces of transparent fishing line. "I'll cut. You tie."

John studied her. "Do you ever think about children?"

"Every day. Have you forgotten that I'm a teacher?"

"I think about children."

"You should, too" she teased. "After all, you are a pediatrician."

"No. I mean, our children."

"Our hypothetical children?"

"The ones we'll have someday. Do you ever wonder what they will be like?" He was prepared for her usual line of defense that she wasn't ready for children, yet.

Without a saying word, Kathryn picked up a snowflake from the basket and began to write. With an impish grin, she handed the snowflake to her husband.

"Like this one?" she asked.

He read the words. "Baby Sullivan Number One."

Instead of responding to his look of bewilderment, she picked up a new snowflake and wrote more words.

"Or this one?" Her eyes twinkled as she handed him the second snowflake.

"Baby Sullivan Number Two."

John looked confused at first, but then slowly, ever so slowly, the realization dawned. Tears of elation sprang to his eyes. Deep inside, a giggle began. It started at the ends of his toes and escalated until he threw back his head and howled with laughter. It was the kind of laughter that produces a full body shake.

"You're pregnant with twins."

Kathryn beamed.

"When are we expecting?"

"The first of August."

Before she could say another word, he caught her up in his arms, twirled her around, and smothered her face in a plethora of kisses.

The glowing embers in the fireplace were still emitting a surprising amount of heat throughout the house when they climbed into bed later that night. Kathryn tossed the quilt toward the end of the bed and lay down beside her husband.

"Penny for your thoughts," she whispered.

"At a time like this, I wish my mom was still alive."

Her voice was filled with compassion. "I know."

However, she didn't know; she couldn't possibly know. Life had always been kind to Kathryn Clarke Sullivan, adhered to her calendar, played by her rules, and certainly had never taken anyone she loved. The only thing she knew for certain was that she was pregnant with her husband's children, and she was deliriously happy.

CHAPTER TWELVE

THE BIRTH OF GRANDCHILDREN WAS the impetus that Kathryn's father needed to retire from South Carolina's judicial system. With their social calendar intentionally cleared the last half of July, and the entire month of August, her parents anxiously awaited the momentous news of the twin's impending arrival. They had their luggage packed and loaded into the trunk of the Chrysler, ready to travel to Asheville the moment they received word that their daughter was in labor.

Kathryn prided herself on being punctual, so no one, except possibly the obstetrician, was surprised when she gave birth to the twins on her due date. Six and half months after cutting paper snowflakes, thirty-one pounds and a single stretch-mark later, she carried two bundles out of the hospital. Jack was wrapped in blue, and Harper was snuggled in pink.

Her parents were a tremendous help that first two weeks home from the hospital. Night feedings, diaper changes, trips to the grocery store, and piles of laundry were handled smoothly with four pairs of adult hands; so efficiently, in fact, that Kathryn had the misconception that she could handle the workload alone. After the obstetrician gave her permission to resume driving, she insisted upon her parents' return to Charleston.

Her mother was visibly upset. "The twins are only two-weeks old."

"John is here to help me."

"Only until the day-after tomorrow. How are you going to manage when he goes back to work?"

"If I can handle a classroom of fifteen active kindergarten students,

I'm sure that I can manage two newborns. It's not like they are going to run into the street and get hit by a car."

"You don't have any idea of the work involved in caring for twins. Your grandmother stayed with me the first two months when you and your brother were born."

"Harper and Jack will be fine."

"I'm not worried about the babies. I'm worried about you."

Kathryn's father intervened on her behalf. "Nancy, it's time for us to go home. I'm ready to sleep in my own bed. Besides, our daughter and her husband need time alone with their new babies. What do they call it these days? Bonding? Like the mother duck and her babies."

"I'll agree to go, only if my daughter promises to call when she needs help."

"I'll call."

"You promise?"

"I promise."

"OK. I'll start packing." Her mother pursed her lips. "But I still think that we are making a big mistake."

KATHRYN WAS CONSUMED IN DOUBLE cycles of diapers and feedings. Dirty laundry piled up on the floor; toilets were left un-scoured; food spoiled in the refrigerator; and dust accumulated everywhere. She lost track of the season, the month, and the time.

The day for the twin's four-month check crept up quietly behind mounds of dirty diapers and took her completely by surprise. They arrived thirty minutes late for their scheduled appointments.

Stricken with embarrassment, she jiggled the baby buggy with the toe of her penny loafers. The infants were napping, scarcely aware of the agitation packed into the steady jiggle of their mother's foot.

"I-I'm sorry we're late," she stammered.

The twin's pediatrician flipped the pages on their charts as he entered the examination room. "It's no problem. I had a baby with croup this morning, which set me back twenty minutes, and I am still behind schedule."

Robert Rhodes, John's senior partner and best friend, planted a kiss on Kathryn's forehead and straddled the stool beside her. He set the clipboard down on the exam table and looked at her. The clothes that she wore hung loosely from her frightfully thin frame, and the carefully applied makeup didn't conceal the dark raccoon circles around her eyes. He removed his glasses and cradled them across his outstretched leg.

She flinched under his scrutiny.

"My dear, you can't keep going at this rate. You need help with the twins."

"Has John talked to you?"

"He didn't have to say a word to me." Robert laughed. "The white coat, which he's wearing for Monday morning's hospital rounds, looks like it has been wadded on a closet shelf for months."

"With the twins, I don't have time to iron."

"No one expects you to iron. But you do need to find some help."

"Did John tell you about Thanksgiving dinner?"

"The canned Spam?"

"It went well with the frozen pumpkin pie."

After a hearty laugh, his tone grew serious. "Kathryn, you cannot go on like this. John is worried about you, and so am I." He shifted on the stool. "Please forgive me, but I have to ask. Is this a matter of pride?"

Her throat tightened. "My mother said that I didn't know the work involved in taking care of twins."

"Who does?" he asked. "There is an exponential difference between taking care of one and two babies. Admitting that you need help isn't a sign of weakness. It is the reality of being a new mother, especially the mother of twins."

"OK. I give up. I'm throwing in the towel."

He raised his eyebrows.

"I promise," she conceded softly. "I'll call my parents."

"I'm not saying that you have to call your parents. Just get some help. You can always hire a housekeeper or a nanny."

"No, I can't," she sighed. "I promised my mother that I would call her, as soon as I needed help."

"Then your parents, it is." He picked up the charts. "Now let's take a look at these sleeping babies. Who should I wake-up first?"

HER PARENTS ARRIVED TWO DAYS later with all the fanfare of Cunard's *Queen Mary 2* docking in Liverpool on her birthday tour. Leather suitcases, packages wrapped in brown paper, two hanging clothes bags, and gifts purchased from an exclusive children's boutique in Charleston were hauled from their gold Chrysler.

They easily settled into their roles as grandparents, housekeeper, and butler. Her father went to the grocery store, while her mother fed the babies and put them down for a nap.

For the first time in months, Kathryn began to relax. She was folding diapers at the kitchen table when her mother kissed her on the cheek. "Why don't you take a nap while the twins are sleeping? You look exhausted."

Kathryn was yanking the quilt over her shoulders when her mother tapped at the bedroom door. "Are you still awake?"

"Come in, Mother."

Her mother lugged an assortment of shopping bags, all shapes and sizes, into the bedroom. "Before you go to sleep, I want you to take a peek at these gowns."

"Right now?"

"It will only take a minute."

Kathryn stared at the gowns, which her mother pulled from one of the shopping bag. Pure white, crocheted with matching bonnets, they looked like baptismal gowns.

"Thank you," she said stiffly. "They are lovely."

"What's wrong?"

"It's just that they are," she hesitated, not wanting to hurt her mother's feelings, "well...uh, identical."

Her mother was incredulous. "Of course they're identical. You have twins."

"I'm not dressing the twins alike."

"So I have noticed."

"Mother, I want them to be individuals."

"I always dressed you and Kevin alike."

"I know. My point is--"

Her mother changed the subject. "See if you like these outfits. They aren't the same." She opened another shopping bag.

Kathryn looked at the outfits in her mother's hands. They were adorable infant gowns, long-sleeved with Peter Pan collars, obviously purchased from an expensive children's boutique. One was blue, and the other one was pink. Otherwise, they too were identical.

Before she could comment, her mother began foraging through the largest shopping bag. "Close your eyes, dear. I brought a special treat for you."

She pulled out a plush full-length, terrycloth robe, pale pink, with deep pockets and wide cuffed sleeves. Beautifully scripted in white floss on the upper left were the initials *kSc.*

Realizing that her mother was totally unpredictable, Kathryn's heart softened. One minute her mother was the bane of her existence, like a brier jabbing into her foot; the next minute, her mother was a gentle and soothing balm for all of life's troubles.

When she awakened from a luxurious nap, John was sitting beside her, kissing the palm of her hand.

"How are the babies?" she asked.

"They're absolutely fine. Your father is entertaining Jack with his rattle while your mother finishes giving Harper a bottle."

"What time is it?"

"It's about five o'clock."

"You're home early."

"My last patient canceled." John reached inside his coat pocket. "Guess what? I have an early Christmas present for you."

"Christmas is still two weeks away."

"I know, but I want you to open it now."

Simple but elegant, the message inside the card was a heart-felt declaration of his love.

Christmas 1964

Dearest Kathryn,

You are one-of-a-kind... the only one for me.

I am forever yours,

John

Kathryn suspected that the tiny gift box in John's hand contained a charm commemorating the twins' births. A charm such as a pair of booties or a baby's bottle or possibly a buggy with wheels that actually turned. Never in her wildest dreams would she have imagined that the small box wrapped in silver and tied with a red bow contained two separate charms. They were both snowflakes, translucent, similar but certainly not identical.

A SUDDEN CHILL SUGGESTED THE need to nudge the thermostat a few degrees higher. The basement furnace groaned as she notched the thermostat further to the right until it settled on a comfortable, seventy-four degrees.

Once again, she spoke to John as though he was sitting at the kitchen table. "I know it's warm in here, but my joints ache more than usual today. I've not been feeling well since you've been gone."

She touched the snowflakes on her bracelet. "It's ironic, don't you think? I spent years establishing an identity to call my own. However, when you died, a part of me died with you."

CHAPTER THIRTEEN

GLUED TO THE TV FOR two days, the nation cheered wildly on April 17, 1970, as *Apollo* 13 completed its most crucial mission, using the lunar module as a "lifeboat" to re-enter the Earth's atmosphere and splash down in the Pacific Ocean. Less than two weeks later the nation was stunned when guardsmen at Kent State fired into a crowd of students protesting our invasion in Cambodia, killing four students and wounding nine others. The Beatles rocked the world May 8th with its release of another smash hit while rumors spread about their impending break-up.

Spring, 1970, marked a time of change, and Kathryn was begging for a change in her corner of the world as well.

The seams on their two-bedroom home were ready to burst. Off the chart in height and weight, Jack looked more like a stocky third-grader awaiting his next growth spurt than a first-grader who had just turned six the previous summer. Harper was pencil-thin like Kathryn and easily the tallest girl in her class.

It was no wonder. Measuring six feet and four inches in his stocking feet, John's father was affectionately known throughout the farming community of Asheville as a gentle giant. His ways were simple and unsophisticated; his business dealings fair. Towering over most men, not only in height but in character, he was what the Appalachians referred to as "all wool and a yard wide." He was genuine from head to toe.

Kathryn opened the back of her station wagon. "William, I'm sorry to clutter your attic with these boxes. We don't have any room to spare."

"I'm glad to help." John's father lifted a cardboard box from the back of the car..

His third-floor attic was her repository, crammed with a crib, high chair, stroller, and boxes upon boxes of clothes. Like a squirrel storing nuts for the winter, she stockpiled items in the hope that John and she would someday have another child. Unfortunately, pregnancy was eluding her.

After William closed the attic door, they walked down two flights of stairs.

"May I offer you a glass of sweet tea?"

"Just half of a glass. I'm taking the children out for ice cream this afternoon."

"When is the last day of school?"

"Tomorrow. That's plenty of ice for me," she said.

"Do I have the pleasure of having the entire family for Saturday morning breakfast?"

"We'll all be here."

"French toast and scrambled eggs?"

"It sounds delicious." She watched him pour the tea. "What can I bring?"

"Just your work gloves. We've a full day's work ahead of us."

"Before I forget, the children asked if they can feed the baby ducks while John mucks out the barn."

He set the pitcher on the counter. "Sure. Just remember--"

"No bread; only dog food."

"I've taught you well."

"Or maybe, I'm just a quick learner."

As they sipped their tea, they chatted about the fungus that seemed to be attacking the tomato plants, the boards in the hay loft that needed replacing, and the number of hours that John was working each week.

"The practice is booming, and money is good," she said. "Did John tell you that his partner bought a new house on the east side of town? I haven't seen it yet, but I hear that it's lovely."

William set down his tea glass. "Have either of you thought about buying a new house?"

"Why? Are you tired of the paraphernalia that I'm storing in your attic?"

"That's not what I'm suggesting. Those boxes are welcome to stay in the attic until I'm in my grave, and you decide to sell this place," he said. "I can't help but wonder if your house is big enough to accommodate a family of four, especially at the rate that the twins are growing."

"We are definitely cramped; that's for sure. I've tried talking to John, but he refuses to consider another house until we have more cash in the bank."

"More tea?" he asked.

Kathryn shook her head. "I've had plenty, thank you."

"When John was a little boy, we scrimped and saved for everything we got. The first few years after Rose died were especially difficult. I cut back on my hours at the mill in order to be home with the boys by nightfall."

She was silent.

He took a sip of tea. "I always told my boys that borrowing was a sign of impatience."

"Your son learned that lesson well."

"Maybe too well," he said pensively.

Jack and Harper were tucked in their beds for the night, their voices melting into whispers. Kathryn curled up beside John on the love seat in the living room.

"I had an interesting discussion with your father today."

"Where did you see him?"

"I hauled those boxes of clothes out to the farm."

"And?"

"He asked me if we ever talk about buying a new house."

His silence was deafening.

"I heard that the school board is looking to hire a handful of kindergarten and first-grade teachers next year. It would be a way for me to supplement our income."

"I don't want my wife working."

"John, I just don't understand why you are being so unreasonable."

"There's nothing unreasonable about a man not wanting his wife to work."

"We have outgrown this house."

As John leaned forward, his eyes filled with tears. "I remember racing my brother home from the bus stop every afternoon. We pushed open the back door and yelled, 'Mama. We're home.' Then we hung our jackets on the coat rack and kicked off our shoes. My mother was always in the kitchen anticipating our arrival. Her hair was tied in a bun, and she wore a faded yellow apron and a wonderful smile. Mama had a smile that would light up the world."

Kathryn said nothing.

"On the table were peanut butter and jelly sandwiches and glasses of milk. Iced cold. She must have poured the milk the minute the school bus came down the street. Every afternoon, the three of us sat at the kitchen table and told silly stories. Our laughter filled the room. It was the best part of my day."

He cleared his throat.

"Mama got sick when I was in the third grade. Trevor was only in the second grade. We raced from the bus stop every afternoon and hung our jackets on the rack; but, Mama wasn't waiting in the kitchen anymore."

Kathryn placed her hand on his arm.

"My job was to get the peanut butter out of the cabinet, because Trevor wasn't tall enough to reach the jar, even with the footstool. We carried our sandwiches to her bedroom and sat beside her on the bed. We didn't laugh much that year. By the time I was in the fourth grade, my mother was gone."

Kathryn clasped his hands.

"That's why I'm being unreasonable," he said. "I don't care if we live in a shack or a palace. I want you here, at home, when Harper and Jack get off that school bus. I want peanut butter and jelly sandwiches, oatmeal cookies, ice cream, or whatever you want as long as the three of you are together, laughing. I don't want our children alone."

He removed his hands from her grasp and wiped away the tears from his eyes.

"I know that we need a bigger house. We'll have one soon enough; I promise you."

Saturday promised to be a magnificent day at the farm. Lining the driveway along the pasture fence was a row of dogwoods. The rays of the morning sun coursed through their branches. A single shaft of sunlight streamed through an opened barn door, brilliantly illuminating the three stalls on the right side of the barn. The only light reaching the stalls on the left side--where John and his father worked side by side pitching hay--was from a sixty-watt bulb suspended by a thin wire.

Kathryn paused outside the barn door, eavesdropping on a conversation between her husband and her father-in-law.

John jabbed his pitchfork into the hay. "Dad, is something wrong?"

"Nope," William said. "My belly's full, and I've got a roof over my head."

"You got that furrow between your brows, the one you always get when something's bothering you."

"Son, take this pitchfork. It's bigger."

"Thanks."

"I've been thinking of ways to save space in this barn. We can board two of the horses in a single stall."

"Dad, what has gotten into you? You know there isn't enough room for two horses in one stall."

John's father pulled a handkerchief from his back pocket and wiped the sweat from his brow.

"I guess you're right. A horse needs space to call its own. And so do your children."

With no more words to say, William Sullivan stuffed the handkerchief into his pocket, hoisted a saddle from the rack, and walked through the opened door into the blinding sunlight.

John heard his father call to the twins, who had just finished feeding the goats scraps of French toast and scrambled eggs left over from breakfast, "Which of you, ornery munchkins, wants to saddle Belle?"

Pulling the pitchfork out of the hay, John jabbed the prongs into the stall's soft soil, wrapped his hands around the pitchfork's handle, and leaned forward with all his weight. He wiped the sweat from his brow and breathed in the fresh hay's delicious, sweet-smelling aroma. His dad was right. If the twins were expected to feed the goats and saddle their own mare, they deserved separate bedrooms.

CHAPTER FOURTEEN

John called Martha Howard on Monday morning with the news that their home was for sale. Not only was she the mother of one of his patients, Martha was heralded as one of the best real estate agents in both Asheville and the surrounding area. Competitors likened her to a blood hound which, with its nose to the ground, could sniff out sales on houses yet to be shown.

It seemed surprising when the months of July, August, and September passed without a single offer on John and Kathryn's house. After all, the home was adorable, immaculate, in a great neighborhood, and reasonably priced.

Whack. Kathryn's floured hand hit the lump of bread dough. Placing the heel of her left hand on the back of her right one, she kneaded the dough with a steady rhythm, using the force of her arms to compress the dough away from her and then fold it back over itself. One partial turn and she began the whole process over again. The lump of dough didn't stand a chance against her fury.

"John, it was humiliating. The man's only remark about our home was that the color scheme seemed antiquated."

"Antiquated? The walls are off-white. How is that antiquated?" he asked.

Using the back of her hand, she pushed a strand of hair away from her face. "You should have seen his bow tie. It was chartreuse."

"Kathryn, you need to forget it. By the way, what's for dinner?"

"Tuna noodle casserole." She folded the dough and gave it another hard whack. "I will never relinquish my home to such a crotchety, garish old man. If only I had Mother's horn-rimmed reading glasses, the ones with the turtle shell, I would have--"

John stood up. "You would have what?"

"I would have glared at him, right over the rims. You know; the way my mother does when she is disgusted with a salesman."

"I know the look, alright," he muttered.

"And I would have said, 'My home is very livable, thank you very much.'"

Finally tired of the whole charade, he threw his hands into the air. "Who cares about the color of the man's necktie? We're selling a house, not neckties."

She swiped at another strand of hair. "I hate having our house on the market. When is it going to sell?"

"It's never going to sell, if you keep scaring off the buyers."

"What is that supposed to mean?"

"We've already lost two potential buyers, because you followed them around the house playing tour guide."

"Where did you get that idea?"

"From the real estate agent."

"Well, I've never heard of anything so crazy."

"Martha has two showings scheduled tomorrow. One is at ten o'clock, and the other one is at noon. The first one is a young couple, no kids, who want to buy a starter home. The second couple is older. Martha thinks that they are looking for an investment property."

"Does she realize that tomorrow is Saturday? What are the children to do for two hours while she is showing the house?"

"Martha doesn't want us at home tomorrow."

"Any of us?"

"No."

"Where does she expect us to go?"

"Anywhere, but here."

"And where do you suggest?"

"I've already given it some thought."

"And?" she asked.

He brushed the flour from her cheek. "Trust me. I have a great idea."

"Why do I think that it's a surprise?"

"Because it is." He kissed her on the cheek; then, he picked up his newspaper and walked out of the kitchen.

And for the first time since morning, she smiled.

Carloads and busloads of tourists travel every year to Pisgah National Forest to revel in the rugged beauty of the Blue Ridge Mountains. The area touts well-mapped hiking trails, gorgeous waterfalls, and scenic vistas. Tourists are invited to visit the Cradle of Forestry, spend an afternoon white-water rafting, or slosh knee-deep in icy steams in hope of hooking a trout.

John didn't have any of these activities in mind as he packed the family station wagon the following morning. On the back seat was an old milk crate heaped with metal pie pans and plastic margarine dishes and pieces of screen mounted on wooden frames. Jammed on top of the crate was a duffel bag, filled with hats, suntan lotion, and extra sets of clothes for the twins. Sitting beside the milk crate was a cooler of peanut butter sandwiches and grape soda. The twins sat on the middle seat, clutching their beach towels. On the floor of the front seat, straddled between Kathryn's feet, was a bag of fresh apples.

From Asheville, John drove south on the Blue Ridge Parkway toward Pisgah National Forest. Without warning, he pulled off into a parking area alongside the road.

"Out of the car, everybody," he said. "We're here."

Jack peered out the window. "Where are we?"

"Looking Glass Falls. Don't forget your towels. You're going to get wet."

Having unloaded the car, he herded his family downstream, far from the deep pool at the base of the falls, where they could plant their feet in the gravel creek bed and not be knocked off balance by the current. He amazed the twins by crawling along the bank on his hands and knees and pointing out areas where swift flowing spring rains and

72

melting snow carved away softer rock. He explained that these areas were prime examples of weathering and erosion. With tremendous patience, he taught them how to use their pie pans to scoop out sediment from the creek bed and to pour the contents directly onto the screen. He demonstrated how to lower the screen into the water and gently swishing away the soil and dirt.

"Sparkles, Daddy, look." Harper pointed to tiny specks scattered on her screen.

"Those are flecks of mica."

"What's this?" Jack yelled over the roar of the waterfall, which plunged more than sixty feet in a single drop. Balancing the screen in both hands, he splashed his way across the stream.

"Look at the brown and gold. That's topaz."

John was happy to see that his son was enthralled with their adventure. Unlike other boys his age, Jack was bored by outdoor activities, especially sports. He was a born reader, which is not a bad thing in itself; however, as a pediatrician, John was genuinely concerned that his son didn't get enough fresh air or exercise.

It tickled John that Kathryn had stopped worrying about the bread dough embedded beneath her nails and had started enjoying the family adventure. With the sun was directly overhead, and the children grumbling about being hungry, he decided to let her slosh downstream while he set up their picnic lunch. He had barely opened the largest cooler when he heard her scream.

"John. Hurry!"

Panic cut him to the core. That day in Pisgah National Forest, John Sullivan outran, out-powered, and out-jumped the best that any comic book superhero has to offer.

He was gasping for air. "What?"

"Just look."

There in Kathryn's screen, amidst the gravel, was a magnificent sapphire, deep royal blue, pure in both color and clarity.

"Don't ever scare me like that again," he shouted. Then he turned on his heel and trudged back upstream, forgetting to comment on her spectacular gemstone.

They spent the remainder of the afternoon hiking the trail to Looking Glass Dome. Then, as the perfect ending to a beautiful day, they took a couple of trips down Sliding Rock. Luckily for the twins, their life jackets were in the back of the station wagon. Though Harper and Jack had completed two summers of swim lessons and were fairly proficient in the water, Kathryn was aware of the deep pool at the bottom of the rock and insisted that they wear life jackets.

As John unloaded the cooler and gemstone mining equipment, and the twins raced into their bedroom to change out of their wet clothes, Kathryn headed to the laundry room. It was a tiny porch, off the kitchen, which John enclosed after the twins were born. Prior to that, Kathryn had been making weekly trips to the laundromat on the other side of town.

As she passed through the kitchen, she noticed a piece of yellow scratch paper sitting on the tile counter. It note from their real estate agent: *Call me when you get home. I have a contract in hand, which needs your consideration. Martha.*

That evening, John and Kathryn stood in their living room, dumbfounded by the contract that Martha presented them. The older couple in search of investment property offered two thousand dollars less than the listing price but promised cash in hand if they agreed to a late March closing.

John was trembling with excitement. "Tell them that it's a done deal."

OCTOBER AND NOVEMBER WERE A forgotten memory as Kathryn and John feverishly squeezed house hunting into their already demanding schedules. Before they knew it, the Christmas holidays were knocking at their door.

The Christmas Eve service at St. Paul's Cathedral was glorious but long. By the time Harper and Jack changed into their new flannel pajamas and set out a tall glass of milk and plate of sugar cookies for Santa, they were giddy with exhaustion.

The next morning, Kathryn lay tucked in the crook of John's arm, enjoying a brief moment of solitude before the sun peeked above the horizon. She was prepared for the festivities to begin. The Christmas tree stood in the corner of their living room, decorated with tiny pinecones and sand dollars and antique ornaments bequeathed to her from a great aunt. Lying beneath the tree's boughs were piles and piles of beautifully wrapped presents.

She hoped that Jack and Harper would sleep until at least eight o'clock. However, her hopes were dashed at six-thirty when the creak of bedsprings, footsteps scurrying back and forth to the bathroom, and muffled giggles told her that the children were wide awake.

John's rule was unbending: no peeking at the stockings on the mantel or at the presents under the tree until the little hand was pointing to the seven, and the big hand was pointing on the twelve. Except for trips to the bathroom, the children were basically cloistered in their bedroom on Christmas morning until seven o'clock.

Neither a minute too late nor a minute too soon, Jack and Harper tumbled into their parents' bed, bouncing and shouting, "Merry Christmas."

Abhorring the frenzy which erupts in most American households on Christmas Day, Kathryn made an attempt to maintain some semblance of order. While she helped Harper and Jack take down their stockings from the mantelpiece, John hauled an armload of dry firewood from the back porch and stacked it on the fireplace grate.

With the twins seated cross-legged on the floor, their stockings in their laps, she asked, "Are you ready?"

Jack clapped, and Harper cheered.

"Do you remember the rules?"

"We're not allowed to peek inside our stockings until you say, 'Go.'"

"Correct." She counted slowly, "One...two...three...go!"

An assortment of trinkets and candies tumbled from Harper's stocking onto the hardwood floor. Enchanted, she plowed through her pile, squealing about a new plastic jump rope and the fake fingernail polish, a large box of crayons and the chocolate reindeer.

Everything about Jack was methodical. Sitting on his knees and readjusting his glasses, he patiently waited for his sister to finish. As her squeals of delight died down, he began removing one item at a time from his stocking. His eyes sparkled when he saw an inflatable galaxy beach ball hidden in the assortment of miniature toy cars and chocolate candies.

Harper was the impatient and impertinent one. "It's taking Jack too long. Why can't I open Santa's presents?"

Kathryn snapped her fingers. "That's enough complaining, young lady."

Jack was the first one to open a gift from Santa. His loud outburst over a backyard telescope caught the entire family, including his twin, completely by surprise. Harper hugged the giant stuffed palomino pony and promised never to let it go. Their mouths dropped open when John rolled two bicycles with training wheels from the laundry room.

Family tradition dictated that John's gift for Kathryn was the last gift of the morning. Snuggling beside the children on the love seat, she read his card aloud.

Christmas 1970

Dear Kathryn,

Sharing life's surprises with you makes everyday a delight.

Yours eternally,

John

Inside the box from Nora's Jewelry store was a royal blue sapphire, pure in both clarity and color, beautifully set in silver.

John looked sheepish. "I hope that you don't mind, but I raided your dresser drawers."

She was stunned. "Is this the sapphire that I found in the creek?"

"It is," he answered. "I hope the setting's okay."

"It's gorgeous, absolutely gorgeous." She left the love seat and hugged him. "Now, I have a little surprise for you."

Motioning for the children to get up, she reached between the two cushions of the love seat and withdrew a tiny box. The box's size, the silver foil, and the red bow were surprisingly reminiscent of a gift bought from Nora's Jewelry store.

He was completely baffled. Christmas and birthday gifts from Kathryn basically resembled her approach to life--practical and predictable, no risks and no surprises. Floor mats for his truck, golf umbrellas, and new hedge trimmers were specific examples.

"What's this?"

"Open it."

"Daddy, what is it?"

"I don't know. Let's take a look."

He tore off the wrapping paper and removed the lid from the box, all the while casting questioning glances in Kathryn's direction. Smiling, she stood with her arms wrapped around the children.

A puzzled look on his face, he removed the gift. Sparkling in the light of the tiffany lamp was a charm. It was an iridescent snowflake.

Elated, John rushed over to Kathryn and plastered her face with kisses. Laughing, he kissed Harper and Jack.

"Daddy, what is it?

His voice quivered. "We're having a baby."

The twins whooped with excitement as they jumped up and down. John dragged Kathryn to the middle of the room and twirled her under his arm. Theirs was the perfect life.

AS SHE REPLACED THE CARD inside its rightful envelope, Kathryn chastised herself for acting like a sentimental old fool.

She twisted in her chair to see the clock over the stove, and then she began to cry. The face of the clock blurred through a film of tears. Was it twenty minutes until eleven or twenty minutes until twelve? Her tears made it difficult to distinguish the time, but then again, it really didn't matter.

She twisted back around in her chair and looked at the blue sapphire on her bracelet. The gem was still stunning and flawless, even after nearly forty years.

Why hadn't their perfect world remained similarly untainted and unscathed?

Facing John's empty chair, she implored, "You were the amateur geologist. Why didn't you warn me that life would erode the soft places of my heart?"

CHAPTER FIFTEEN

A S WINTER RELINQUISHED ITS ICY grip on the mountains and gave way to yellow daffodils and pink crocuses poking their heads through the ground, Kathryn and John began to get nervous. Only one month remained before the contract on their home would be signed. They needed to find a house to buy; otherwise, their family of four, soon to be five, would be rendered homeless.

Kathryn sat perfectly still in the front seat of the car, lips pursed in a thin line and eyes staring straight ahead. Compared to the emotional turmoil attacking her stomach, the baby's movement at twenty weeks was only a flutter. She smoothed the brown leather gloves draped across her lap. The gloves, mirror images of each other, lay perfectly matched on top of her bulging abdomen.

She admired the way that Martha expertly backed her flashy red Fiat out of the driveway. There wasn't anything subtle about their real estate agent. Less like a statement and more like a billboard, everything surrounding Martha shouted financial success. An agent of Martha's caliber and expensive tastes obviously hauled in a tremendous paycheck.

She took one final glance at the house for sale and sighed; it was the third house of the morning, and by far, the best.

John fidgeted nervously in the backseat as the Fiat turned onto the main thoroughfare. As they passed by the second traffic light, he poked his nose through the space between the driver and front passenger seats. "What did you think of that house?"

"There's no need to discuss it. The house is definitely out of our price range." If Kathryn hadn't been so agitated, she would have laughed at his mediocre attempt to appear nonchalant.

"That's not what I asked."

"What do you want me to say, John?" she snapped. "It's gorgeous, stunning, perfect, what I've always wanted." Her voice trailed off.

Shifting her gaze, she peered out the passenger window. Tears of frustration coalesced like raindrops converging into dark thunderclouds. She appreciated that for once Martha was being discreet, staying focused on the road and remaining silent.

The house, a Tudor revival, was the complete package. Every square inch dazzled Kathryn. The front gables over the arched windows reminded her of something from a fairy tale. She was enchanted by the steep roof lines with multiple breaks and varying pitches. Decorative half timbers on the exterior and large grey stones were suggestive of post and beam construction from the Middle Ages.

The interior of the house was as intricate as the exterior. Each room downstairs, including the master bedroom, had ten-foot ceilings and beautifully hand crafted crown molding. The foyer, kitchen, and utility room floors were laid with large gray slabs of tile imported from Italy. She was stunned by two stone fireplaces, one in the living room and one in the family room; both lined by built-in mahogany book cases. There wasn't a single detail that had been overlooked.

Martha explained that the house was new, built by a local contractor in the hope of wooing his wayward wife back home. Unfortunately, both the house and the contractor were unsuccessful. She served him divorce papers the day before the tile was to be laid. The house went on the market two weeks later.

While Kathryn admired the builder's attention to detail, John looked at the practical aspects of the home. The utility room off of the two-car garage had cabinets to the ceiling. There were laundry shoots from the second floor into the basement, and a sprinkler system had been installed in both the front and back yards. Located in an excellent school district, the house was definitely a good investment. One day, it would have a great resale value.

From his back seat position, John took a deep breath. "Do you want the house?"

Kathryn twisted around as far as possible within the confines of her pregnancy and Martha's tiny sports car. Tears splashed over her lower lashes.

John directed his next statement toward Martha as she shifted the Fiat into third gear. "Offer the listing price and ask how fast we can close the deal."

MARCH ARRIVED LIKE THE PROVERBIAL lion. John and Kathryn were caught up in a whirlwind of deadlines. Loan approvals, appraisals, and inspections had to be completed by the last day of the month. Within twenty-four hours, they bought one home and sold another. Their limited belongings, packed in cardboard boxes and vegetable crates from the corner market, plus their few pieces of mismatched furniture were hauled to the new house in a horse trailer borrowed from John's father. By the end of the first week of April, the move was complete.

There was a drastic difference in square footage between the old and new houses. The furniture that fit comfortably in the nine hundred square feet on Laurel Avenue was swallowed up by a house with thirty-five hundred square feet. Scantly furnished with few rugs and no curtains, the upstairs echoed. Every movement, every whisper, and every giggle of the twins reverberated down the winding staircase to the tiled foyer and into the master bedroom.

Kathryn didn't have the luxury of being concerned with unfurnished rooms or the lack of upstairs window treatments. During the course of their move, she quietly slipped into her third trimester. Swelling each time the baby stretched for more room, her growing abdomen was a constant reminder that she had less than three months to transform one of the extra bedrooms into a suitable nursery for the baby.

She spent the last two weeks of April rummaging through wallpaper stores in Asheville, frantically searching for a colorful border to brighten the baby's room. Upon Harper's insistence, she chose a pastel print showcasing Noah and his ark. The ark was filled with four silly animals: a pink and white polka-dotted giraffe; a solid-yellow duck with a bright-orange beak; an exuberant brown monkey, looking very much like Curious George; and a goofy elephant, pale blue with green and white gingham ears.

John painted the nursery a lovely shade of yellow and pasted the wide border above the wooden chair rail. After sewing a frilly set of yellow curtains for the room's only window, Kathryn hooked a rug with a scene of Noah's ark for the nursery floor.

A stuffed bear, soft and cuddly with button eyes and an adorable sailor's suit, was the nursery's finishing touch. Jack named him, "Willy Bear." Propped in the corner of the crib, Willy Bear seemed to be waiting patiently for the baby to make his or her grand entrance--an entrance that was to come sooner rather than later.

CHAPTER SIXTEEN

IT WAS THE SECOND WEEK of June. Kathryn shifted uncomfortably in her captain's chair at the kitchen table, rubbing her lower back as she checked over the final notes for the evening's charity auction. In only two hours, John and she would be hosting the gala event, an annual black-tie affair jointly sponsored by the arts guild and historical society. Proceeds from the auction would go toward upgrading the downtown business district.

She contacted the caterer earlier in the week with the final head count. One hundred fifty-two adults would be in attendance. Items for the silent auction were numbered and arranged on tables draped in crisp white linens. Yesterday's crisis was averted when the auctioneer miraculously recovered from a severe case of laryngitis. Starching John's white long-sleeved shirt, pressing the cummerbund of his black tuxedo, and getting dressed were the only things left for her to do.

Continuing to rub her lower back, she peered out the kitchen window toward the side yard. The hillside was magnificently cloaked in mountain laurel and purple rhododendron. A breeze left over from last night's storm dislodged a handful of cherry blossoms and sent them floating gracefully toward the ground. She felt a pang of regret as she considered the florist's bill for the evening. The ox-eyed daisies and purple irises that were interspersed on the hillside would have made beautiful floral arrangements for the night's venue.

The next hour passed quickly. Having finished the ironing, she lay down on her side with her back wedged against the family room couch for a half hour nap.

John had taken Harper and Jack to his father's farm to spend the night, so the house was quiet. As she dozed off to sleep, she remembered the children chattering like squirrels, deliberating about what to pack in their overnight bags. Boots or gym shoes for riding Belle? Carrots or lettuce leaves for the baby rabbits? Mason jars or empty peanut butter jars for catching fireflies?

The sound of John's truck pulling into the garage awakened her. As she lay on the couch waiting for him to stroll through the door, Kathryn rubbed her hand back and forth across her belly, trying in vain to ease a strong Braxton Hicks contraction that suddenly gripped her. Her abdomen felt as hard as a rock.

John leaned down and kissed her forehead. "Time to get up, sleepy head. We need to be out of here in thirty minutes or less."

Thankful that she didn't have to climb the stairs to get to their bedroom, she heaved herself off the couch and waddled her way down the hall toward the vanity in their master bedroom. Yesterday, full of energy, she carried multiple loads of laundry up and down the steps. Today, the same climb would be brutal.

Kathryn helped John fasten his cufflinks. Then, she awkwardly stepped into her gown.

"Would you zip my dress?"

"I would be delighted."

After a bit of tugging to get the zipper closed, John slowly and deliberately turned her around. Gazing at her from arms' length, he drank in her beauty. Nothing went unnoticed--her hair swept up in a French braid, the strand of cultured pearls, or her protruding stomach covered in a black-and-white gown made of silk jersey.

"You look ravishing," he said hoarsely.

"I look like a beached whale." She massaged her lower back. Another Braxton Hicks contraction, this one was worse than the last. Her belly was as hard as a bowling ball.

"No, you are tantalizing."

"John, look at me. I look like an orca, dressed in a strand of cultured pearls."

"You look like a woman who is beautiful with child."

"I wasn't this big with the twins."

"Actually, you were bigger."

"I didn't gain forty-two pounds with Harper and Jack."

He knew that once she introduced the issue of weight gain, the conversation had reached a dead end. He picked up the beaded evening bag and black shawl, which sat on the end of their bed. "Are you taking these?"

She nodded.

He glanced at the clock beside the bed. "We need to go. I'll get the bedroom lights."

An impressive structure, built from granite boulders that had been hauled up the side of a mountain, Grove Park Inn was a perfect venue for the auction. With the sun setting over the mountains, casting vibrant shades of purple and orange across the valley, John and Kathryn graciously greeted guests in the hotel lobby and directed them toward the silent auction down the hall.

After a time, the crowd coming through the front door thinned.

John turned toward Kathryn and noticed a drawn look on her face. "Are you okay?"

"I'm fine. My back is just a little sore from standing; that's all. I'm going to slip into the ladies' room for a moment."

She crossed the tremendous lobby and was passing by one of the huge stone fireplaces when she heard a familiar voice warmly call her name. She turned to see Martha, their real estate agent, hurrying in spiked heels to catch up with her. Martha was as flamboyant as ever in her strapless gown and long silk scarf. "How is the house?"

"It's wonderful."

"You know that you have all the women here green with envy."

A sharp pain stabbed Kathryn in the back.

Keeping her eyes peeled for a potential client, Martha readjusted the strap on her heels. "John is the most dashing man in the lobby, and you look absolutely sensational."

Searing pain again jolted her back, and her abdomen tightened into a huge contraction. She grabbed for the fireplace to catch her balance and was aghast when water splashed on the floor between her feet.

"Martha," she cried. "Get John. Hurry."

The next fifteen minutes were a blur. The contractions were now coming one right after another. Unwilling to make a scene, she begged John not to call an ambulance. Trying not to moan, she steadied herself on the edge of an oversized wooden rocking chair as they waited for the valet to bring the car around to the front of the hotel. Relief washed over her when John lifted her into the back seat of their old Buick.

He maneuvered the car down the winding mountain road with the flashers going. "Kathryn, don't push. I'm driving as fast as I can."

Frustrated by the long line of traffic at the bottom of the hill, he slammed his hand against the steering wheel. Minutes passed as they sat at the stop sign, waiting for an opportunity to merge. He glanced at her in his rear-view mirror and noticed the beads of sweat forming on her brow.

"Hold on, honey. You can do this. Just a few more minutes."

"John---"

The desperation in her voice told him that she didn't have a few more minutes. He had to find a place to stop, the sooner the better, preferably a place with good lighting. He spied a run-down gas station on the right, barely a hundred yards away. A neon sign, blinking TEXACO, seemed to be the only light available.

John pulled into the gas station's parking lot. Noticing that a side door was propped open and a light was shining inside the garage, he jumped from the car and ran to the opened door.

A young man with long, shaggy hair straightened up from a car engine and wiped his greasy hands on an orange rag sticking out of his pants pocket. "We're closed."

"Get on the phone and call an ambulance. My wife is having our baby."

Choosing to ignore the young man's look of disbelief, John raced back to Kathryn's side. He positioned her on her back, so that he could examine her. As he lifted her gown above her knees, his worst fears were realized. Delivery was imminent. The baby was crowning, and Kathryn was ready to push.

The gas-station attendant sauntered to the car, still wiping his hands on the rag. "The ambulance is coming."

"There's no time." John slung the jacket to his tuxedo over the front passenger seat and began removing his cufflinks. "We're having a baby, and I need your help."

Suddenly, the young man looked like a frightened, little boy. "I don't know nothin' about babies."

"Don't worry. I'm a doctor," John said. "I need you to find a flashlight, string, scissors and clean rags. Got it?"

Neither he nor Kathryn was willing to acknowledge that the last baby delivered by his hands had been in medical school.

"A flashlight, twine, scissors, and rags," the young man repeated. "I got it."

"Clean rags. Please."

Two more contractions swept over Kathryn by the time the attendant sprinted into the garage and returned with the supplies. This time his hands were clean.

"Hold the flashlight steady, right there," John instructed. You're doing great."

The light wavered back and forth with each tremble of the young man's hand.

"Alright, sweetheart. Give me a strong push with the next contraction."

Kathryn uttered a loud groan. In the distance, the wail of an ambulance could be heard.

THE NEXT MORNING, SHE SAT up in the hospital bed and brushed the French braid out of her hair. Laying the brush in her lap, she stared in wonder at her infant son, swaddled in a pale-blue nursery blanket and cradled in John's arms. It was one of those rare moments in life when everything felt right with the world.

"I cannot believe that I gave birth to our son in the back of the old Buick. And to think that Martha said that I was the envy of every woman at the auction."

"You did a great job."

"In front of God and a service-station attendant at Shell. What will my mother say when she hears the whole story?"

"Texaco."

"What?"

"It was a Texaco station."

"I can see the headlines now: Grease monkey helps orca give birth in an abandoned gas station."

Neither Kathryn nor John could stifle their giggles. They threw back their heads and roared with laughter, releasing the pent-up emotion from the evening's dramatic delivery. As their silliness began to fade. John reached up and kissed the tip of her nose. "I adore you."

She beamed with joy. "I adore you, too."

There was a gentle rap, and the door opened.

"Excuse me, Ma'am."

"Yes?"

"How's the baby?"

She didn't recognize the young man standing at the door. He was dressed in jeans and a pressed shirt, and his long hair was slicked back in a ponytail. In his right hand was a small bouquet of ox-eyed daisies.

"Kathryn, it's our hero from the Texaco station," John exclaimed.

The young man walked across the room and handed her the bouquet of flowers. "My mama sent these."

"That is very kind," she said. "They're beautiful. Please tell your mother that I said, 'thank you."

"How's the baby?"

"He's perfect."

The young man shifted his weight uncomfortably from one foot to the other. "Well, uh, I need to go."

"What's your rush?" John asked. "Do you want to hold the baby?"

"I'm not too good with babies."

"You could have fooled me last night," he said. "Sit here in the chair and support his head like this. Like you're cradling a football."

Kathryn set her brush on the nightstand. "My name is Kathryn, and my husband's name is John. I'm afraid that we don't know your name."

"My real name is Timothy, but my friends call me Wart."

"May we call you Timothy?"

The young man nodded, never removing his eyes from the newborn. "What's his name?"

John looked curiously in Kathryn's direction. They were so busy moving to a new house and planning the auction that they never decided upon a boy's name.

"It's Timothy," she said. "No nicknames, just Timothy." At that moment, the floodgates of her heart burst open with love for her husband, her newborn son, and the Texaco attendant whose not-so-steady hand on a flashlight ushered her son safely into the world.

BABY TIMOTHY CHANGED DRASTICALLY THE first six months of his life. By the time that Christmas rolled around, he looked less like the scrawny dark-haired newborn, pictured six months earlier in the local newspaper, and more like the Gerber baby. He was pudgy with wisps of curly blonde hair and blue eyes, which intensified in color when he laughed or cried.

Unaware of traditions and charm bracelets but delighted by ornaments and Christmas tree lights, Timothy bounced in his jump seat on Christmas morning. The twins snuggled on the couch with Kathryn, anxiously awaiting the last gift of the morning.

The words on the Christmas card echoed through the living room as she read John's note aloud.

Christmas 1971

Dearest Kathryn

I checked twice. There wasn't anything about grease monkeys and orca whales in the headlines.

Your loving husband,

John

Kathryn opened the gift and laughed.

Harper tried to see in the box. "What is it?"

"An orca."

"What's an orca?"

Absorbing and retaining facts like a human sponge, Jack quickly answered. "It's a killer whale. It can weigh up to six tons."

"That's weird."

"It's not weird. An orca can grow to be twenty-three feet in length."

Harper snapped at her twin. "I wasn't talking about a real orca. I was talking about Mama's charm."

Jack rolled his eyes.

"Daddy, why did you buy a killer whale for Mama's bracelet?" she asked.

John winked at Kathryn. "It's something special between your mama and me."

Kathryn stood. "I need to put the ham in the oven. Timothy and his mother will be here at two."

She walked from the room, but not before casting a loving glance in John's direction. Despite its brevity, the glance spoke volumes. It was a love story upon which the ink had yet to dry.

SHIFTING IN THE KITCHEN CHAIR, Kathryn stretched her back. The young man with stringy hair and grimy hands now owned two gas stations near Charlotte, North Carolina. Just last week she received a Christmas card from him. It was rich with news about his wife's remission from breast cancer, the birth of their first grandchild, and his work at a local homeless shelter.

Kathryn couldn't help but smile as she clasped the killer whale dangling from her Christmas bracelet. She cherished the love language that John and she once shared, a language in which the word *orca* summoned memories of a summer evening. A black-and-white silk gown. A service-station attendant dressed in greasy coveralls. And the cry of a newborn baby splitting the night air.

CHAPTER SEVENTEEN

JOHN SLID A METAL SPATULA under a pancake and flipped it. "Hey, where is everybody? Breakfast is ready."

Clad in blue jeans and a plaid long-sleeved flannel shirt with Kathryn's cotton apron secured around his midriff, he looked more like a Red Skelton TV character than one of Asheville's more prominent pediatricians.

"Super Boy is here to save the day." Five-year-old Timothy skated across the kitchen floor in stocking feet. His arms were bent, displaying biceps that were only a figment of his young imagination.

"I'll be right down, Daddy. I need to find another ribbon for my hair." Harper's sweet voice melted her father's heart.

Jack appeared in the kitchen doorway. With his leather slippers scuffing the tile floor, he walked over to the table and poured himself a glass of milk.

Kathryn called from the top of the stairs, "Does anyone know where Timothy left his boots?"

John grabbed a pot holder. From the oven, he removed a warming tray, which held a thick slab of bacon cured on his father's farm, cooked brown and crisped to perfection. "Timothy, go help your mother find your boots. Kathryn, do you want anything to eat?"

"Just coffee and juice. Please keep Timothy with you. I'll find his boots."

Wooden chair legs scraped the kitchen floor as the children, who had picked up their breakfast plates from the counter, scooted in as close as they could get to the kitchen table.

Jack reached across the table. "Pass the syrup."

"Hold your horses," Harper retorted.

"Can't any of my children say, 'please?'"

A toothless grin spread across Timothy's face. "More juice pleeeese."

John grabbed another carton of orange juice from the door of the refrigerator. "The three of you are eating us out of house and home." It was no wonder. At age twelve, the twins were knocking on the door of middle school, and Timothy was already in kindergarten.

Harper slammed her elbows on the table. "Joey Miller says that I can't be a doctor."

John poured the juice. "Who's Joey Miller?"

"He's a really smart boy in our math class."

Jack looked up from the morning paper. "He's not that smart. He only got a 98 percentile on Mrs. Black's last test."

"How do you know?"

"Because he was bragging about it in our study hall. Didn't you hear him?"

"What did you get?"

"A point higher than Joey Miller."

"I only got a 95," Harper admitted. "I missed the decimal problem."

"Who wants more pancakes?"

Timothy held up his plate with another toothless grin. "I do. Pleeeese."

Harper dragged the conversation back to Joey Miller. "Daddy, can a girl become a doctor?"

"Of course. A girl can be anything she wants to be."

Harper smirked. "Joey Miller isn't as smart as he thinks, then."

John walked to the staircase leading up to the second floor and shouted, "Kathryn, are you coming down soon?"

"In just a minute." Little did he know that she was on her hands and knees, searching under Timothy's bed for his missing boots. Why did it have to be this morning, of all mornings, with her parents coming tomorrow and only four days until Christmas? Kathryn had no time to fool with her son's irresponsibility.

Completely unaware that his mother's frustration level had reached its breaking point, Timothy stared into space, totally engrossed in the oversized bite of a pancake stuffed inside his cheek. It was a sumptuous bite, dripping with melted butter and maple syrup.

John could hear the frustration in Kathryn's voice and knew that it was time for him to intervene. He walked back to the kitchen. "Son, when did you last see your boots?"

"Um. . . " Timothy looked to the ceiling for an answer. He knew that his father had asked him a question, but what the question entailed, he was not sure. His mind had been daydreaming about superheroes saving the world from an attack of the giant pancakes.

A few minutes later, Kathryn joined her family in the kitchen; instinctively, she reached across the table with a paper towel torn from the dispenser and wiped a coating of syrup off his face. "Timothy, I have searched your entire bedroom. Where did you leave your boots?"

"I don't know."

John wearied of the incessant struggle between his wife and son. "It's not that wet outside. His gym shoes will be fine."

"Do you know how dirty---" Her sentence was stopped in midair by the shake of John's head. It was not often that he overruled her by exerting his authority; however, when he did, she listened.

She took a sip of orange juice. "Any ideas for this year's Christmas tree?"

Timothy was the first to offer a suggestion. "It should be green."

"Green, it will be." Laughing, Kathryn fluffed the loose curls which covered Timothy's head. She regretted the day after day tussle that occurred between the two of them.

"Perfection," Harper announced. "It's simple. I want perfection."

John slid the last pancake onto Jack's plate. "What does a perfect tree look like?"

Timothy reached his hands, sticky with maple syrup, above his head. "It goes up and up and up and up, a million-billion-billion miles high."

Jack reached for the syrup. "That's impossible. That would be 10^{24} miles high."

"It should be a perfect cone, full on the bottom and pointed on the top," Harper said.

"With no bare spots," Kathryn added.

Jack cut his pancake. "What about a Norfolk Island pine?"

John placed the skillet in the sink. "Everyone, finish your breakfast. We don't want to keep your grandpa waiting."

The morning chores were completed in a record amount of time. The breakfast dishes were washed, dried and back in the cupboard; the kitchen floor was neatly swept. The children, with their teeth brushed and their beds made, were warmly dressed and buckled in the car within an hour. Timothy, of course, was wearing sneakers instead of boots.

The blinker of the station wagon signaled a right-hand turn as John pulled off of the paved highway onto a gravel road leading to his father's farm. The gravel road, Rose Lane, had been named for John's mother shortly after her passing.

"I've got the gate." Jack hopped out of the car and pulled a black knit beanie down over his ears. "Meet you at the barn."

Timothy began to whine. "I wanted to get the gate."

"Stay put," Kathryn ordered.

John turned the car to the right, veered down a sharp incline which ran along the white fence bordering the horse pasture, and pulled into the barn's wide driveway.

"There's Grandpa." Impatiently, Timothy knocked on the window to gain his grandfather's attention.

John's father secured the hitch of his flatbed trailer to the back of the old John Deere tractor before straightening and acknowledging his family's arrival. Selecting a Christmas tree from the woods above the horse pasture was a time-honored tradition, and there was no room for mishap or accident due to neglect.

"Timothy, what is your mama feeding you? You've grown a foot since last weekend."

"Pancakes and bacon."

"Mornin', Grandpa." Jack was panting after his hike down Rose Lane. The black beanie had been removed from his head and was now stuffed in his jacket pocket.

"Good morning, Jack. I see that you had gate duty again today."

"Yes, sir."

"Where's my granddaughter?"

Climbing from the car, Harper held up a pink hair ribbon. "Here I am. I was looking for my other ribbon."

"Grandpa, did you make hot chocolate?" Jack asked.

"It's on the stove. Cups are on the counter," he answered. "Be careful; it's steaming."

Kathryn nodded her consent, and the children scurried up the steps of the old farmhouse.

For the adults, the next ten minutes was a bustle of activity. John's father hauled chainsaws and gas cans from the barn, and John hoisted them onto the flatbed trailer. Kathryn gathered the woolen blankets from the house. John was loading the last of the ropes when the children returned from the old farmhouse. To no one's surprise, Timothy sported a chocolate mustache.

Perched on the tractor, John's father waited for the others to get settled in the back of the trailer. Harper and Timothy snuggled under the blankets with their parents. Jack adamantly denied being the least bit chilly and sat at the end of the trailer. His long legs dangled off the edge.

The morning's frustrations long forgotten, there was a notable lilt to Kathryn's voice as she sang the traditional cue. "Dashing through the snow...."

John's father put the tractor in motion.

With the entire family singing Christmas carols at the tops of their voices, the tractor pulled them along the gravel road, around the pasture, and up the steep grade. Sully and Savannah, the farm's two English setters, and Johnson, a chocolate brown lab, barked excitedly as they raced alongside the tractor.

Timothy scooted out from under the army blanket and jumped to the ground almost before the tractor came to a complete stop. "What about this tree?" He pointed to the closest tree in proximity. It was a tall, scraggly pine tree with huge gaps between its branches.

"Yuck," Harper carped.

Jack added to his twin's sentiments. "Can you say, 'Charlie Brown Christmas tree?'"

"Hush, you two," Kathryn said. "Timothy, we have plenty of time this morning. We don't have to take the first tree that we see. Let's find a tree that is greener than this one."

"Okay, Mama."

They stomped through the woods for nearly an hour before deciding upon a gorgeous twelve-foot blue spruce located at the edge of the woods.

John's father tugged on a pair of work gloves. "I've had my eye set on that tree for years. I knew that one day it would be a beauty.

"Dad, we don't have to take this one if you want it."

"It's yours for the taking."

Tender with affection for her father-in-law, Kathryn hugged his arm. "Thanks, Dad."

"Let's get a move on," John prodded. "We've got a Christmas tree to cut down, and it's a big one."

Buzz-buzz-buzzzz.

It took longer than either John or his father expected for the chainsaw to cut through the base of the tree. Finally, the magnificent tree crashed to the ground. Together, the family dragged the Christmas tree out of the woods, and into the clearing where the flatbed awaited their delivery.

It was after twelve o'clock noon when they pulled the tractor into the barn and loaded the tree on top of the station wagon. John and Kathryn declined Grandpa Sullivan's invitation to join him for left-over pot roast.

Disappointed, the children climbed into the station wagon and quickly rolled down their car windows for one last shout. "Bye, Grandpa. Bye, Sully. Bye, Savannah. Bye Johnson."

Kathryn hollered over the clamor coming from the backseat. "Dad, are we still on for dinner with my folks tomorrow night?"

"I wouldn't miss it for the world."

"Then, we'll see you at six o'clock."

Twenty minutes later, the station wagon reached the top of their driveway. Blocking their entrance to the garage was a big Chrysler.

Timothy knocked on the passenger window. "Grandma and Grandpa Clarke are here!"

Kathryn let out a gasp. "What are they doing here already? I don't even have fresh towels in the bathroom."

"The house is fine," John said. He drew in a long, deep breath and braced for an inevitable storm.

CHAPTER EIGHTEEN

Having inherited her mother's propensity for timeliness, Kathryn intentionally slammed the car door and marched up the steps. She swung the front door open and found her parents standing in the foyer. The thin layer of dust covering her baseboards, a slight crease marring the dining room tablecloth, even Harper's copy of *Little Women* sitting on the hardwood steps leading upstairs, seemed to blazon her shortcomings as a homemaker.

"What are you doing here?" she demanded. "We didn't expect you until tomorrow."

Her mother kissed her cheek. "Oh, you know your father, always in a hurry to beat the holiday traffic. I hope that you don't mind that we made ourselves at home."

Any chance to express her displeasure was quickly dispelled when the children stormed the front door. Engulfing their grandparents in a plethora of heartfelt hugs and kisses, they nearly knocked a glass of iced tea from the judge's hands.

Her parents' early arrival dropped the proverbial wrench into Kathryn's well-organized schedule. By the time lunch was finished, she was overwhelmed with the disorder in their home.

"Timothy, clean your mess at the table. The plate goes in the dishwasher. Don't forget to throw your napkin in the trash."

"Yes, ma'am."

"Harper, pull the bowl of gingerbread dough from the refrigerator."

"Yes, ma'am."

"Jack, you need to cover the kitchen table with wax paper."

"Ma'am?"

"Cover the kitchen table with wax paper. Then, the three of you can roll-out the dough for the gingerbread house."

"Yes, ma'am."

"Remember to measure the walls carefully. We don't want a repeat of last year's disaster."

Harper pulled a massive stoneware bowl from the refrigerator. "Grandma Clarke, did you hear about our two-dimensional gingerbread house?"

"Not to my recollection."

"Jack measured wrong, and the walls of our gingerbread house collapsed."

"It wasn't my fault. You used too much flour."

John crossed the room and grabbed a handful of homemade cookies from the Christmas tin sitting on the kitchen table. "We created a replica of Santa's house buried beneath the snow. Only the roof was showing. It was really quite clever."

Kathryn stared at the stack of cookies in his hand. "Are you going to eat all of those cookies?"

"Every morsel."

"What about hanging the holly?"

"Dessert, first."

"Don't forget to hang it over the mantle and on both bannisters. Daddy can help you."

Her mother finished wiping the counter. "What can I do to help?"

"I still have to make benne seed wafers for the neighbors. Can you get the eggs and butter out of the refrigerator? There should be a fresh lemon in the bottom drawer."

Her mother placed the items on the counter. "Where is your cast-iron skillet? I'll toast the sesame seeds."

"I toast them in the oven."

"You mean that you bake them?"

"On a cookie sheet."

Her mother shuddered in horror. "I can't imagine."

"Five minutes in a three hundred fifty degree oven and they're golden brown."

"But your great-grandmother's recipe--"

"Mother, let's be honest. The original recipe came from Africa hundreds of years ago. Chances are that they roasted them over an open fire."

"It grieves me to think that you would alter the recipe," her mother argued. "Great-grandmother loved you so much."

"Fine," Kathryn snapped. "You make the cookies while I clean the upstairs bathrooms."

How was it that her mother had the uncanny ability of always having the final word? It was never lengthy, mind you, just a few words craftily constructed; a barb intentionally dipped in poison. A poison called guilt.

As she climbed the front staircase, Kathryn hollered over her shoulder, "The cast-iron skillet is in the laundry room closet."

"Where? Oh, never mind, I'll find it."

The judge tied a piece of holly to the bannister. "Did you ever see such stubborn, pig-headed, and strong-willed women as the likes of them?"

"Let's add an extra sprig of holly right here." John purposely avoided the question.

"Did I ever tell you about the Battle of Sullivan's Island?"

"Yes sir, you did." He handed the judge another sprig of holly. "Numerous times, in fact."

"Do you realize that Fort Moultrie remains standing to this very day because of our glorious state tree? Those palmettos cushioned the blow and smothered the bombs before they could explode."

"Daddy, I can hear you downstairs."

"I know that you can hear me, baby girl. But, when are you going to listen?"

"I don't know, Daddy. I really don't know." She carried fresh towels into the upstairs bathroom and slammed the door shut.

They made it through the remainder of the day without further incident. It was past ten o'clock before everyone, including the children, retired for the night, and she had time alone to talk with John.

Kathryn brushed the luxurious brown mane cascading beyond her shoulders. "She brings the worst out in me."

John hanged his bathroom towel on the rack and looked at her reflection in the mirror. Tonight, his eyes did not feast upon the stunning curves veiled beneath a thin nightgown; instead, he searched her face, like a physician palpitating for the pain. "Do you know what your father said today?"

"Please, not another history lesson from the war."

"Your father said that there were too many women in the kitchen."

"Might I add that we were in my kitchen?"

"That's not my point."

She stopped brushing her hair. Anger flashed through her eyes as she turned on him. "Then what is your point, John?"

He pulled a chair into the vanity and sat down. "Do you remember this morning's discussion about Christmas trees?"

She bit her bottom lip.

"Timothy wanted a giant tree. What did he say, a million-billion miles high?" he asked.

"Yes. And Harper insisted upon perfection," Kathryn grumbled. "She is so much like my mother; it scares me."

"My point is that the most beautiful tree is the last one standing at the end of the day," he said. "It is always the one that bends before the storm."

"So ultimately, we are talking about the palmettos at Fort Moultrie."

John took a deep breath before continuing. "Your father is right. When you and your mother get together, there are too many women in the kitchen. Neither of you is willing to bend."

"Women in our family aren't capable of bending."

"Oh, you're very capable of bending," John said soberly. "Obstinacy is the brace that keeps both of you standing."

She rubbed her hands over her eyes. "This incessant battle with Mother is exhausting."

"Then stop fighting with her."

"How?"

"Bend." And with that final word, John gathered her in his arms and passionately kissed away the pain of a tedious and difficult day. Breakfast pancakes, Timothy's lost boots, and a tree in the woods seemed a lifetime ago.

THE NEXT FOUR DAYS WERE more than tolerable; they were actually a great deal of fun. The benne seed wafers were packaged and delivered to all neighbors. The tree was decorated, and the greenery was hung. A three-dimensional gingerbread house with candy cane shutters and a gumdrop roof graced the dining room table. Christmas morning arrived with everyone in a joyous mood.

With the stockings emptied and the presents beneath the tree unwrapped, the children piled onto the couch with their grandparents. They watched their grandfather finagling with the remote control dump truck that Santa left for Timothy. The twins looked up as John walked over to the mantle.

"It's time for your mama's gift."

Propped against the brick of the fireplace were a white envelope and a small jewelry box. All eyes focused on John as he lifted the card and gift from the mantle. He placed the items on Kathryn's lap, squeezed her hand, and whispered into her ear, "Just between us."

Christmas 1976

My dearest Kathryn,

It doesn't matter how tall or how green or how perfectly shaped. The most beautiful tree in the world is the one which bends, for it is the one which remains standing at the end of the day.

I love and adore you,

John

Knowing that some things are meant to be shared privately between husband and wife, she ignored the children's pleas for her to read the card aloud. Instead, she assuaged their curiosity by allowing them to open the gift. Harper held up the charm for everyone to see.

"What is it?" Timothy scrunched closer to his sister for a better view.

"It's a tree."

"A Sabal palmetto," Jack said.

"A what?"

The judge was delighted. He settled against the couch with his arms folded across his chest, and a smug grin plastered across his face. "A Sabal palm. None other than the state tree of South Carolina."

Kathryn glanced at the clock over the stove and chided herself for procrastinating. There was simply no reason to sit here any longer. She stood up from the kitchen table and twisted side to side. Her back was stiff from sitting too long.

Thank goodness for everyone concerned, the tug-of-war battle between Kathryn and her mother lessened after that particular Christmas. While nothing was ever confirmed, John and she had the distinct feeling that her mother received a history lesson from the judge, sometime after the holidays.

She regretted that her mother wasn't around any longer to help her make benne seed wafers. Alone, she gathered canisters and jars from the baking cabinet and dairy products from the refrigerator. Last but not least, she made her way to the laundry room closet and found the cast-iron skillet on the third shelf. Her mother was right; she never should have deviated from her great-grandmother's recipe.

CHAPTER NINETEEN

THE GRANDFATHER CLOCK CHIMED TWELVE. Frantically, Kathryn toggled the switch on her countertop mixer, trying to coax the old appliance to crank. Contending with arthritic joints, the mixer sat on metal haunches and refused to budge. It was a prehistoric dinosaur given to her as a wedding anniversary present from John. Was it the fifth or sixth anniversary? She couldn't recall.

"Give me just two batches of benne seed wafers," she pleaded, "and I promise that you can retire. I'll buy a new mixer after the holidays."

Frustrated, she unplugged the electrical cord, bent it back and forth a few times, and returned it to a different outlet. This time when she jiggled the switch, the mixer sputtered. It coughed and hiccupped and slowly began to turn. Finally, it gained enough momentum to settle into a steady whine.

Kathryn was proficient at multitasking decades before the word made its way into Webster's dictionary. Arthritis slowed her movements, but certainly not her mind. She creamed the butter, measured the sugar, sifted the flour, and whisked an egg. She was attentive to the sesame seeds sizzling and popping on the stove. Their delicious aroma, nutty with a hint of butter, delighted her olfactory senses.

For years, she had been fascinated by the way specific aromas could trigger memories, arouse emotions, and even elicit physical responses. The briny, sweet aroma of discarded shrimp shells instantly transported her back in time to languid summer days spent at their Edisto Island beach house. The earthy smell of wet leaves on a cool, dew-filled morning kindled her desire for autumn. Ironically, but not surprising to others who knew her well, the scent of cut roses rendered her nauseous.

The potpourri of Christmas fragrances--the woody scent of freshly hewn balsam and pine, the citrus aroma of pomanders covered in whole cloves; and the sweet smell of peppermint bark--ushered in countless wonderful memories of Christmases past. As she stood in the kitchen, inhaling the delicious smell of toasted sesame seeds, she was transported back to her grandmother's white clapboard house on Azalea Lane.

Grandmother Clarke's home rested in the shade of an enormous live oak tree. Its limbs, bent and twisted, scraped the ground and ascended again over a picket fence, which separated the yard from a dirt road running alongside the house. The only entrance to the yard was through a solitary gate. Its hinges, rusted from years of exposure to rain and humidity, groaned each time a visitor arrived or departed.

She distinctly remembered one cold December morning; it was the winter that she was seven or eight. Draped in her grandmother's apron, she climbed on a wooden stool in the kitchen. A whiff of the wood-burning stove, coupled with the smell of benne seed wafers baking in the oven, made her giddy with excitement. Christmas was just around the corner.

She couldn't have been happier. Spending a day with her paternal grandmother was idyllic. Even at this tender age, she was aware that choosing favorites among her grandmothers was forbidden. But could she help it if she adored Grandma Clarke's little white clapboard house, especially the way it slanted to one side? Could she help it if the austere and inflexible world of her maternal grandmother, the pristine existence of it all, from the marble floors to the perfectly folded bathroom tissue, terrified her?

While she mixed cookie dough in the warmth of the kitchen, her twin brother resumed an imaginary game of cowboys and Indians in the live oak tree. Periodically, Kevin would sneak into the kitchen, just long enough to steal a dollop of dough from the large mixing bowl sitting on the counter. Kathryn knew that it would only be a matter of time before her grandmother caught him.

On one of his more adventuresome trips indoors, Grandma Clarke yelled, "Kevin, if I see you snitch one more bite of dough; I'm going to knock you silly."

He foolishly tested the limits by sticking his hand back into the mixing bowl one more time. Without so much as pausing to wipe her greasy hands across her apron, Grandma Clarke snatched up the wooden rolling pin and chased him through the screen door.

A few minutes later, she returned. A thin film of perspiration beaded above her upper lip. "That boy wears me plum out." She straightened her apron and patted the sides and back of her hair bun. "Now where was I?"

Rumor had it that the elderly Mrs. Clarke regularly chased her disobedient grandson out of the garden, over the picket fence, and down the dirt road.

Kathryn was dropping a spoonful of dough onto a cookie sheet when the front doorbell rang. Beckoned to abandon her childhood memories of rolling pins and white picket fences, she wondered, "Who could be at my front door on Christmas Eve?"

Combing her fingers through her hair, retying the apron around her waist, she made her way down the hall to the front door. Envied by the neighbors for its statement of grandeur, Victorian in style and made of solid mahogany, her front door was a tremendous source of pride. An oval glass window, beautifully etched in mountain laurel branches by a master craftsman, graced the top half of the door. A key dangled from the lock of the deadbolt.

A quick glance through the front door window gave her a start. Either the window's etchings were obscuring her line of vision, or the limbs of an evergreen tree were smashed up against the front door's window pane. Out of the corner of her eye, she caught sight of a pink mitten poking through the branches. Baffled, she partially opened the door.

"Surprise!" Abigail shouted. "Aren't you excited? Now Santa can put presents under your tree. And I can help you decorate it."

A voice sounded from behind the tree. "Abigail, you need to move."

"Yes, Daddy."

"Kathryn, where do you want me to put this tree?"

"Brian, is that you under there? Where are my manners? Please come in." She opened the door completely. "Give me a moment to think. Let's put the tree in the living room like I always do, by the bay window facing the road."

Before he had a chance to move the tree from the front porch into the foyer, Abigail walked into the house and started toward the staircase.

"Just where do you think you are going, young lady?"

The child halted in mid-flight. "Daddy, I have to get the ornaments."

"Not in those wet galoshes, you don't."

With a grunt, Abigail plopped down in the foyer and tugged, first one boot and then on the other. She left both boots stranded in the middle of the floor and bounded up the steps.

Brian carried the tree into the foyer. "How did she get to be so headstrong?"

Kathryn chuckled. "I have lived next door to your family long enough to know the answer to that question, and it certainly isn't your lovely wife."

He held up his free hand. "Guilty as charged."

"Your daughter is a carbon copy of you."

"True."

She pointed to the tree. "What is all of this?"

"Abigail is adamant that you decorate for the holidays."

"I know. It's so sweet of her, but--"

"But what?"

"It's already Christmas Eve. I decided not to decorate this year. I'm not in the mood."

He furrowed his brow. "May I be perfectly honest with you?"

"Of course."

"For once, Sarah and I agree with our daughter," he said. "Christmas was always such a special time of the year for your family. It might be good for you to spruce up the house a bit."

Abigail hollered from the top of the stairs. "Mrs. Sullivan, what are beach ornaments?"

Kathryn held her breath when she heard Abigail's foot hit the top step. The box of ornaments to which Abigail was referring was not only wieldy; it was filled with ornaments that were extremely sentimental. "Be careful coming down those steps," she cautioned. "On second thought, do you want me to carry it down for you?"

"No, ma'am. I'm being careful."

Steadying the box in her arms, securely planting each foot before moving onto the next step, Abigail descended the hardwood stairs. Both adults breathed a sigh of relief when she reached the bottom.

Brian shifted his weight. "Are you ready for me to put up the tree?"

"Ready as I'll ever be." Kathryn pulled a flannel blanket from the hall closet. "We'll need this to protect the living room floor. Let me get the Christmas tree stand and a stack of old newspapers from the garage. I'll show Abigail some of those beach ornaments while you put up the tree."

An odd sensation fluttering in the pit of her stomach accompanied her to the garage. The feeling was unsettling, yet strangely comfortable. New, yet surprisingly familiar.

"Could this be the rekindling of my Christmas spirit?" she wondered as she picked up the Christmas tree stand.

CHAPTER TWENTY

RIAN AND ABIGAIL WERE WAITING in the living room when Kathryn returned from the garage. They quickly set to work, bantering like three old washwomen hanging out laundry on a windy day. Kathryn and Abigail covered the hardwood floor with a thick layer of recycled newspaper. Then, they topped the newspaper with the plaid blanket. Brian balanced the evergreen in the tree stand, at first tilting it to the right, then a tiny bit to the left, back and forth, back and forth again, until the tree stood straight and tall, like a sentinel posting guard at the bay window.

Early in their marriage, Kathryn convinced John that a woman has the prerogative of changing her mind, primarily about those things which are of little importance to a man, things like the latest spring fashions or the placement of patio furniture or the alignment of the Christmas tree. Therefore, before he tightened the metal screws on the Christmas tree stand, she always inspected their tree for flaws.

Keeping in line with years of tradition, she positioned herself as inspector general directly under the chandelier at the center of the room. She expected, as usual, to be impressed. Traditions change, and impressed she was not. She gasped in dismay at the pitiful tree in front of her. Aberrant branches jutted out in all directions. Huge gaps wider than the Grand Canyon exposed the main trunk.

"It's a Fraser fir," Brian offered sheepishly.

Good decorum says that one shouldn't laugh a gift horse in the mouth, or a Christmas tree between its branches, so Kathryn said nothing.

"It is the only decent one that we could find at this late date," he explained. "The other ones were extremely dry."

Abigail wrinkled her nose. "They all looked dead to me."

"This is a Charlie Brown Christmas tree if I've ever seen one," Kathryn said.

Brian and Abigail giggled, and soon all three of them were enjoying a good laugh. Not the side-splitting kind of laughter that gets out of control and leaves your belly aching, but the kind of laugh that refreshes one's soul like a drink of cool water from a babbling mountain brook.

When their laughter subsided, Kathryn's voice became subdued. Tears stung her eyes. "It's perfect, really. Thank you for your kindness."

Brian discreetly steered the conversation toward the box of ornaments that Abigail left lying on the living room couch. "Why don't the two of you look through the beach ornaments while I trim these unruly branches?"

Abigail's excitement was barely containable. Sitting cross-legged on the floor with her hands on her knees, she stared wide-eyed into the box. The ornaments, individually wrapped in pieces of white tissue paper, were aligned in perfect rows.

Randomly, Kathryn removed an ornament from the first row and unwound the tissue paper. "Let's look at this one." It was a perfect sand dollar, bleached white and tied with a red satin ribbon.

"Can we please look at another one?" Abigail begged.

Kathryn reached under the top layer of shells and pulled out another ornament. She unwound the tissue, revealing an exquisite three-inch shell with a blue whorl smack-dab in the center. Having washed ashore on Edisto Beach after a tropical storm, this shell was a family favorite. John had carefully drilled a hole through the edge of the shell and attached a tiny swivel and hook so that it could be hung from the tree.

Abigail's eyes grew wide. "What is it?"

"It's a shark's eye."

"A real shark's eye?"

'No. It is a shell. Its real name is the Atlantic moon snail."

"Mrs. Sullivan, you know everything about the beach, don't you?"

She laughed. "Hardly."

Abigail pointed to another shell in the box. "Could we look at this one?"

"Sure. Let me take off the tissue."

The child clapped her hands in delight at the sight of Santa Claus, rosy cheeks and all, painted in the center of a shell.

"Do you know what kind of shell that is?" Kathryn asked.

"Nope."

Once again, Brian's voice was heard from behind the tree. "Young lady, do you speak to adults like that?"

"Sorry," Abigail said. "No, ma'am."

"It's an oyster shell," Kathryn said.

"Where did you get it?"

"Every October, when I was a little girl, my parents hosted an oyster roast for the community. I collected the shells and used them to make Christmas ornaments. It became a tradition with our own children, as well. This particular ornament was painted by my daughter when she was in middle school."

"Is there anything else in this box?"

"More ornaments from the beach."

"Can I go upstairs and get the other boxes of ornaments?"

"You can. You have already shown me that you are capable," she replied. "The real question is, 'Are you permitted?'"

"Ma'am?"

"I am saying that I will give you permission if you use the word *may* instead of *can*."

"That's what my teacher says when I have to go to the bathroom," Abigail said.

"You must have a very good teacher."

"May I go upstairs?"

"Yes, you may. Be sure to turn on the hall light, so that you don't stumble."

"Yes, ma'am."

The next box of ornaments, which Abigail carried downstairs, was marked: ORNAMENTS--HANDLE WITH CARE. It contained heirlooms that were either fragile, irreplaceable, or both. Carefully packed in this box were handcrafted crystal snowflakes, the last two from a set of six; colorful baubles imported from Germany in the early twentieth century; delicate glass blown spires from her parents' trip to Italy; and the angel tree topper, which belonged to her maternal grandmother. Kathryn judiciously set the box aside and sent the child upstairs for another box.

Abigail appeared a few minutes later. Tucked under her arm was a box marked ORNAMENTS/ FAMILY MEMORIES.

Kathryn's worry about broken ornaments was alleviated. The ornaments in this box were made of unbreakable materials. Each one, however, was a family keepsake with its own unique story. This box was sure to hold a child's attention longer than the two previous boxes.

Abigail was immediately drawn to the wooden rocking horses bought to commemorate the twins' first Christmas. Jack's horse was painted white with tiny blue flowers, and Harper's horse was painted white with tiny pink flowers. Timothy's baby ornament, a darling brown teddy bear with a dark-green bow tied around its neck, was buried somewhere in the bottom of the box.

The seven-year-old picked up a Christmas tree that Jack made from green construction paper when he was in the second grade. The glitter had fallen off decades ago, leaving gobs of dried glue stuck to the branches. A dilapidated star, faded yellow, clung to the tree for its life. Without a second glance, she discarded the homemade Christmas tree on the living room floor and picked a red, wooden apple from the box. "What's this?"

"An apple a day keeps the doctor away," Kathryn sang. "A student gave that to me more than forty years ago."

Obviously unimpressed, Abigail rummaged through the box until she found something else to interest her. She held up a shiny, gold ornament. "Mrs. Sullivan, is this the Biltmore House?"

Kathryn nodded. "You took a class trip there before Thanksgiving, didn't you?"

"Yes, ma'am. I liked the big staircase."

"My children always loved the bowling alley."

Abigail looked baffled.

"Didn't you see the bowling alley in the basement?" Kathryn asked.

"There's a bowling alley?"

"And a swimming pool."

"My class never went in the basement." A look of disgust crossed Abigail's face. "Peter Glass, the mean boy in my class with red hair, well, he threw up on the stairs--right by my feet. It was orange."

Brian stepped out from behind the tree. "That's enough about Peter Glass and his stomach virus."

"Daddy, I told you it wasn't a virus." She was indignant. "My teacher said that he ate a giant bag of cheese puffs."

"Virus or cheese puffs, I am sure that Mrs. Sullivan doesn't want to hear the sordid details about Peter Glass."

"She might."

Sighing, Brian placed the tree clippers on the floor. As he straightened, he rubbed his chin. "Kathryn, would you excuse us? I need to speak to my daughter in private about slandering the reputation of her classmate."

She watched admiringly as Brian escorted his only daughter from the room. He was a devoted and caring father. Having journeyed the difficult road of infertility, nearly devastated by multiple miscarriages before God mercifully granted their prayers for a child, Brian and Sarah were committed to the task of raising their daughter.

She was immensely relieved to have the two of them temporarily distracted in another room of the house. Quickly, she sifted through the box. Like a covert operation, she located and removed an ornament with a slip of her hand, sliding it into the slit of her apron pocket. She didn't mean to be devious, but there were some things that she just didn't feel like explaining, especially not this Christmas Eve.

Abigail walked into the living room holding Brian's hand. Her exuberant personality was only slightly deflated. "I am sorry that I talked ugly about Peter."

Kathryn drew the child to her and hugged her warmly.

Brian stood back and examined the Fraser fir. "What do you think about your Christmas tree now?"

From her seat on the couch, Kathryn gave the Fraser fir the once-over and offered him an honest assessment. While it would never be chosen for the White House or Central Park or even the Biltmore Village, the tree was surprisingly lovely.

Abigail picked up Harper's wooden rocking horse. "Can I start hanging the ornaments?"

"No, ma'am," he said. "It's time to go home."

"Who's going to decorate Mrs. Sullivan's tree?" she cried. "Santa will be here tonight."

"Your mother suggested that instead of Mrs. Sullivan coming to our house for dinner, we could bring dinner over here, around five o'clock. That would give us enough time to eat and decorate the tree before we go to church. That is, if it is fine with you, Kathryn."

"Once again, I am beholden," she answered.

"That's a fancy way of saying, 'thank you.'" The child's air of authority made both adults laugh.

"If you have a broom, I'll sweep up these pine needles before I go," he said.

"I can sweep this little bit. You've done enough already."

"If you're absolutely sure--"

"I'm positive; truly, I am."

"Then we'll be on our way. Grab your boots, little Miss Dictionary. And don't forget your mittens."

Brian and Abigail exited the front door, but not before a blustery wind showered the foyer with tiny bits of ice and snow. Fearful that she might slip on the wet floor, Kathryn gripped the inside door knob and lowered herself to her knees. As she gathered the skirt of her apron to wipe away the melting snow, her hand brushed against the pocket. Inside the apron pocket was the ornament, which she had intentionally hidden from Abigail's view.

She sat on the tile floor and rested a moment or two. Then, she withdrew the ornament. It was a miniature pillow, three inches square, covered in white satin. Delicate pink rosebuds were embroidered on all four corners. Stitched across the front of the pillow was the phrase: *Rose's First Christmas 1978.*

Kathryn rubbed her forehead, wondering if she would ever tell Abigail the story about her precious daughter.

CHAPTER TWENTY-ONE

THE LAST TWO TRAYS OF cookies sat cooling on wire racks beside the stove while the dishwasher hummed its way through an extra rinse cycle. With a glass of milk left on the kitchen table, neglected and growing warm, Kathryn cradled the ornament from Rose's first Christmas in the palm of her hand. The miniature satin pillow was still pristine, as unspoiled and untouched as her memories of Rose. Memories which began a year and a half before her beautiful daughter ever entered their lives . . .

A tidal wave of disbelief washed over Kathryn and engulfed her in an incredible sea of sadness. At the age of forty-two, she sat on the edge of a hospital bed, on the fourth floor's labor and delivery ward. She stared intently at the lines etched into the palms of her hands, but her eyes registered nothing. For the first time in her life, she experienced true emptiness.

Two months earlier at John's request, she reluctantly scheduled a routine physical with her gynecologist to discuss the stages of menopause and possible hormone-replacement therapy. Kathryn's mother began missing her monthly cycles at the age of forty-five, so why should Kathryn be surprised if she began doing the same? She was only three years younger. Not surprisingly, the thought of entering menopause at the age of forty-two didn't fluster her in the slightest. With three beautiful children and a husband who adored her, Kathryn's world felt complete.

She tried to convince John that her fatigue was the result of over-commitments on her part. As the elementary school's PTO president, the historical society's auction co-chairman, and the Girl Scout cookie sales coordinator for the western half of North Carolina, her calendar was crammed full. In addition, she was a consummate tennis player and the mother of three active children who just happened to own two mares, which boarded at their grandpa's farm. John readily agreed that her schedule was ridiculous; however, his concerns remained unabated. He nagged until she grudgingly canceled the spring PTO board meeting and scheduled an appointment with the gynecologist instead.

For Kathryn, the drive after her doctor's appointment was a total blur. Like pieces of wet laundry inside a dryer, gaining momentum with their initial ascent and hanging suspended for a brief moment before toppling headlong to the bottom of the cylinder drum, her thoughts and emotions tumbled with the news: She was eight weeks pregnant.

Her thoughts were barely focused on the road as she maneuvered the station wagon through the late-afternoon traffic. She took the most direct route to John's office. Her hands were clammy, and her throat was dry.

As she pulled between freshly painted yellow lines in the parking lot, she took a deep breath. "How do I break this news?"

Everything in her world was about to change. Her favorite heels, Italian imports that accentuated her shapely calves, needed to be traded in for a nice pair of flats, or possibly plain white tennis pumps, depending upon the amount of swelling in her ankles. Salt was now officially off her list of acceptable foods.

Her Italian heels as she walked down the hallway. She spied John sitting at the nurses' station, his fingers tapping on the countertop, his head bent over a patient's chart. Funny, but she had never noticed that his hair was streaked with such a significant amount of gray.

He looked up from the chart. "Kathryn, what is it? Are you okay?"

She tried to answer, but the words were stuck in her throat.

"Do you want to sit down?"

She shook her head.

"What did the doctor say?"

"He said--"

"Sweetheart, whatever it is," he declared, "we'll handle it together."

"What about two o'clock feedings?" she asked.

"Anything. We'll get the best doctors, whatever you need."

And diapers."

John gasped. "What did you say?"

"Two o'clock feedings. Messy diapers."

"You're pregnant?"

"Eight weeks."

"At our age?"

"You mean at my age." Her tone was defensive. "Women older than me have babies."

"I know. It's just that--" he said. "Sit here. On second thought, maybe I need to sit down."

He rubbed his temple between his hands.

A nurse appeared at the counter. "Dr. Sullivan, your well-baby check is ready in room two."

"Thank you. I'll be right there."

Kathryn began to cry. "You've made yourself perfectly clear. You either think that I'm too old to have a baby, or you don't want this child."

He reached for her hand, but it was too late. Turning on her heels, she fled down the hall and exited through a side door. She decided not to breathe a word to the children about the pregnancy. They would find out soon enough.

An hour later, chagrinned and looking like a naughty puppy with his tail tucked between his legs, John walked through the mud-room door. In one hand, he carried a dozen red roses, and in the other, a grocery bag filled with dill pickles and vanilla ice cream.

"Could I have another chance?" he begged.

"What do you mean?"

"Could you tell me the news like I've never heard it before?"

"What news?"

"Please don't tease me. I feel wretched enough as it is."

She whispered in his ear, "Do you mean the news that I'm pregnant?"

"We're pregnant," he whispered back.

Kathryn giggled. "And to think that I was worried about developing a middle-age spread."

Laughing, John lifted her off her feet and slowly twirled her around the kitchen floor to the sound of an imaginary waltz.

Together, they made the transition, shifting gears from thinking that they had advanced beyond the child-bearing years to being exhilarated by the fact that Kathryn was pregnant. Jack, Harper, and Timothy were thrilled about the prospect of having a new addition join their family.

Family and friends were mindful of the fact that, because of her age, this pregnancy was considered high-risk. The obstetricians, her mother, the women at the tennis club, and even the butcher at the corner market nagged her about eating a well-balanced diet, taking prenatal vitamins, and resting more. Unconcerned, Kathryn basked in the glow of pregnancy and flippantly assured those who were concerned that she would never do anything to jeopardize the health of her unborn child.

Infused with renewed vigor as the first-trimester exhaustion subsided, she poured herself into plans for renovating the upstairs nursery. She spent countless hours examining wallpaper samples, debating between pastels or primary colors in stripes or prints. One print, in particular, caught her eye. It was called "Country Gardens." With colorful spring flowers, rolling green meadows, and white picket fences, its tranquil scene reminded her of paintings by Monet.

Unfortunately, her fairy tale ended.

Early one morning, not long after John left the house for rounds at the hospital, a severe cramp rippled across her lower back. Kathryn gripped the bathroom sink. By the time she reached the phone in the bedroom, her pair of panties was soaked in blood.

For the next twenty-four hours, John did not leave her side. Labor and delivery nurses, speaking in hushed voices, came and went with each shift change. John's father visited just long enough to deliver an overnight bag and homemade cards from the children.

Her breakfast tray remained untouched the following morning. After changing from the hospital gown into a fresh set of clothes, she sat alone on the edge of the bed, awaiting her discharge summary. A wheelchair passed by her opened door. Its occupant was a woman half her age, dressed in a loose UNC sweat suit and maternity jeans. Cradling her newborn son, the woman beamed.

Acutely aware of the cramping in her now empty womb, Kathryn looked at her watch. In a few moments, a nurse would rap on the door and escort her downstairs to where John was waiting patiently with the car. And she would go home quietly with nothing left from the pregnancy except an exorbitant hospital bill, three unopened rolls of wallpaper, a new pair of flat shoes, and an illogical, but incredible sense of personal failure.

CHAPTER TWENTY-TWO

KATHRYN SLIPPED HER NIGHTGOWN OVER her head. "I want another child."

After rinsing his mouth with water, John set his toothbrush down by the edge of the sink and turned around to face her.

"I can't explain it," she said. "I thought that our family was complete, but that was before I got pregnant. The loss of the baby left a hole in my heart."

He gathered both of her hands in his. "It's common for a woman who has suffered a miscarriage to experience a tremendous sense of loss. I don't think that we should make a decision about another child right now."

"Why not? I thought you were excited about the baby."

"I was. But I don't want this decision to be fueled by your raging hormones and fluctuating emotions. Let's just give it a little time."

"Two weeks," she bargained.

"Two months."

"One month," she begged. "I'm not getting any younger."

"What about considering adoption?" he suggested.

"Adoption?"

"To be honest, I'm worried about another high-risk pregnancy."

"I've never thought about adopting."

"Think about it for the next month." John kissed the tip of her nose; then, he walked out of the bathroom.

It didn't take a month for her to decide. By the time Kathryn finished brushing her teeth, she had made her decision.

The mounds of paperwork, as well as the home visits, were expedited by their willingness to adopt a special-needs child from another state. Fifteen months after the miscarriage, Kathryn and John flew to upstate New York to meet their new daughter.

The flight home with a screaming infant and a three-hour layover in Atlanta left Kathryn exhausted. She contemplated an afternoon nap while the baby slept; however, she needed to finish unpacking before the children came home from school.

She could hear her mother speaking with Kevin on the phone. Her family, especially her brother, never understood their reasons to adopt a child; much less one who was born north of the Mason-Dixon Line and saddled with health issues.

A successful cardiologist with a lucrative practice in Charlotte, her twin's biggest worry was a possible rain delay between the ninth and tenth hole of his Friday afternoon golf match. She knew that while he adored his eleven-year-old son, the thought of being saddled again with diapers, car seats, and late-night feedings was as foreign to him as missing a round of golf.

"They arrived about an hour ago. Your sister looks exhausted. But what else would you expect? A new baby at her age."

Kathryn's mother tilted the phone, balancing it between her shoulder and cheek, as she wrestled a roasting pan into the oven.

"Sorry about the clatter, dear. I promised Jack that I would make a pot roast and whipped potatoes for tonight's dinner."

"There are complications for sure. To what extent, I don't know. They said that they would explain everything to us later. John has gone to the office to check his mail, and your sister is putting the baby down for a nap. I promise to have her call you this weekend. I'm glad the storm is clearing. Stay under par. Bye, bye."

Kathryn walked into the kitchen. "Where's Daddy?"

"He's in the family room, asleep in the recliner," her mother replied. "By the way, your brother called. I told him that you were putting the baby down for a nap, and that you would call him this weekend."

"I don't know how to thank you and Daddy for watching the children while we were gone."

"It was our pleasure. I have a few more t-shirts to fold, and then the laundry will be done."

A large wicker basket sat on the kitchen table filled with underwear, socks, sheets, and towels. Propped on top of the clean laundry, Timothy's toy bear looked very much like a traveler waiting for the next train.

Kathryn picked up the bear in her arms and cradled him tightly against her chest. His adorable blue sailor's suit had long been discarded, and his fur, once soft, was now nappy and rough to the touch. Multiple washings over the years lightened the bear from a rich brown to the color of green tea. His arm dangled by threads. A small tear in the cloth marked the place for a missing eye button.

"Did anything exciting happen while we were gone?" she asked.

"Let me think. Harper is utterly dumbfounded by the fact that she wasn't chosen as editor for the middle school newspaper, and Jack has fallen head over heels in love with one of the little girls in the neighborhood."

"Jack? Who is the lucky little girl? Is she cute?"

"A bit of a bookworm. Perfect for Jack, though. Ginny something or another."

"Virginia?"

"That sounds right."

"Virginia. Our son has a crush on Betty Lou and Harold Keefer's daughter?"

"Horn-rimmed glasses, dark stringy hair, and knobby knees"

"That's Virginia."

"By the way, did I mention Timothy's gym shoes?"

"What about them?"

"They have been missing in action for three days!"

"Why am I not surprised?" Kathryn hugged Willy Bear. "I hope that the children behaved."

Her mother stared in mock surprise. "My grandchildren? They were perfect angels, of course."

"Seriously, Mother."

"I am being serious; your children are always well behaved."

Kathryn became more specific. "Were there any skirmishes or major battles that I need to know about?"

"Two skirmishes; one battle."

"Whose fault was the battle?"

"Actually, it was Willy Bear's fault."

"Willy Bear?"

"It was nothing really. Jack and Harper were playing keep-away with Willy Bear."

Kathryn sighed. "I can hear Timothy now, screaming bloody murder."

"The screaming didn't escalate until Jack referred to Willy Bear as a piece of rubbish and threw him in the garbage can."

Kathryn held the bear at arm's length and gave him a long, hard look. "He really is a pitiful looking bear."

"A pitiful bear whose worth is measured in Timothy's love. Which is in itself, immeasurable."

Carefully considering her mother's words, Kathryn clutched the ragged bear to her chest. "So you rescued Willy Bear from the garbage can."

"Jack fished him out. That is, after your father held court."

She cringed. "I'll bet Daddy wasn't whistling Dixie that day, was he?"

"You can say that again." Her mother pulled up a kitchen chair. "Now, enough of such talk about teddy bears and trash cans. I want to hear about my new granddaughter."

Kathryn laid Willy Bear back on top of the laundry and settled into a kitchen chair across from her mother. "She could be the poster child for trisomy 21. Flat facial features--"

"Trisomy 21? I thought she had Down syndrome."

"One in the same. Trisomy 21 is the medical term. Everything about Rose--"

"So you did decide to name her after John's mother?"

Kathryn nodded. "Please don't say anything to his father when he comes over tonight. We haven't told him yet."

"My lips are sealed. Is he coming for dinner?"

"I suppose so. Like I was saying, everything about her is typical for a child with Down syndrome: flat facial features, small head, and a protruding tongue. Unfortunately, the extent of her malady is much more involved than the orphanage led us to believe. She is four months old, and she can't even hold her head up by herself."

Her mother didn't respond.

"Mother, I know that you want to say, 'I told you so.'"

"You have me all wrong; you always have. I'm not about to say any such thing. Furthermore, I didn't ask for a health report. You whisked her upstairs to the nursery before we even got to take a peek at her."

"I'm sorry, Mother. I just wanted to put her down for a nap."

Nancy's tone softened as she reached for her daughter's hands. "Please introduce me to my new granddaughter. Not through a medical report, but through her mother's eyes. Your eyes. Does she curl her toes when she takes a bottle? Does she like to be bundled tightly or loosely? Does she respond to your voice?"

"Most of the time, she seems unresponsive."

"What does John say?"

"He is concerned by the distant, faraway look in her eyes. He suspects that she may be deaf. Yesterday, when I was giving her a bottle, her pudgy little hand latched onto my finger, and my heart melted. Oh Mother, she's broken; yet, she's so beautiful."

"And you love her. In the same way that Timothy loves Willy Bear."

"Just like Willy Bear--" Kathryn's voice trailed off.

"What's wrong, dear?"

"What if I'm not up to the task?"

"What task?"

"What if I'm not able to care for a handicapped child?"

"Listen to me carefully. When you and John informed us of your intentions to adopt a child, I asked you if you had truly considered the far-reaching ramifications of this decision. What you never gave me a chance to say before you became angry with me and stormed out in a huff was this: You are the most amazing, committed, devoted mother whom I have ever known. If a handicapped child--or special needs or whatever you want to call her--has any kind of chance in this world, it would be with you as her mother."

Kathryn began to cry. "How am I going to prepare the children for Rose's limitations? We cannot even begin to know her degree of retardation. You know how cruel this world can be. What if someone pokes fun at her?"

"Trust your instincts. When the time comes, you'll know the right thing to say."

They heard Timothy open the front door and dump his Spiderman book bag on the stairs. "Nana, I'm home. Can I have some chocolate cake?" He was still wiggling out of his Cowboys sweatshirt when he entered the kitchen.

"Mama, you are home." He tossed the sweatshirt in the chair and wrapped his arms around her waist as if he would never let her go. "You were gone ten whole days."

Tears streamed down her cheeks as she ran her fingers through his hair. "I know, sweetie. I missed you so much."

"I missed you, too, Mama."

Kathryn peered at her mother over the top of Timothy's head and smiled. She knew exactly what she would say when the time came.

CHAPTER TWENTY-THREE

Thirty minutes after Timothy arrived home, a school bus squealed at the bottom of the hill, its breaks long past the need for a check-up. Unless Jack tarried at the bottom of the hill giggling with Virginia Keefer, the twins would be joining them in a matter of minutes. Breathless, they walked through the front door at the same time John came in through the mud-room door. The family had such a grand homecoming that even the judge rallied from reading the stock reports to join the fun.

"Mama, where's the baby?"

"She's napping."

"Did you decide on a name?"

"We are calling her Rose, after my mother," John answered.

"When can we see her?"

"In a few minutes. Your dad and I want to talk to you before we go up to the nursery. Everyone, grab a seat."

Kathryn picked up Willy Bear. "Do you remember the night that we discussed Down syndrome?"

The children nodded their heads.

"You mean trisomy 21?"

Kathryn pursed her lips. Her oldest son was as predictable as the phases of the moon. Whether they were talking about Christmas trees or medical maladies, Jack insisted, to the point of irritation, upon exact locution. She often worried about his need to be precise.

"Rose's limitations are much more extensive than we were led to believe," she said.

Timothy wrinkled his nose. "What does that mean?"

"When a baby comes into my office for a check-up," John explained, "I make sure that the baby has reached or is reaching certain milestones. For example, a normal four-month-old baby has head-control and can track sounds. Does this make sense to you?"

Harper was impatient. "What does this have to do Rose?"

"Your sister is not a normal four-month-old. Developmentally, she is very far-behind. She is more like a two-month-old baby than a four-month-old. Some of it is caused by Down syndrome; however, some of it may be failure to thrive."

Jack's ears perked up. "What's that?"

"It means that, in the orphanage, she didn't receive the love and stimulation that she needed."

"She's going to be okay, isn't she?"

"At this point, we really don't know."

"Maybe you should have picked out a different baby."

"Timothy, hush," Harper reprimanded. "It's not like Mama and Daddy went to the dime store."

Kathryn looked at the children. "Timothy makes a very good point; a point that this family needs to discuss."

She held up Willy Bear for everyone to see. "In many ways, Rose is like Willy Bear. Instead of being round, the back of her head is flat. Her ears are teeny tiny, and they fold over slightly at the top. She has a fat pink tongue that sticks out--"

"Just like Willy Bear," Timothy said.

"That's right. Just like Willy Bear."

"Now see how Willy Bear's arm is floppy." She demonstrated by bending the stuffed bear's arm back and forth. "Rose's whole body is floppy, because she has poor muscle tone. You are going to have to be very careful when you hold her."

"She's in the right family. I'm the only boy in my PE class who can't flex his biceps."

Everyone laughed at Jack's assessment of his fourteen-year-old physique, or lack thereof.

Kathryn handed the bear to Timothy. "Why do you love Willy Bear?"

"Um."

"Is it because he's perfect?"

The twins giggled.

She repeated the question. "Timothy, why do you love Willy Bear?"

"Because, he's my bear."

Kathryn smiled at him. "Exactly, and it's the same with Rose. We love her, because she is ours to love."

John slapped his hands across his knees. "How would the three of you like to meet your baby sister?"

The children raced up the stairs, sounding like a herd of elephants. They vied for the best position around the crib. Kathryn's fears melted away as she watched Timothy peer through the slats and the twins look over the rails. Their faces were filled with wonder.

Timothy scrutinized Rose. "She doesn't really look like Willy Bear."

"She's beautiful," Harper said, breathlessly. "May we touch her?"

Kathryn nodded. They took turns stroking Rose's arm.

Whispered in hushed tones, the children's comments blended into a magnificent lullaby, a lullaby that Rose would never hear if John's suspicions were correct.

Leading with his big toe, one step at a time, Jack was tentative carrying Rose downstairs to the family room. He settled into the glider, crooning softly as he rocked her back and forth. Then it was Harper's turn to hold her.

"Mama, tell Timothy to stop shouting Rose's name. He's going to scare her."

Kathryn and John knowingly exchanged glances. This was as good a time as any to share their suspicion.

John began. "One of the complications of Down syndrome can be hearing loss. Chances are that Timothy isn't going to scare her."

Harper looked at Rose. "You mean she's deaf?"

"We won't know for sure until a specialist tests her."

Jack was intrigued. "How are we going to talk to her?"

Kathryn wiggled her fingers. "We'll learn sign language."

"Cool. Wait until I tell Ginny," he said.

Kathryn's mother could be heard, rummaging through the pots and pans.

Timothy plugged his fingers in his ears. "You mean that Rose can't hear Nana making all that noise?"

The racket in the kitchen ceased. "Timothy Sullivan, your baby sister may be hearing impaired; however, my ears work fine."

Everyone laughed. Even the judge looked up from the Wall Street Journal, slid his reading glasses down his nose, and grinned.

Routine swept in the next morning like the southwest wind coming off the mountain slopes. With bagged lunches stuffed in their book bags, Kathryn shooed the children off to their respective bus stops. John left hours earlier to make hospital rounds. Moments later, clean-shaven and dressed in khakis, the judge hurried down the steps with a suitcase in each hand.

Kathryn met him in the foyer. "Do you have to leave so soon?"

"Your family needs time to get adjusted," he said. "Besides, we'll be back at Christmas. It's barely two months away."

Her parents had been gone less than five minutes when an old Ford truck climbing their steep drive shifted its gears into low. The truck's rusty door hinges creaked as William stepped out and pulled an oversized shopping bag from the floor behind the driver's seat. An unfortunate victim of gout, a casualty of last night's pot roast and gravy, he limped gingerly up the stone steps.

"Can't stay but a moment," he said. "I just wanted to drop this off for my new granddaughter."

"I can't begin to imagine."

"Open it."

A kaleidoscope of colors greeted Kathryn; varying shades of pink, blue and green interwoven in a familiar pattern on a background of pale yellow. Even before she asked, she knew that this was the quilt which William kept at the foot of his bed. From past conversations, she knew that the quilt had been a wedding gift from Rose's grandmother and that the interlocking rings had been stitched with fabric saved from the dresses that Rose wore as a young girl.

"William, this was your wedding quilt. I can't accept this."

Her father-in-law rubbed his jaw. "I don't see that it's yours to accept. It's a gift for little Rose."

"Are you sure?"

"John's mother would want her to have it."

Kathryn remembered the cherry jewelry box that now housed John's Christmas cards. "Where have I heard that before?"

"I've got to get these pumpkins to market." William hobbled down the porch steps. "Give my new granddaughter a kiss for me."

"I'll give her a kiss on each cheek. Thank you, again." She waved as his truck pulled down the drive.

WITH TWO NEW ADDITIONS, THE family Christmas photograph quickly became one of Kathryn's favorites. Rose, who was responding favorably to the love and attention afforded her, was snuggled with the wedding quilt on Kathryn's lap, while Willy Bear made a comical debut sitting on top of Timothy's head.

That year, the note in John's Christmas card was brief. A single sentence, it spoke volumes.

Christmas 1978

My dearest Kathryn,

Like Willy Bear, she is perfect.

Forever yours,

John

The charm was a silver teddy bear with a yellow ribbon around its neck.

AWARE OF A CLOCK TICKING, Kathryn studied the teddy bear charm. She squeezed her eyes shut and then opened them again for another perusal. A fleck of yellow paint chipped from the bear's ribbon sadly reminded her that nothing in life remains forever.

Not long after the Christmas photo was taken, Timothy lost Willy Bear. The entire family searched for him. They shoveled junk out of Timothy's closet; turned the house upside down; climbed the loft in Grandpa Sullivan's barn; dug through the dumpster behind the grocery store; and even scoured the shelves at the Salvation Army. No idea was considered too obvious or too obscure.

There was no rhyme or reason. Willy Bear was gone.

CHAPTER TWENTY-FOUR

Soggy from an early morning drenching, the mountains of Western North Carolina looked dismal the first week of February. The afternoon temperature had barely moved above freezing. Ominous black clouds, which blanketed the mountains, threatened another insufferable downpour. Strong gusts of wind cut across the French Broad River valley with a deafening roar.

Encumbered by three-year-old Rose and an overstuffed diaper bag, Kathryn shouldered her way out the front door. She realized, way too late, that her thin raincoat was insufficient for the winter chill. The day's schedule, ominous as the clouds, didn't afford her the time to change. It was already past noon, and she had promised John's father that they would arrive at the farm for their weekly visit with the horses before one o'clock.

As she set the diaper bag on the floor of the Buick and buckled Rose into the car seat, Kathryn smiled. She tucked a few wisps of her daughter's auburn hair beneath the hood of a new snowsuit. Pale pink, the snowsuit highlighted not only Rose's dazzling blue eyes and adorable dimples; it showcased her sweet innocence.

Because her daughter's growth was stunted, buying a new snowsuit that was a size larger than last year's, was a personal victory for Kathryn. Contributing to Rose's small stature were abdominal issues specific to Down syndrome and poor muscle tone, both of which hindered her ability to eat. Also problematic was the atrial-ventricular defect, for which she had endured extensive cardiac surgery at the age of ten months. It caused her to tire quickly, even when eating.

Kathryn was painfully aware that Rose's medical complications were much more problematic than most children with Down syndrome; however, like a mother lioness on the prowl, she bristled whenever the pediatric cardiologist used terms like *heart failure* and *failure to thrive* in reference to her daughter.

Exuberant with laughter, brilliant with white flecks on the periphery of her irises, Rose's eyes danced when Kathryn played a quick game of peek-a-boo before closing the car door. Peek-a-boo was only one of the therapeutic activities played during the morning. Desperate that her daughter would someday walk, she had hired the best physical therapist in Asheville to design an exercise program for Rose, one that would strengthen the child's floppy muscles and develop her skills.

Searching for any sign of cognition in daughter's almond-shaped eyes, Kathryn formed a *u* with the pointer and middle fingers of her right hand. She placed her thumb against her right temple, bent the fingers down and straightened them again, repeating the motion twice. "Horse," she said. The extent to which her daughter comprehended verbal or sign language was a lingering question for their family, friends, and even the professionals; however, it wasn't a question for Kathryn. She had to believe in Rose's ability to learn. For if she didn't believe, who would?

As they reached the end of the driveway, Kathryn noticed that one of the white pines had been uprooted by the wind, either the night before or earlier that morning. It lay across the split-rail fence with multiple branches spilling onto the road. A dump truck crept by with its orange lights flashing, liberally scattering salt in anticipation of a hard freeze later that night.

News of her father's stroke scrolled repeatedly through her mind like a long list of credits being displayed across a movie screen. It still seemed inconceivable to her that the judge had suffered a major stroke on New Year's Day. They had celebrated Christmas together in Asheville, and everything seemed fine. Everything, that is except a bitter altercation with Kevin. She could still hear her twin's insistence that they institutionalize Rose.

"What about your volunteer work? When do you have the time?"

he asked. "Have you done anything outside this home in the three years that Rose has been here?"

She slipped on an apron and matching oven mitts. "I'm very active working with parents of children with trisomy 21. I received a call just yesterday from a new mom who was panicked about trying to get her newborn to take a bottle. I told her how to stimulate the sucking reflex by stroking the cheek."

"That's precisely my point. You are totally unengaged from life unless it involves Down's syndrome."

"It's Down syndrome, without the possessive, and whether you approve or not, my life is about Down syndrome." She removed a warm pecan pie from the oven.

"What about the rest of your children?" he persisted. "The twins and Timothy? Particularly Timothy. He's crying out for your affection. Is this what they want?"

"Timothy is fine except for an occasional lost shoe," she answered defensively. "The children love their baby sister."

"That's not what I asked." He slammed a fist on the counter. "Do you not realize or are you too proud to admit that Rose is a burden upon this entire family? Forget that she is in diapers and will be forever. She is not going to improve. You said it yourself; her heart is extremely enlarged. If by some miracle, she does survive, are you going to leave the burden of taking care of her to your other three children? How fair is that?"

"Please lower your voice," she snapped.

"Why? Are you afraid that Rose will hear me? Even with state of the art hearing aids, the little girl is practically deaf."

Neither of them realized that John was standing in the kitchen doorway.

"Our daughter is severely hearing impaired, but the rest of this family is not," he seethed.

"John, be reasonable," Kevin begged.

"I am being reasonable. This is our home, and you have overstepped your bounds. This nonsense is going to stop."

With his voice booming, Kathryn's father barreled his way into the kitchen. "Where is everybody? And where is my pecan pie?" Whether the interruption was intentional or not, the judge's timing could not have been better.

She grabbed a knife. "Daddy, I'm slicing it right now."

"Good. My mouth's a watering for some homemade pie. Have I ever told you that your mama keeps me on a strict diet?"

The laughter, which ensued at the sight of him dramatically patting an overextended paunch, dissipated the brewing family storm, and the remainder of the day passed without further incident.

It seemed hard to believe that her father, always so animated and boisterous, truly the life of any party, now lie in a nursing home with his gaze averted to the left, his right extremities limp, and the left side of his face drooping. Kathryn spent the first week after the stroke by her mother's side, and Kevin was there the second week. After four weeks in the Medical University Hospital with little hope for improvement, he was moved to a nursing home. Because her mother insisted upon keeping an hourly vigil at the facility, Kathryn felt that a return visit to Charleston was imperative. If her schedule went according to plan, she would be leaving in the morning.

"Old MacDonald" blared from the tape deck. She treasured these times in the car with Rose--away from the distraction of telephones, washing machines, grocery lists, and as much as she hated to admit it, the sound of the other three children demanding her attention.

If only Kevin could see Rose's reaction when they turned onto the gravel road leading to the farm. Delighted by the vibration of the rocks under the tire treads, the three-year-old pumped her black-and-white saddle oxfords up and down and rocked from side to side within the confines of the car seat. Kathryn wholeheartedly believed that Rose would surprise the experts who were so quick to label her uneducable.

Aloft at varying heights, like kites on a windy day, a handful of buzzards circled overhead. "Looks like something is dead in the pasture," she said to John's father as she stepped out of the Buick.

"They have been circling for more than an hour. They were there when I came out of the barn."

"How's Bess?" she asked.

"That ole mare, she's as gentle and sweet as my little Rose."

With a coat, the color of chocolate, and a flaxen mane and tail, the mare was as striking in appearance as she was gentle in nature. William and Bess were instrumental in helping Rose overcome the tactile sensitivities that are often inherent in children with Down syndrome. Coaxing her not to flail against the different sensations, William patiently guided his granddaughter's pudgy hand along the mare's flank and through her mane. The greatest victory was the day that Rose lay her cheek against Bess' sleek coat and gurgled with delight.

As he carried Rose to the barn, William asked Kathryn about her father's condition.

"Basically, he's unresponsive. Now I'm worried about Mother. She's exhausted, but Kevin and I can't convince her to leave his side."

"Is there anything that I can do?"

"I am supposed to leave in the morning, but I still have to get to the grocery store and to the pharmacy," she said. "Do you mind looking after Rose this afternoon?"

"It would be my pleasure. Leave me the car seat, and I will bring her back around five."

"Are you sure that it's no problem?"

"Absolutely. What about Timothy?"

"I'll be home from the grocery store in time to pick him up from cub scouts."

Kathryn had the groceries on the shelves; medicines picked up from the pharmacy; ten-year-old Timothy home from his den meeting; and a load of laundry in the washing machine when William, punctual as usual, rapped on the door. It was five o'clock sharp, and Rose was sound asleep in his arms.

"How did she do?"

"Fine--" He sounded hesitant.

"But what?"

"She seemed to tire quicker today than usual."

"Rose or Bess?"

"That ole mare never tires."

"I was just teasing," she said. "I knew that you meant Rose."

"I wonder if she senses that you are leaving again."

"That is very possible, or maybe it's the weather. This dreariness certainly drains me."

He rubbed his chin. "Let's hope so."

Kathryn invited him to stay for meatloaf and mashed potatoes, but she wasn't the least bit surprised or offended when he declined her offer. Her father-in-law strictly adhered to farmer's hours, awakening each morning at four, eating the main meal at noon, and retiring to bed at eight. After laying Rose in her crib and guiding Timothy step by step through a "yucky" division problem, her father-in-law was gone.

She was hanging up Rose's snowsuit when John called to say that he had four more patients in the waiting room, and that he would be late for supper the second time this week. Flu season had packed a mighty punch during January, and the epidemic wasn't showing any signs of diminishing in February.

The following morning, John sat on the edge of the bed, pulling on a dark-blue sock, as Kathryn packed foundation crème and eye shadow in her well-stocked cosmetic bag.

"No one in the nursing home cares what you look like," he said.

Without saying a word, she jammed another tube of lipstick into the case.

"I didn't mean to make you angry. I'm just being practical."

"I'm being practical, too." Her voice was strained. "I can look my best, even when it's not the way I feel."

Laying the free sock on the bed, he gave her his full attention, if only for a few moments. "How are you doing?"

"I'm miserable," she answered. "I feel as though I am living with one foot in the mountains and one on the coast."

"I guess that leaves you sitting smack-dab in the Piedmont."

"Ha. Ha. Ha," she said. "It's just that--"

"Honey, I'm sorry, but I've really got to leave. I'm already twenty minutes late." He pulled on the other sock, slipped on his shoes, grabbed a tie, and kissed her good-bye. "Hang in there. I'll call you at the nursing home tonight."

A growing uneasiness gnawed at her gut as she finished packing the children's school lunches. Jack, Harper, and Timothy all vied for one last kiss before grabbing their book bags and heading out the front door to catch the school bus.

She was checking the list of emergency phone numbers when Lois, a trusted family friend who had been John's head nurse before being forced into early retirement by her husband's unexpected triple bypass, tapped on the kitchen door. Lois was Rose's one and only baby-sitter, outside of their immediate family.

"Brrrrr. It's freezing out there." Lois pulled off her scarf and gloves. "Are you all set?"

"I don't know. Rose woke up this morning with the sniffles. She doesn't have a fever, but she is definitely lethargic. John is grappling with the worse flu season that this area has seen in years, and Timothy has a social studies project due on Friday."

Lois held up the coffee pot. "May I?"

"Go ahead. Here's a cup. Rose is so susceptible to bronchitis, especially when she comes down with a cold. Maybe I shouldn't go."

"She will be fine. I will keep a close watch on her. If there is a question, I'll call either you or John."

"She'll moan if she doesn't feel well."

"I know. I've watched her now, how many times?"

"You'll call if anything--"

"I'll call. Now shoo before you change your mind. I'll put your suitcase in the car while you say good-bye to her."

Incredible sorrow washed over Kathryn as she cradled Rose in her arms and sang "Old MacDonald" one last time. The dog barked; the cow mooed; the pig oinked; the horse neighed; the duck quacked; and the chicken clucked before she could tear herself away from her precious daughter.

How could Rose, who couldn't comprehend simple words or commands and was dependent for every basic need, understand that she had to leave for yet another week?

CHAPTER TWENTY-FIVE

THE HEAVINESS IN HER HEART eased as Kathryn dropped out of the mountains and crossed into the state of South Carolina. She ran through a mental checklist. She needed to stock her mother's pantry with groceries; enlist Uncle Bob to escort her mother home; and pick up a bouquet of daisies, her father's favorite, before going to the nursing home.

It was after four o'clock when the elevator doors opened on the third floor. The pungent odors of disinfectant and urine greeted her. With trembling hands, uncertainty marking every step, she carried the vase of daisies down the hall and into her father's private room. She placed the vase besides an assortment of colorful greeting cards arranged on the dresser. Neither the flowers nor the cards alleviated the stark contrast of harsh white walls against the black-and-white tile floor. In her opinion, softer tones such as a subtle avocado or warm beige would have been much more soothing for the patients and their families.

One glance toward her mother confirmed her worse fears; her mother was on the verge of collapse. A chiffon blouse hanging loosely from her frame made her appear frail and vulnerable, like a broken little bird. Her lips, thinly set as she looked out the window, appeared incredibly pale without the usual pink lipstick. Even her hair seemed uncharacteristically disarrayed.

There was a gentle rap on the door. Kathryn smiled and beckoned her uncle to enter.

"Mother, I'm going to stay this week with Daddy. You need to go home with Uncle Bob and get some sleep. Aunt Harper already has clean sheets on the bed for you."

Her mother, without making eye contact or uttering a single word of protest, gathered her winter jacket from a narrow closet and walked out of the room. Uncle Bob followed closely behind her, shaking his head in disbelief.

After the door closed behind them, Kathryn sat beside her father and picked up his limp right hand.

"Hello, Daddy. I'm going to stay with you while mother gets some rest."

He gazed to the left, and a tear slipped down his right cheek.

She nestled her head against his chest, taking comfort in the steady rhythm of his heart. She chatted with him, easily, like she had done as a little girl. "The twins are camping next weekend in Pisgah National Forest with the Wilderness Club, and Timothy has signed up to play soccer this spring. Rose still has a bit of the sniffles, but she'll be fine."

Exhausted, she slept soundly by his side until the late-afternoon sun slanted through the window and awakened her. She shifted to a rickety leather recliner crammed in the corner of the room and absentmindedly thumbed through a cooking magazine. From time to time, she glanced sorrowfully at her father, who was now a shell of the man whom she once knew.

She was sitting in the recliner the next morning, enjoying a cup of coffee from the nurse's station, when the telephone on the nightstand started to ring.

"Hello?"

"How is your father?" It was Lois.

"No change. How is Rose today?"

"Well, that's what I am calling about. She has a low-grade fever, so I gave her some liquid acetaminophen."

"The sniffles?"

"Definitely a cold, which may be moving to her chest. She seems to be having trouble clearing the congestion."

"There is a bulb syringe in the top left dresser drawer for her nose."

"I've been using it all morning."

"Have you called the doctor?"

"The earliest appointment is three o'clock. They are being slammed with the flu."

One of the aides tapped softly on her father's door and signaled that it was time to check his vital signs.

"Lois, I'm sorry, but I have to go. Please call me after her appointment."

Sporting striped pink knee socks with tennis shoes, braids tied on the ends by lime-green ribbons, the red-headed nurse's aide could have been a character out of a children's novel. As she leaned down to secure the corner bed sheet, a handful of ballpoint pens spilled from her apron and clattered across the tile floor. Two pens rolled under the hospital bed; another scooted under the wooden chest of drawers. Flustered, the young girl gave Kathryn a weak smile, stuffed the run-away pens back into her apron pocket, and scurried from the room.

Quickly, Kathryn's thoughts shifted from pink knee socks and rolling ball point pens to the possibility that Rose was developing a respiratory infection. Poor muscle tone made it difficult for her daughter to cough productively and clear mucous from her lungs. John's partner would know to administer antibiotics as soon as Rose showed any sign of infection, fever being a major indicator.

She busied herself the next two hours, fluffing her father's pillow and adding fresh water to the daisies--whether they needed it or not. The oil painting hanging on the wall definitely needed straightening, and she was glad to oblige. It seemed ironic to her that the artist had painted a father and his young daughter, strolling together through a breathtaking field of white and yellow daisies.

John called on the phone while she was writing a note to the children. The tone of his voice caused her immediate alarm. It was the same tone that he used when Jack, at the age of eleven, shattered both leg bones in a freak hiking accident; the same tone that he used when Rose went into cardiac arrest two days after having open-heart surgery; and the same tone that he used a month ago when her father suffered a devastating stroke.

"How's Rose?" she asked. "Did she get an antibiotic? I meant to remind you that penicillin sometimes gives her diarrhea. Did--"

John was curt. "Rose may have pneumonia. Her fever has spiked to 104 degrees, and her breathing is labored. I've called her cardiologist, and he is admitting her to the hospital tonight for observation."

Panic seized her. "I can't come home right now. I don't have anyone to stay with Daddy, and I don't trust his nurse's aide. Mother is exhausted--"

"Calm down. I don't want you on the road tonight anyway." His voice softened. "Lois is staying at the house with the kids while I stay at the hospital with Rose. I'll call you in the morning."

"If there's a turn for the worse--"

"I'll call. I promise," he said. "I love you."

"I love you, too. Bye."

Kathryn set the phone down and began searching for something to occupy the time. With her mind darting like water bugs across the pond, finishing the note to the children was out of the question. An unopened package of peanut butter crackers caught her attention, but food was the last thing that she wanted. After smoothing her father's bed sheets and wiping his face with a wet washcloth, she stood by the window and aimlessly fiddled with the blinds, opening and closing them, as though she were sending Morse code across the parking lot. She finally collapsed on the rickety old recliner, overwhelmed by the sheer weight of stress gone unchecked.

At some point in the night, a loud rap on the door awakened her. The afghan was bunched on the floor beneath her feet, and she was shivering.

"Excuse me, Mrs. Sullivan. You need to wake up." It was the night duty nurse.

Rubbing her eyes, she tried to push away the fog that was clouding her mind. "What time is it?"

"Five o'clock in the morning. Your husband has been trying to reach you. You didn't answer the room phone, so he called the front desk."

"Did he leave a number?"

"It's by the phone at the nurses' station. Just dial direct. I'll stay here with your father while you make your call."

Kathryn's mind cleared as she walked the short distance down the hall. By the time she dialed the number, and the hospital operator transferred her call to the pediatric floor, she was fully awake. Frantically, she strummed her fingers on top of the desk at the nurses' station and waited for John to answer.

His voice sounded hollow. "I tried to call, but you wouldn't answer."

"I'm here now."

"There were complications--"

"Complications? What sort of complications?"

"Her heart and lungs just couldn't fight anymore."

Kathryn struggled to understand the meaning of John's words.

"Anymore?" she screamed into the phone. "What do you mean anymore?"

He began to sob. "Rose is gone, Kathryn. We've lost our little girl."

Unable and unwilling to comprehend the news, vaguely aware of the night duty nurse holding her, she stared at the black-and-white floor in total disbelief. Again, she wondered why the interior designer chose such stark colors when a subtle avocado or warm beige would have been so much more soothing.

Stricken with grief, she endured the arduous journey home in the back seat of Uncle Bob's car. Someone must have driven her car, but she didn't know who.

John nudged her the next morning. "Kathryn, it's time to wake up. We need to pick out a dress for Rose to wear."

"I need to go shopping."

"Surely, there's something in her closet--"

"I want to go shopping; it's the only going-away outfit that my daughter will ever wear."

Holding hands, they wandered among the store racks until Kathryn spied the perfect dress. It was an all-white linen christening gown with a lace Peter Pan collar and tiny cap sleeves.

She held up the gown. "This one is sweet, just like Rose."

John began to cry.

For the next three days, they were accosted by decisions that demanded their attention, each one categorized under the label *funeral arrangements*. When visitors to the house inquired about her well-being, she merely shrugged.

The morning after the funeral, Kathryn sat at her vanity like a marble stature, extremely pale and drained of emotion. She reached for her foundation crème and blush.

Harper walked into the room, crying softly. "Mama, do you have time to talk?"

The doorbell rang.

"Not now. There's someone at the front door." She stood up from the vanity. "Get ready for school, Harper. You look a mess."

Without acknowledging the look of anguish on her daughter's face, she exited the room.

A few moments later, she carried a Pyrex dish covered with aluminum foil into the kitchen. John was reading the morning newspaper.

"Are you going to work today?" she asked.

He shook his head. "Another casserole, I see."

"Just one more thank-you note to write. Why does everyone insist on bringing us a meal?"

"Is that a rhetorical question?"

"We've lost our daughter," she said. "I haven't forgotten how to cook."

"People want to help; I suppose."

"The only thing that will help is to have our daughter back."

After placing the casserole dish on the kitchen counter, she began rummaging through the refrigerator. Pushing a gallon of milk to one side and a carton of eggs to the other, she removed a half-eaten apple pie and left-over lasagna from the bottom shelf.

"Do you mind? I'm trying to read the newspaper. "

"I'm not stopping you."

"The clattering of dishes--"

"Have you looked at this refrigerator? It can't hold another thing," she complained. "What am I to do with another chicken noodle casserole? I know, bake it at three hundred fifty degrees for thirty minutes, just like the last four casseroles drenched in cream of mushroom soup." Sarcasm dripped from her tongue, but she didn't care.

It was precarious, but she cradled the Pyrex dish on top of a ham at the back of the refrigerator. She returned the pan of lasagna to the bottom shelf and tossed the apple pie into the garbage.

Concerned, John removed his reading glasses and set them on top of the newspaper.

"I'm sorry that I sounded so ungrateful." She closed the refrigerator door.

"You didn't sound ungrateful. You sounded angry."

Being placated by one's husband was even worse than being criticized. Her ire was mounting. "You have always said that the first stage of grief is anger."

"It is, but--"

"But what, John?" she demanded. "Tell me."

"Kathryn, we need to talk about Rose's death."

Ignoring the chair that he pulled out for her, she remained standing by the refrigerator. "And say what? That she's in a better place? Or that we had more time with her than anyone suspected? I heard you say that at the funeral."

"Let me explain--"

"Maybe it was enough time for you, John, but it certainly wasn't enough time for me," she snapped. "Save your platitudes and your explanations for someone who cares to listen."

Tormented by a myriad of questions, which had no answers, she shook uncontrollably. Her mind screamed, "What if I hadn't driven Rose to the farm in such rainy weather? What if I had never gone to Charleston?" Terrified of losing her composure, she turned on her heels and left John sitting alone in the kitchen, looking terribly hurt and confused.

Six weeks after the funeral, with Kathryn and her mother at his side, her father died quietly in his sleep. The family's grief, like the well pressed black attire worn at his funeral, was dignified and reserved.

In the dark period that followed, Kathryn thrust herself into a frenzied cyclone of activity. Casserole dishes were scrubbed and promptly returned to the neighbors. Wallpaper, stripped and replaced, transformed Rose's room into a comfortable guest bedroom. Asheville's art council, historical society, county library, and garden club all benefited from her need to stay busy. Her greatest solace, however, came from a backyard English garden that she lovingly created in Rose's memory.

THE MONTHS PASSED, AND CHRISTMAS morning arrived. While John and the boys constructed a model rocket, Kathryn and Harper snuggled together on the couch.

"Hershey, come here," John called. "What do you have in your mouth?"

Hershey, a black lab puppy rescued from Asheville's Humane Society, was temporarily residing in their home until John's father finished building a new doghouse. The mischievous puppy slinked around the corner.

John followed the pup from the room, only to return a few minutes later. "Guess what he had this time."

"More wrapping paper?"

"Ribbon?"

"Plastic?'

John shook his head. "A cow."

"A cow?" Kathryn was incredulous. "Not the wooden cow from your father's Nativity set?"

"Did Hershey eat it?" Timothy asked.

"Only its ear."

"What am I going to tell your father when he comes today for Christmas dinner?" she asked.

John laughed as he walked to the fireplace. "I'll tell him that his puppy prefers beef to poultry. Now, enough talk about Hershey and the cow. Are you ready for the last gift?"

The children were still giggling about a chewed-off ear when Kathryn read John's card.

Christmas 1981

My dearest Kathryn,

Our years with your father and Rose enriched my life immeasurably. I will never stop loving them, nor will I ever stop loving you.

Eternally yours,

John

Like the dress that they selected for Rose's funeral, the charm was perfect. It was a silver rose. A single petal was missing.

Kathryn reached for the box of tissues from the kitchen counter. Her tears flowed unsparingly, like a stream of hot water from the bathtub faucet.

CHAPTER TWENTY-SIX

EIGHT YEARS AFTER HER DEATH, the English garden planted in Rose's memory was a masterpiece. Like a picture painted by Monet, a kaleidoscope of colors from spring until early fall, it meandered along the brick walkway leading from the stone porch to the vegetable garden. Lavender and phlox created a plush border along the edge of the walkway while an abundance of snapdragons, irises, daffodils, and daisies filled the space between the walkway and the split-rail fence.

Purple irises and yellow daffodils were swaying in the breeze as Kathryn traipsed down the walkway, admiring the vibrant colors of spring. It was a lovely morning. The skies were clear, and the temperatures hovered in the low seventies.

By the time she sank back on her knees, tucking a strand of gray hair behind her ears, the sun had moved directly overhead. She surveyed her work with a tremendous amount of satisfaction. The lawn and gardens were beautifully manicured. Without a single dandelion or stray leaf in sight, the backyard offered an attractive and spacious venue for Timothy's graduation party.

Years ago, Kathryn accepted that, in the academic world, her youngest son was a square peg being forced to fit into a round hole. Capable of fixing anything mechanical, Timothy excelled under his grandfather's tutelage on the farm. Unfortunately, these skills didn't carry over into the classroom. The high school's two-year foreign language requirement caused him the greatest anguish. In order to earn a passing grade in Latin and subsequently receive a high school diploma, he spent four grueling hours a week with a dedicated tutor. The tutor was a retired Latin teacher, old-school but born with the patience of Mother Teresa. If for the tutor's sake alone, Kathryn wanted everything to be perfect for the evening's festivities.

Showered and changed into a lightweight shift, she eyed the clock over the stove. Quickly, she washed down a peanut butter sandwich with a glass of milk. It was already one-thirty, and time was fleeting. She had two hours to arrange fresh flowers, bake a caramel cake, and clean the guest bathrooms. The caterer was scheduled to arrive at three.

The band was checking its sound system and tuning the guitars when she ventured outside at five o'clock. She blinked in amazement at the stunning transformation. Steaming trays of roasted pork loin and Greek potatoes filled a banquet table on the porch. Stationed at both ends of the table were huge whiskey barrels packed with iced sodas and bottled waters. Teakwood tables and chairs, set on the stone porch and down the brick walkway, were covered with white linen tablecloths. Each table was adorned by a transparent champagne flute holding two or three yellow daisies.

Delighted, she clapped her hands together and acknowledged the caterer with a nod. Then she returned indoors to finish frosting the caramel cake.

Distracted by the sound of heels clicking on the tile floor, Kathryn glanced toward the hall. Standing in the kitchen doorway was her daughter, looking more like a runway model than a third-year medical student. Whether it was the attractive Italian cut suit, which accented her long slender legs, or the presence of her handsome new beau, Chadwick O'Leary III, Kathryn wasn't quite sure.

"Mom, the vase of purple irises on the dining room table is simply gorgeous," Harper said.

"Thank you. They're homegrown."

Her daughter picked up a handful of butter mints. "Why didn't I inherit your green thumb? Even the silk flowers in my apartment turn brown."

"That's dust, dear. If you stayed home long enough to clean your apartment--"

"With classes, when do I have the time?"

"I'm just teasing," Kathryn said. "Honestly, when it comes to growing plants, your father and grandfather taught me everything that I know."

"Speaking of Daddy, where is he? I thought that he would be home by now."

"He called about ten minutes ago and said that he was leaving the office. I asked him to stop at the gas station and pick up another bag of ice." She dipped the spatula into frosting bowl. "I hope that it's okay with you that I enlisted Chad to help Timothy. They are in the driveway, waiting to park cars."

"Where did Jack go? I thought that he was supposed to help Timothy."

"He should be here soon. Ginny needed a ride from her parents' house."

"Mom, I have a question for you."

"I'm listening."

"Is Jack ever going to propose?" Harper crunched on a mint. "I almost feel sorry for Ginny."

"I suppose that your brother wants to be sure before he commits to marriage."

"They've been dating since the eighth grade. That's thirteen years. How much more time does he need?"

"That's not for us to decide."

"Well, if he's not careful, I may beat him to the altar."

Kathryn raised her eyebrows.

The door to the mud-room opened and closed, and the sound of heavy footsteps carried through the house. "Where is everyone?"

"We're in the kitchen, Daddy."

John dropped his briefcase on a chair and kissed both women on their cheeks. "How are my two favorite women?"

"Good." Rotating the cake a quarter turn, Kathryn dipped the spatula into the frosting. "Do me a favor and put your briefcase in the hall closet before the guests arrive."

Like an obedient puppy, he obeyed.

He returned to the kitchen and enfolded her in his arms. "What do you want me to wear for the party?"

"I laid out a pair of khakis and your golf shirt, the yellow one with thin purple stripes."

"Speaking of purple, did you notice the irises on dining room table?" Harper asked. "They're gorgeous."

John winked at his daughter. "Nothing can be as gorgeous as your mother."

"I'd be careful, Mom. That's a pick-up line, if I ever heard one."

Kathryn squirmed from his embrace and waved the spatula under his nose. "You are as subtle as a two-ton truck, John Sullivan. Even our daughter can read right through your tactics."

"What?"

"You are conniving for a taste of my homemade toffee icing."

"Can you blame me?"

Whether his question was rhetorical or not, it didn't matter. The doorbell rang, interrupting any further conversation about toffee icing or purple irises.

John looked at his watch. "What time does the party start? It's not even six o'clock."

"It's probably Mother. She was determined to come early in order to help." Kathryn jabbed the spatula into the bowl of frosting and began untying her apron.

Seconds later, her mother marched into the kitchen, a picture of fashion dressed in a smart linen pantsuit and low heels. Parading behind her was Kevin's wife, Pam.

"Hello, dear. What can we do to help?"

"Nothing, really," she answered. "I'm about finished."

Pam set her purse on the counter. "I hope that you don't mind, but

Timothy told us to come inside. Everything looks fantastic, especially that cake."

"Thanks. Wait until you see what the caterer did with the backyard."

"Where's Kevin?" John asked. "Did you leave him at some abandoned rest stop along the way?"

Pam popped a Greek olive in her mouth. "Tempting, but no. He's in the driveway, chatting with the new graduate. By the way, who's the gorgeous hunk with Timothy?"

Harper blushed. "That's Chad. He's with me."

"Tell me more." Pam was intrigued.

"He's from a wealthy family in Virginia."

"Old money?"

Harper nodded. "What else can I say? He's brilliant and witty and charming. We were assigned to the same gross anatomy table our first year of medical school."

"Is it serious?"

Kevin barged into the kitchen. "Are you ladies talking about the young man with Timothy? He can't possibly be in medical school."

"And why not?" Harper demanded.

He grabbed a handful of nuts from the counter. "John, did we ever sport tans like that when we were in medical school? Whatever happened to pasty white?"

"I believe that things are different these days."

Harper rolled her eyes. "Let me guess. The two of you walked ten miles in the snow to get to your gross anatomy class."

"No snow. Maybe a hurricane or two." Kevin munched on the nuts. "I remember spending six months in that building on Calhoun Street without seeing the light of day."

"Are you talking about B building?" she asked.

"Is that old dungeon still standing?"

"The hospital labs are housed there now."

Conversation shifted to Timothy and his plans for the future.

Kathryn finished frosting the cake. John's father joined them in the kitchen. Followed by Jack, Ginny, Timothy, and Chad.

Spontaneously lifting her glass of sweetened iced tea, Kathryn offered a simple toast. "I want to congratulate Timothy on this fine achievement, and I want to thank our family for being here to celebrate his graduation."

Everyone cheered and patted Timothy on the back.

John and Kathryn intermingled gaily with the guests on the back porch. Despite her apparent ease, she kept a watchful eye in anticipation of any need that might arise. Additional chairs, dessert plates, spilled punch, mosquito spray, and bored relatives fell into the realm of her responsibility.

As she wandered among the tables, she noticed her eldest son sharing a piece of caramel cake with his girlfriend. Dressed in khaki pants and a white oxford button-down shirt rolled up at the sleeves, Jack appeared every bit the part of a graduate student. His passion for the mountains had carried him to the Rockies where he was pursuing a doctorate in geology at the Colorado School of Mines. Ginny was also pursuing her doctorate in Colorado.

From the side of the porch, Kathryn observed Timothy proudly introducing his two grandparents, John's father and her mother, to the Coast Guard recruiter. It was hard to imagine that in three months' time her youngest son would be leaving for boot camp. His beautiful curly locks would soon be gone, as would his civilian status. She noticed a drawn, tired look on her father-in-law's face and couldn't help but wonder if the reality of Timothy's enlistment was causing him angst. The thought was puzzling, because William was the main person who encouraged Timothy to join the Coast Guard.

Needing to enlist his aid lighting the outside lanterns, she searched the crowd for John. She saw him standing in the yard beside one of the teakwood tables, pathetically cornered by Timothy's senior English teacher. Kathryn waved the box of matches in his direction. Looking like a whipped pup, he shrugged helplessly. She would have to light the lanterns by herself.

"May I offer a hand?" a male voice asked.

She was surprised to see Kevin standing beside her. "Thank you. Has anyone told you recently that you are a gentleman and a scholar?"

"Only when I left the waiter at the club a thirty percent tip."

"I can only imagine."

"By the way, what are the chances of you and John joining us at Edisto Island for a long Fourth of July weekend? No children. Just the four of us, like old times."

"I don't know if John can afford any more time off work."

"I checked the tide chart, and there's a spring tide the third of July."

She knew that spring tides occur when there is a new moon. Perfectly aligned, the sun and the moon exhibit the greatest amount of gravitational pull causing high and low tides to peak. High tides reach all-time high, and low tides drop to an all-time low. Female loggerhead turtles are known to choose this time to slog onto the beach, drag their massive bodies past the high-tide mark, and lay a hundred or more ping pong sized eggs.

"I must admit that it's tempting," she said. "The Fourth of July at the beach, warm sand between my toes, and mama loggerhead turtles."

"Don't forget, homemade ice cream and steaks on the grill."

"Okay. You've convinced me. Let me talk it over with John."

She intentionally waited until the next morning to discuss it with him.

John shook his head. "You know that I don't have any vacation time left. I've already scheduled a week's vacation in the fall to fix things around this house."

"Please, John," she begged. "Just two or three days. It will be fun."

"What about my dad?" he asked. "We always spend the holiday picking watermelons at the farm. It's been our tradition for years."

"He'll surely survive one year without us; besides, Timothy will be here to help him."

"I don't know."

"It will give the two of them time together before Timothy leaves for boot camp."

"Let me think about it."

She could tell, by the way he walked out of the bedroom, that he was annoyed.

It took two days of persistent cajoling on her part to erode his line of resistance. Enticed by her assurances of time together without Kevin and Pam, allured by the thought of two pairs of bare feet imprinted in the wet sand, John finally acquiesced.

CHAPTER TWENTY-SEVEN

THE MONTH OF JUNE WAS soon a forgotten memory, and they found themselves enjoying a leisurely drive to Edisto Island. They arrived late Friday afternoon just in time to dine on Kevin's famous shrimp fajitas and to hear him brazenly gloat about the thirty-inch spot-tail, which he reeled in earlier that day.

The following morning, Kathryn and John held hands like two young lovers strolling along the water's edge. They laughed at a lone sandpiper dodging the waves in what looked like a child's game of tag. To the delight of any avid beachcomber, they discovered a smorgasbord of seashells. Scattered among the cockleshells and coquinas were moon snails, whelk egg cases, olive shells, and jackknife clams. John happened upon a pen shell, completely intact, with a gorgeous iridescent center.

"Are you glad we came to the beach?" she asked.

He flipped a dead jellyfish over with his toe. "I'm glad, but--"

"But what?"

"I'm still worried about Dad and Timothy." He squatted down to examine a channel whelk. "There's a ton of watermelon to be picked, not to mention the okra and the tomatoes."

"We can help pick when we get home on Tuesday; that's really the Fourth of July, anyway."

"Dad was determined to finish picking before the holiday, and you know how fastidious he can be."

"Trust me; they'll be fine." She grabbed his hand and pointed toward a tidal pool. "Let's look at the horseshoe crab over there."

Like the ingoing and outgoing tides, one day flowed into the next. Mornings were spent lazily combing the sand for shells. Avoiding the afternoon heat, Kathryn sipped freshly squeezed lemonade and chatted with Pam on the screened-in porch. Meanwhile, John joined Kevin on the beach, casting his line and his luck into the surf until the biting midges, known by the locals as no-see-ums, drove him indoors. After sundown, both couples armed themselves with flashlights and ventured to the beach in search of ghost crabs, translucent little critters scurrying sideways across the sand.

Temperatures soared into the upper nineties on Monday afternoon, making the atmosphere conducive for a late-afternoon thunderstorm. Cumulous clouds and the sound of thunder convinced John and Kevin to reel in their lines, long before the midges had a chance to bite.

"It's going to be a great night for loggerhead turtles," Kevin announced.

Kathryn cringed as a flash of lightning cracked directly overhead.

"Mark my word. It will clear out of here in thirty minutes or less," he said.

Pam passed around a plate of sharp cheddar cheese and crackers. "Have you heard that the female loggerhead turtle sheds tears while she lays eggs?"

John munched on a saltine. "Those aren't tears. She is secreting salt, which accumulates in her body."

"Well, I like to think that she is crying over the fact that nature calls her to abandon her eggs."

"Spoken like a true romantic," he teased.

"I'm being serious."

"I know that you are." He smiled as he reached for another cracker. "I have a ton of mothers in my practice, just like you."

Pam persisted. "It amazes me that the babies dig their way out of the sand and find their way to the water."

Kevin interrupted her. "Not all of them. Kathryn, do you remember when we found those hatchlings near the dune?"

"I remember that it was incredibly sad. There were five baby turtles under the sea oats, all dead."

"Lights from the beach houses disoriented them. Instead of heading toward the water, they headed toward the dunes."

"Strawberries, anyone?"

"I'll take one," Kathryn said.

Kevin wiped out an oversized, stainless steel pot. "Speaking of nests, how are the two of you going to survive an empty nest when Timothy heads to boot camp?"

"Easy. We're going to garden, hike, and travel," John answered. "All those things that we've never had time to do."

"Personally, I prefer not to think--" Before Kathryn could finish her sentence, the phone rang.

"Hello," she answered.

Timothy was hysterical on the other end of the line.

"It's Grandpa," he screamed. "He's collapsed."

"Have you called an ambulance?"

"Y-yes ma'am. They're on their way now." He was sobbing. "Mama, I don't know what to do."

"First, you have to calm down." She snapped her fingers at both John and Kevin, signaling that she needed help. "Timothy, listen to me. I'm going to hand this phone to Daddy, and Uncle Kevin is going to pick up the phone in the living room. They are going to tell you what to do."

John and Kevin proceeded to talk Timothy through CPR until the paramedics arrived. Despite the valiant effort of everyone involved, resuscitation failed.

Kathryn and John's drive home to Asheville that night was interminable. The sunset receded behind the Blue Ridge Mountains as they crossed into North Carolina, and darkness fell before they reached the farm.

As they climbed the steps of the old farmhouse, the front door opened. Robert and Gail Rhodes, John's most senior partner and his wife, stood at the door.

"It's my fault," Timothy cried. Before anyone could press past the doorway, he crumbled into John's arms.

"It's not your fault. Grandpa's heart has been ailing for years," John said. He firmly guided Timothy to one of the ladder-back chairs at the kitchen table. Kathryn subtly acknowledged Robert and Gail's motion that they would be leaving.

"Grandpa kept wiping his brow, but I coerced him to keep working. I called him 'ole m-man,'" he sobbed.

Unable to locate a tissue, Kathryn grabbed a paper towel for him to wipe his nose. Then John and she waited quietly for him to collect himself enough to continue talking.

"I carried the last two watermelons to the truck while he went in the house to shower. The water ran for a long time, so I checked on him. That's when I found him on the bathroom floor."

Timothy digressed, alternating his words and his tears. He rambled about the breakfast waffles being burned on the edges and rabbits worming their way underneath the chicken wire and the water dripping in the shower. He apologized for not picking any tomatoes.

"Forget the tomatoes," John said sternly.

Exhausted, Timothy curled up on grandfather's feather bed and cried himself to sleep. Kathryn tiptoed quietly into the bedroom and covered him with the extra quilt that William kept folded at the foot of the bed. Tidying the room, she picked up the clothes that her father-in-law had worn to pick the watermelons, a filthy long-sleeved shirt and a pair of denim jeans, and dropped them into the clothes hamper. Then she found fresh sheets for the bed in the guest room.

As if in respect for its fallen master, the old farmhouse kept a silent vigil. Kathryn listened intently for the creak of the kitchen floorboards or the flush of a bathroom toilet, but she heard nothing. Instinctively, she knew that John had carried his despair to the sanctity of the barn.

Her eyes adjusted to the darkness as she walked down the gravel drive and crept undetected through a barn door left slightly ajar. Like a fifty-pound bag of potatoes, slumped over in the darkness, John sat on the floor of the only empty stall and bawled. Unable to bear his anguish, she escaped silently into the darkness.

CHAPTER TWENTY-EIGHT

ORE THAN VIGILANT, KATHRYN WAS obsessed with the farm after William died. She single-handedly hauled the truckload of watermelons to the farmer's market the morning of the funeral. She battled tomato rot, cabbage worms, and bunny rabbits with the doggedness of a stalwart General Patton. Cucumbers and okra, picked and pickled by the quart, lined the pantry shelves. The horses were never without fresh hay, and the cow never bellowed in need of milking. By the time growing season waned, the dark circles under her eyes were noticeable.

Goldenrod bloomed along the highway and attracted the monarch butterflies traveling south on their winter migrations to Mexico. Autumn's foliage appeared at the mid-to high elevations the week after Labor Day, delighting the tourists and surprising the locals. Nighttime temperatures began their steady descent. Kathryn realized with sadness that nature was marking time for Timothy's departure.

It was September twenty-second, and all eyes were focused on South Carolina in the aftermath of Hurricane Hugo. Making a midnight landfall at the Isle of Palms with winds in excess of 130 mph, the storm ravaged coastal communities from Charleston to Myrtle Beach. Scenes of towering pine trees snapped like toothpicks, homes flooded with plough mud from the horrific storm surge, and fishing vessels deposited in the center of the road left Kathryn riveted to the television set. She received word during the afternoon that her mother and Harper were shaken but fine.

Unable to view anymore devastation, she turned off the TV and lugged Timothy's wicker laundry basket upstairs to his bedroom. She inventoried the contents of the basket one last time. There were ten pairs of government-regulated white underwear; ten pairs of government-regulated white socks; and ten government-regulated white V necked t-shirts, squarely folded and ready to accompany him to Camp May, New Jersey. To her dismay, the homemade caramel cake and oatmeal cookies, which she planned to pack for him, were not acceptable for basic training. Such items were listed by the Coast Guard as contraband.

Three days after Hugo swept through the Carolinas, Kathryn stood in the airport terminal in Asheville and watched her youngest son cross the threshold into manhood. With his duffel bag slung over his shoulder, Timothy boarded a plane to Philadelphia. Another passenger following in line behind him, a man in a dark suit, blocked her view. With her faced pressed against the glass window pane, she whispered one last, "I love you."

Having waited for his plane to taxi and lift off the runway, John and Kathryn walked slowly through the terminal. Each was absorbed in his or her own thoughts.

John was the first to speak. "We just saw Bernoulli's principle at work."

She was confused. "What did you say about somebody's principal?"

"Bernoulli's principle, that's what makes those big planes fly."

Kathryn sighed. "Is this what it feels like sending a son off to war?"

"It's boot camp, not war."

"To me, it feels like war."

Kathryn felt him squeeze her hand. He commiserated with her sense of loss.

John's vacation plans the following week were foiled by Hurricane Hugo. Instead of trimming the hedges and fixing the shed, they loaded the trunk of the Buick with a chain saw and bottled water and headed to the coast.

They were aghast at the devastation caused by the storm. The major thoroughfares had been cleared; however, downed power lines and trees still blocked the side streets leading to her mother's home. Stacks of rubbish, shattered glass, ruined furniture, torn shingles, tree limbs, and a cracked toilet were heaped along the curb.

It took them four days to clear a path through the debris deposited around her mother's house. Snapped in half by the hurricane's fury, two huge pines lay sprawled across the driveway. The magnificent oak tree, in whose shade Kathryn had spent countless childhood hours swinging, was uprooted by the storm. Without water to bathe or air-conditioning to combat the sweltering heat, they returned to Asheville on Sunday afternoon, desperately needing a shower.

THE MONTHS ON THE CALENDAR flipped over quickly. Every free weekend was spent in Summerville helping her mother restore the yard. They cheered at Timothy's graduation from boot camp in October and hiked the Rockies with Jack and Ginny in November.

Family and friends were amazed by the ease with which Kathryn and John adjusted to life without children at home. Taking their hectic schedules into consideration, they were simply too busy to notice that the children were gone. That is, until December twenty-fifth.

John awakened Kathryn at eight o'clock Christmas morning with a steaming cup of hot chocolate. Miniature marshmallows floated at the surface.

"Merry Christmas, sleepy head," he said cheerfully.

"No coffee?" she asked.

"We're starting a new Christmas tradition."

"I hate new traditions," she groaned.

This was their first Christmas alone in twenty-five years. Significantly low temperatures, colliding with a storm moving across the mid-Atlantic region, dropped record snowfalls on the South Carolina coast and rendered Harper and Kathryn's mother snowbound in Charleston. Jack was skiing with Ginny in Aspen, and Timothy was newly stationed on a buoy tender in Astoria, Washington. It was the first Christmas without John's father, and his presence, of course, was sorely missed.

"What about mixing a new tradition with an old tradition?" John reached into his pocket.

Her spirits lifted when eyed a gift box from Nora's. The renewed sparkle in her eyes expressed relief that some traditions never change.

Christmas 1989

Dearest Kathryn,

For twenty-five years, you devoted yourself to the raising of our children. You protectively hovered over the nest when they were small and offered them the freedom to choose their own paths when they were grown. Our children have chosen well because of your devotion. They are blessed to call you their mother, and I am blessed to call you my wife.

Always yours,

John

The gift box held a silver charm; it was a loggerhead turtle.

Painfully aware that this would be the first Christmas in forty-nine years without a gift from her husband, Kathryn held the loggerhead turtle charm between her fingers. She pondered empty nests versus empty houses; she contemplated new traditions versus no traditions at all. She envisioned the female loggerhead sitting alone on her nest with salty tears of loneliness slipping from her eyes and cascading down her beak, shedding tears for the hatchling and the mate that life had unfairly snatched away from her.

CHAPTER TWENTY-NINE

SPRING DAWNED GLORIOUSLY ON THE farm the following year. White dogwood petals floated aimlessly to the ground around the old farmhouse. Eight-inch trillium, commonly known as painted ladies, shyly dotted both the front and back yards. Thickets of rhododendron growing wildly on the hillsides above the lower pasture blossomed into a wedding bouquet of colors, just in time for Mother's Day.

Enchanted by the clusters of pink and white mountain laurel, Kathryn and John held hands as they strolled along their favorite horse trail. The trail began at the fence of the lower pasture and twisted and turned through dense foliage for two hundred yards or more until it suddenly opened into a beautiful clearing. At the southern end of the clearing was a deep pond which, fed by a cool mountain stream miles from civilization, remained pristine. The only mark of mankind, an old wooden bench positioned with a prime view of the water, sagged severely on its left side.

Sharing the right side of the bench, Kathryn and John soaked in the beauty of their surroundings. Tremendous majesty and tranquility were found in the stillness of the deep pond. Rays of sunlight sparkled like diamonds on the surface of the water. Gentle kisses of dragonflies failed to disturb the lily pads floating on the water's edge.

John broke the silence with what was becoming one of his favorite sayings, "A penny for your thoughts."

"I was thinking about how quickly our lives keep changing," she said. "I can't wrap my brain around the fact that Harper graduated from medical school last week. Wasn't it just yesterday that I was changing her diapers?"

"And now she's getting married at Christmas. To Chad. What *is* his last name?"

"O'Leary III."

"How can I forget a name like that?"

His disparaging remark left Kathryn dumbfounded. "You don't like Chad?" she asked.

"I don't dislike him." John placed an emphasis on the word *dislike.* "My problem is that they are both entering a very competitive residency program and getting married in the same year. I am afraid that they've proverbially bitten off more than they can chew."

"You know our daughter. Once she makes up her mind, there is no turning back. She's like a two-ton bulldozer."

"Where have I heard that before?"

"In reference to my mother?"

"And who else?"

"Me?"

John reached out to tickle her, and she took a playful swipe at him. Then, he became serious again. "Does Harper's engagement and wedding seem rushed to you?"

"Without a doubt," she answered. "I shudder to think of the work that we have ahead of us between now and December twenty-second."

"My biggest concern is that you are going to shoulder the responsibility for this wedding."

"I'll be fine. Having the wedding here in Asheville makes things so much easier."

"I suppose so."

"I have an off-the-wall question," she said.

"I'm listening."

"Why does the idea of change scare me?"

"You're not the only one," he said. "Change scares everyone."

"But it doesn't scare you."

John chuckled. "It scares me more than you realize."

Carefully, she shifted her weight on the bench. "Give me one example of when you were frightened by change."

"I'll do better than that. I'll give you three." He counted on his fingers, "One, having the twins. Two, buying our dream house. Three, expanding my practice."

"You were afraid of having the twins?" she asked.

"The thought of twins probably terrified me more than the other two combined."

"Why?"

"Two reasons, actually," he confessed. "I was afraid that I couldn't support a family of four, and I doubted my ability to be a good father."

"You didn't act scared. You were a wonderful father from the start."

John stooped to pick up a large rock. "I want to show you something."

"What are you going to do?"

"Watch."

"Please don't throw that in the water."

"Why not?"

"I don't want you to disrupt the pond," she answered. "It seems, I don't know, almost sacred."

"Trust me. You won't be disappointed."

"John, don't."

He hoisted the rock into the pond. Magnified by the element of surprise, the rock's impact created a huge disturbance. The surface was broken, and the sparkle was gone.

"Why did you do that?" she demanded.

"To make a point," he said. "Just watch."

For the next five minutes, they sat on the dilapidated bench with their eyes transfixed at the point of impact. The energy from the rock was transferred in all directions as waves spreading out in a perfect pattern of circles. The lily pads swayed to the rhythm of the waves gently lapping a distant shore, and the dragonflies hovered with excitement, awaiting a new and different place to land. Gradually, the tranquil beauty was restored.

John took both of her hands into his own. "Now I have a question for you. Was the beauty here really lost?"

She was silent.

"It wasn't lost," he said emphatically. "It simply changed."

"And your point is what?"

"It is no different from the changes or disturbances that occur in our lives." His voice was earnest. "When things change, the beauty of life is eventually restored."

"Some people would heartily disagree with you."

"I know, but that is how I believe." He brushed the dirt off his hands and leaned back against the bench.

"John Sullivan, you are a poet, and you don't know it." She smiled and then kissed his cheek. Their lighthearted laughter could be heard echoing across the pond.

CHAPTER THIRTY

JOHN'S PREDICTION ABOUT HARPER AND Chad was correct. As first-year internal medicine residents in Charleston, they were piled under mounds and mounds of work. Kathryn, therefore, shouldered the responsibility for organizing their wedding. Week after week, she mailed samples of color swatches, materials, pictures, and invitations for their approval. John gritted his teeth, but said nothing. The week that she transported samples of wedding cake from Asheville to Charleston, for an official taste test by the bride and groom, nearly sent him into a tizzy.

Major decisions for the wedding were finalized by the end of summer. There was no question in anyone's mind that Harper's wedding, an elaborate black-tie affair scheduled for the twenty-second of December, would be five-star all the way. Thanks to her mother.

Kathryn's amazing attention to detail, from the sconces and pillar candles to the white poinsettias with sprigs of holly, was gone in the blink of an eye. The prime rib dinner and fabulous jazz ensemble were forgotten as soon as the bride and groom drove off in a rented, black limousine. It was well past midnight when Kathryn slipped out of her gold heels, and John removed the cufflinks from his tuxedo.

"I wasn't this tired after giving birth to the twins," she groaned. "Can you help me with the clasp on this strand of pearls?"

"May I remind you," John said as he unlatched the clasp, "that you were quite a few years younger when the twins were born?"

"I was afraid that you were going to say that."

"You did an amazing job planning this wedding."

"Thank you, my dear." She motioned for him to unzip her gown. "I have a question for you. What was it like walking your daughter down the aisle?"

"The only word to describe it is *surreal.*"

"She was a stunning bride."

"I've never seen one prettier, except maybe you." He kicked off his shoes. "What are the plans for tomorrow?"

"Everyone is coming here for an eleven o'clock brunch. I've kept it simple and relaxed. I'm only serving quiche, hot fruit compote, and pastries."

"How many is everyone, may I ask?"

"It's just our family, so there are only fourteen of us. Chad's family won't be here. They are heading home to Virginia first thing in the morning," she said. "On the spur of the moment, I invited Ginny's parents to join us."

"Have you spoken to Jack about his living arrangements with Ginny?"

"No, but I intend to do so tomorrow. I don't approve of them living together in Colorado, and neither does Betty Lou. I just do not understand why he won't propose to Ginny. It's not like they haven't dated each other since the eighth grade."

Kathryn snuggled beside John in bed. As she drifted off to sleep, she was vaguely aware of male voices in the kitchen and the rattle of plates being removed from the cabinet. "Jack and Timothy," she thought. "It's good to have them home."

Five hours later, the alarm clock rang.

John rubbed his eyes. "What time is it?"

"It's five thirty," she whispered. "Go back to sleep."

"Why did you set the alarm so early?"

"I have to get ready for the brunch."

"What happened to simple?"

"I have to make the quiches and set the buffet table."

As she tiptoed from the bedroom, he pulled the covers over his head.

CHAPTER THIRTY-ONE

ASKING IN THE AFTERGLOW OF Harper's glorious wedding, Kathryn relished a morning to herself. She cracked eggs and grated cheese, rolled out pie crusts, and sliced fresh fruit to the tune of Christmas carols playing on the radio.

The menu for the brunch was simple: crab quiche, sausage quiche, and broccoli-cheddar quiche, for anyone who might be a vegetarian. Crabmeat, caught and picked at Edisto the previous summer, thawed in the refrigerator during the night.

By the time that John dragged himself out of bed, the last of the quiches were baking in the oven. With the pastries beautifully displayed on a serving tray and the fruit compote warming in the crock pot, the only thing left to do was set the buffet table.

John was sitting at the kitchen table, laboring over the morning's crossword puzzle, when the boys came downstairs. It was nearly nine o'clock. He peered over his reading glasses. "What is a word that begins with the letter *w* and means ruination?"

Intent upon tidying the kitchen, Kathryn shrugged her shoulders. Timothy rolled his eyes and continued reading the sports section. Jack popped a piece of pastry into his mouth. "Do you have any other letters?"

"The craziest thing is that I have it ending with *oo*."

"Eight letters, right?" Jack said.

John was amazed. "How do you know that it has eight letters?"

"The word is *waterloo*."

Kathryn covered the tray of pastries with aluminum foil. "You are going to be my waterloo, young man, if you don't stop eating the pastry for the brunch."

"One more piece?" he teased.

"Absolutely not."

Jack grew serious. "Ginny and I have something to discuss with the family. Do you mind if she comes over in an hour or so?"

"Not at all."

Ginny arrived at ten o'clock. The knobby-kneed, stringy-haired, bespectacled girl who stole Jack's heart away in middle school had matured into a lovely woman. She was tall and willowy, waif-like, with shoulder-length brown hair and pale-green eyes. Her sunny disposition and warm, genuine smile captivated everyone who knew her. Especially, Jack.

Eagerly anticipating a comfortable family discussion, which centered upon diamond rings and future wedding plans, Kathryn ushered everyone into the family room. She settled next to John on the couch. Timothy reclined in the antique chair with his long legs outstretched and his hands clasped on top of his head. Jack and Ginny huddled side by side on the hearth, looking like two mushrooms clumped together in matching taupe vests.

Jack cleared his throat. "Uh, I really don't know how to say this."

"Just say it," Timothy prodded. "You're always the one with the big vocabulary."

"Well, uh. What I'm trying to say is--" He rubbed his hands together. "Let me start again."

"Jack is trying to say that I am expecting," Ginny announced.

"Expecting what?" Timothy asked.

John looked amazed. "A baby?"

"You're pregnant?" Kathryn's voice squeaked. Clearly, this was not the announcement that she anticipated.

"Whoa. I'm going to be an uncle. When?"

Jack gripped Ginny's hand. "The baby's due date is the first of June."

"But you're not even married," Kathryn protested.

Looking sheepish, Jack reached into his vest pocket and pulled out two thin silver wedding bands. He handed the smaller one to Ginny and slipped the larger one on his left ring finger.

"We've been married nearly a year."

Kathryn was shocked. "Did you get married on a whim?"

"Mom, we had been dating for twelve years. How can that be a whim?"

"When did you get married?"

"Last Christmas. On our ski trip to Aspen."

"Why didn't you tell us?" she demanded.

"We just couldn't find the right time. We didn't want to tell either you or Ginny's parents over the phone, so we waited until after Harper's graduation. But then right after the graduation, she and Chad announced their engagement."

"Does your sister know?"

"I told her Friday night after the rehearsal dinner."

"What about Harold and Betty Lou?"

"We told my parents yesterday," Ginny answered.

Kathryn folded her arms. "I absolutely don't know what to say. I'm in total shock."

A weighty, uncomfortable silence filled the room.

"Dad, you are mighty quiet," Jack said.

"You've caught us completely by surprise; that's for sure," John answered. "Yesterday we celebrated your sister's wedding with tremendous fanfare. Your mom and I were thrilled to give Harper the wedding that she has always wanted. However, I once told your mother that wedding bells don't usher in a marriage, and I still believe that to be true."

All eyes were on John.

"You've just announced that you're married. You've told us that you have a baby on the way. What do you want me to say?" he asked.

Jack gripped Ginny's hand.

A grin spread slowly across John's face. "I am thrilled, son. Congratulations."

Jack breathed a sigh of relief. "What about you, Mom?"

As she looked into her son's eyes, Kathryn experienced a change of heart. She leaped from the couch and hugged Jack's neck. Then, she hugged Ginny. Laughing, she asked, "Am I really going to be a grandmother?"

The remainder of the morning was swept away by a steady stream of congratulations for Jack and Ginny. Each time that their news was shared, another round of handshakes, hugs, and backslaps was offered to the young couple. Kathryn's mother, giddy at the thought of being a great-grandmother, insisted upon buying the baby's layette.

After having their fill of quiche and chatter with the women-folk, the men inconspicuously slipped into the family room for an afternoon of Sunday football. The women tarried in the kitchen, sharing heroic tales about pregnancies, deliveries, and babies. No one, of course, could top Kathryn's story of delivering a baby in a gasoline station.

With a drive to Atlanta still ahead of them, John's brother and his family bid their adieu at half-time. The remainder of the guests lingered until the very last second ticked from the scoreboard. With one final wave, Kathryn closed the front door and breathed a sigh of relief. She would digest the fact that both twins were married, and that she had a grandchild on the way, in time. For now, she needed to sleep.

She awakened early in the morning. Lying beside her, propped on one elbow, John twirled a strand of her hair between his fingers.

"Good morning, sleepyhead" he said.

"I feel like Scrooge, but I have to ask. What day is it? Is it Christmas Eve?"

John chuckled. "No. Christmas Eve was yesterday, and you completely slept through it."

"So it's Christmas?"

"If I say, 'yes," he asked, "will you pay me two pence to buy the turkey, the big fat one, at the corner market?"

Kathryn longingly traced the outline of John's chin with her fingertip. "With the wedding preying on my mind, I haven't slept in weeks."

"It's a good thing that Jack and Ginny eloped. I can't imagine two weddings in the same year."

"It still baffles me that they chose to elope."

"Receiving their doctorates is more important than planning an elaborate wedding."

"Why would they get married and not tell anyone?"

John twirled a strand of her hair. "They were waiting for the right time to share their news. Jack has always allowed Harper to have the limelight."

"I suppose you're right," she sighed. "Do you realize that, in order to keep their marriage a secret, they've been sleeping this week at separate houses?"

"It certainly alleviates your angst about them living together." John kissed her. "Let's hope that our children are as happy in their marriages as we have been in ours."

She stretched her body, fingertips to toes. "I could certainly use a cup of coffee."

"Grab your robe and slippers. I have a surprise for you in the living room."

Unwilling to crawl under the bed to retrieve her slippers, she slipped on a pair of John's moccasins and shuffled her way toward the living room. She was stupefied by the thought that he had planned a surprise for her. With all the wedding arrangements, she had taken only a snippet of time to swing by Sandra's feed store and purchase a new pair of hedge trimmers and coveralls for him.

NOTHING COULD HAVE PREPARED HER for John's surprise. A beautiful fire roaring in the fireplace and the flicker of pillar candles on the mantle gave the room a warm, soft glow in the early morning light. Sitting on one end of the coffee table was the gorgeous hardback book entitled *English Gardens*, a book that she had coveted for years. It was propped against a crystal vase filled with a dozen long-stem red roses. A Blue Willow teapot with two matching teacups, a sugar bowl, and creamer sat on a silver tray at the other end of the coffee table. Leaning against the center cushion of the living room sofa was a white envelope marked *Christmas 1990* and a small gift box. Keeping with tradition, the gift box was wrapped in silver foil and tied with a red ribbon.

Kathryn was speechless. John took her hand and led her over to the sofa.

"Well?" he asked.

Like a fool, she muttered the first thing which popped into her mind. "Tea?"

"You'll understand once you read the card." His grin was wider than the smile on a Cheshire cat.

Christmas 1990

My dearest Kathryn,

Disruption and change continue to introduce new beauty into our lives. A beauty that manifested itself during the events of this past weekend.

Before being swept into the world of in-laws and grandbabies, I want to escort the woman of my dreams to the land of English gardens. Hence, we begin today with a spot of tea.

Love,

John

The charm, a silver dragonfly, stirred special memories of a warm spring day, one large rock, and a lopsided bench overlooking their pond.

FOR SOME STRANGE REASON, IT struck Kathryn that there hadn't been a fire in the fireplace since John died. She didn't know if there was any dry wood in the garage, nor did she know if the flue was open or not.

She looked past the dragonfly to the other charms on her bracelet. A silver morning glory commemorated their glorious trip to England the following year. John proudly toasted her with a tennis racket the year she won the women's doubles tournament, and he sentimentally remembered her mother's passing with a silver sand dollar.

Six of her favorite charms, offered in subsequent years, were silver letters. Each letter was written in cursive: *R, C, S, D, T,* and *W.* The letters celebrated the births of her grandchildren in the order that they were born: Rachel, Caitlyn, Samantha, Derrick, Trey, and William.

All six grandchildren brought disruption and change into her life and introduced Kathryn to a new, beautiful kind of love that she had never before experienced.

CHAPTER THIRTY-TWO

"I HOPE YOU DON'T MIND THAT I stopped by Sandra's to buy a new rake before going to the grocery store." Kathryn's chatter was light as she unpacked the plastic bags heaped on the kitchen counter.

Bleary eyed and still half asleep, John leaned against the doorframe and yawned. Lines from the bedroom pillow creased his left cheek.

She placed a bag of onions under the kitchen sink. "Whew. I have to get out of this sweatshirt." It was late September, and the weatherman stayed true to his promise. The arrival of Indian summer raised daytime temperatures to the upper seventies.

"I was planning on baked chicken for dinner tonight, but I'm not sure I want to start the oven."

"What about a bowl of soup?" he suggested between yawns.

"Is your stomach still bothering you?" Balancing a dozen eggs in her left hand and a gallon of milk in her right, she used her hip to force the refrigerator door ajar.

"Just a little queasy, that's all. The diarrhea isn't as bad."

She set the gallon of milk on the bottom shelf and turned to face him. "This has gone on long enough. We returned from our cruise to Mexico more than six weeks ago, and you still aren't well. Looking back, I'm not sure you felt well before we left. You have been tired for months."

"I know. I know," he mumbled.

"I just wish that you would take care of yourself," she said. "By the way, did you set a date for your retirement?"

The last thing that she wanted to do was to spiral into another heated argument about his retirement, but decisions needed to be made. They were completely at odds. She suggested either an elegant reception or a community drop-in; however, he didn't want anything, nada, not even a plaque engraved with his name.

"I'll make an appointment with the doctor if I'm not feeling better next week," he grumbled.

"John, this has gone on long enough. I'm going to get you an appointment with Tom this week, and that's final." Tom Robinson was a busy internist with a huge practice. His schedule was normally double-booked, and his patients waited three-to-four weeks for routine appointments.

Ignoring John's protest, she smashed the speed dial on her cell phone. She was by-passing Tom's receptionist and going straight to the top. The phone at the other end of the line belonged to Mary Lou, Tom's wife, who just happened to be her co-chair for the silent auction and doubles partner at the tennis club. With Mary Lou's nasty serve and Kathryn's strong defensive back hand, they formed an indomitable team, both on and off the court.

"Tomorrow morning at seven-thirty is perfect. He'll be there," she said. "Thanks, Mary Lou. See you tomorrow at the club."

Kathryn spent the morning competing in a doubles tournament, while John grudgingly kept his appointment with Tom. She was disappointed when he wasn't home for lunch. The Italian subs that she picked up on a whim from the corner deli were causing her stomach to grumble.

"Where have you been?" she asked when he walked into the kitchen. "I was getting worried."

"Tom ran some tests."

"What tests?"

"Just the routine ones, a chest x-ray and an ultrasound of the gut." He grabbed a handful of saltine crackers from the cabinet over the stove. "No sub for me, thanks. By the way, I have a follow-up appointment on Wednesday afternoon."

"Aren't you working on Wednesday?" she asked.

"The appointment is at four-thirty, after I finish seeing patients."

She poured herself a glass of sweet tea. "I'm going with you on Wednesday."

He swallowed a bite of cracker. "How did you and Mary Lou fare today?"

"Superb. Thanks for asking." She wrapped her arms around his neck and hungrily kissed his lips.

Kathryn suggested that John leave his office by three-thirty on Wednesday afternoon, even if it meant shuffling two late-afternoon well-baby checks to one of his partners. Her suggestion afforded him the time to swing by the house, change clothes, and drive across town before Route 81 was clogged with late-afternoon traffic. The clock on the dashboard read four-fifteen as they pulled into Tom's parking lot.

Unlike John's office, which featured Walt Disney characters on its walls, Tom's waiting room was lavishly decorated in rich jewel tones: dark blue, hunter green, and burgundy. There was a stone fireplace at one end of the room, brown leather couches in the middle, and a floor-length mahogany bookcase on the other end. The bookcase was filled with classics such as *Wuthering Heights* and *Robinson Crusoe*.

An article about injuries sustained by professional tennis players caught Kathryn's attention as she thumbed through one of the medical journals, left on an end table in the waiting room. She was reading treatment options for tennis elbow when a nurse, dressed in burgundy scrubs, beckoned them to follow her down a narrow hallway to Tom's personal office. Kathryn couldn't help but notice that the nurse's scrubs and the curtains in the waiting room matched in color.

Totally absorbed in the medical report that he was reading, Tom didn't acknowledge their entrance. His long, spindly fingers readjusted a pair of wire rim reading glasses, which threatened to slide off the end of his nose.

John settled quietly into a handsome leather chair as Kathryn glanced at the latest pictures of Tom and Mary Lou's grandchildren. The rap-tap-tap of Tom's ballpoint pen against the chair's armrest raised the hair on the back of her neck. Mary Lou often complained about Tom's excessive tapping; it was a sure sign that he was extremely agitated and upset.

With one final loud tap, Tom removed his reading glasses and slowly shoved the report to the side of the desk. He rubbed his palms together, leaned forward across the desk, and looked at the two of them, squarely in the eye.

"The fatigue, the nausea, and the diarrhea are caused by a mass growing in your liver."

"Cancer?"

Tom nodded. "I'm pretty sure. I've scheduled a needle biopsy for tomorrow, just to confirm. A bone scan is scheduled for Friday."

Kathryn gasped, and the walls began to close in around her. Desperate for air, she gripped both arms of the leather chair. A voice in her brain began to scream, "I don't have time for this. There's Thanksgiving next month, and then the Christmas holidays. What about the auction?"

The truth is that her heart was wailing, "No, God. Not John. I can't lose him, too."

"...Chemotherapy next week." With a voice droning like agitated bumblebees hovering over the mountain laurel in the spring, Tom talked incessantly about various treatment plans. The droning finally ceased, and Kathryn raised her eyes to discover that he was once again looking over John's report.

"... asymptomatic... remain undetected until they have grown quite large..." She desperately tried to focus on the medical terms that he tossed back and forth like a tennis ball crossing the net. John took her left hand. His grip was crushing.

It seemed as though an interminable amount of time passed before they were released from Tom's office. As she walked out the door, she stopped to organize John's appointment cards and to grab a pair of sunglasses from her purse. "It seems like we were in there all afternoon. I am surprised to see the sun still shining."

John smiled blandly. "Let's go home. We need to call the kids."

IN THE BLINK OF AN EYE, they stopped being the masters of their own schedules. There was a needle biopsy on Thursday, and a bone scan Friday. The first round of outpatient chemotherapy began the following Tuesday; and twice a week, thereafter. Needless to say, the retirement celebration was completely forgotten.

As November nipped at the heels of October, the weather changed drastically. A chilling arctic blast swept down from Canada. Like an angry woman shaking dust from a rug out her backdoor, strong winds stripped autumn leaves from their branches.

Kathryn and John were unaware of autumn's arrival and equally unaware of its departure. Chemotherapy propelled them into a new existence. It was an endless corridor of dazzling white hallways, where time was marked not on a calendar but by a treatment plan, not by the hour but by the dose.

The magazines in the waiting room, primarily *Southern Living* and *Sports Illustrated*, were the only reminders that somewhere outside the hospital's stark walls were frosty mornings and recipes for pumpkin pie. Although John and Kathryn despised chemotherapy for its invasion upon their lives, they clung to it for hope--like two desperate children, wrapped around their mother's leg.

CHAPTER THIRTY-THREE

RUMBLING THAT IT WAS THE Tuesday before Thanksgiving, and the sports section had very few predictions about the college football games, John laid the newspaper down and leaned back in the leather recliner for his afternoon nap. He was snoring within minutes, oblivious that Kathryn was scurrying around their kitchen.

She was attentive to her movements, careful not to slam the kitchen cabinets or jostle the utensils. As she rolled the dough for four pie crusts, she recalled her grandmother's joke that making a great pie crust was like making a fortune. It's all about handling the dough.

She held her grandmother's conviction that the quickest way to ruin a delicious Southern pecan pie was to use a pie crust plunked straight from a grocery store's freezer. Pies worth their weight in calories deserved flaky crusts.

With the mouthwatering aroma of a turkey baking in the oven, she felt alive for the first time in weeks. John was given a one-week reprieve from his treatments, not because chemotherapy adheres to the nation's celebration of Thanksgiving, but because there was a significant drop in his hemoglobin. While the decrease in itself was disheartening, Kathryn was pleased to have a break.

As she pinched the edges of the piecrust, she mentally replayed last week's disappointing phone conversation with Harper.

"Mom, I'm sorry about not coming home at Thanksgiving. It's my turn to have the children, so I promised to take them to Walt Disney World and Sea World. They're almost too big to go to theme parks anymore."

"I can't imagine anyone being too old for Sea World." Kathryn immediately regretted not biting her tongue. While Harper and Chad's separation was an amiable one, she knew that the holidays were particularly difficult for her daughter.

"I'm really sorry, Mom."

"Not as sorry as I am."

"What about Jack and Ginny?" Harper asked. "Can't they come home?"

"I've already asked. The University of Colorado has final exams the second week of December. They both have tests to grade and semester exams to write."

"What about Timothy? Can't he catch a cheap military flight home for Thanksgiving?"

"No, his cutter is getting underway next week. He'll be at sea until February."

"I know that you're disappointed. It seemed like it was more important for the three of us to come home after Dad was diagnosed with cancer than to wait until the holidays."

Kathryn concurred. Having Jack, Harper, and Timothy home before John began his chemotherapy had been remarkable. The five of them stayed up well past midnight, laughing over yellowed photographs assembled in old family photo albums long before scrapbooking became a national trend. Without a doubt, it was a weekend for the memory books.

"The month of June will be here before we know it, and everyone will be at the beach house," Harper said.

"I hope that your father is enough to travel."

"I spoke with the oncologist last week, and he was very upbeat about Dad's prognosis."

"He's upbeat even when your father's blood counts drop." She realized that she was whining, but she was too disheartened to care.

"We'll be together again in June. I promise."

"I hope so."

Her daughter changed the subject. "Have you bought a turkey?"

"Yes. It's a big one, twenty-four pounds." She didn't bother to mention that it was for the homeless shelter. With John eating like a sparrow, she wasn't about to cook a turkey for only the two of them.

Brian stopped by for a visit the following morning. As the pastor of a growing country church, with two morning worship services on Sunday mornings followed by afternoon activities for the youth, he kept anything but banker's hours. Weekdays and evenings were jammed up with committee meetings, Bible studies, hospital visitations, and mid-week services. Despite his hectic schedule, he spent at least two or three hours a week with John, sometimes more. Their conversations, ranging from sports and local politics to God's design for human suffering, kept John's keen mind active and Brian's little black notebook filled with ideas for future sermons.

While Brian visited with John, Kathryn delivered food to the homeless shelter located in a refurbished gas station on the other side of town. On her way home, she stopped by the grocery store for a pound of sliced deli turkey and a carton of milk. She lingered by the mud-room door and eavesdropped on John's animated but friendly banter with Brian. Today, they were discussing government spending and tax hikes.

She waited for a pause in their discussion before carrying the groceries into the family room. Kissing John on the forehead, she said, "It sounds like a Congressional debate in here."

"Wait until our debate really gets started," he said.

Brian looked at his watch. "It will have to wait for another day, because I have a sermon to write."

John joined her in the kitchen after Brian left.

She was warming left-over vegetable soup for lunch when she heard the front door open. "Is anyone home?"

Thinking that Brian had forgotten something, she answered, "We're in the kitchen."

The sounds of whispers and giggles and tiptoes floated down the front hallway.

"Happy Thanksgiving, Nana!"

"Oh my word." She turned from the stove in time to be swallowed in hugs from her Colorado grandchildren. "Rachel… Caitlyn…Trey… I can't believe you're here."

Jack and Ginny stood in the kitchen doorway, smiling.

A loud racket averted everyone's attention. A monstrous yellow lab, overfed and undertrained, thundered into the kitchen, dragging its owner by the leash.

Harper yelled from the front foyer. "Derrick, put Jasper in the back yard. That beast, which you insist on calling a dog, is not going to destroy Nana's house."

Overwhelmed with emotion when Harper and her daughter, Samantha, entered the kitchen, Kathryn tried to formulate her thoughts. "I thought… you said… what about semester exams…Walt Disney World?"

"Small, white lies to keep you from suspecting," Harper answered.

"What about Timothy?"

"That wasn't a lie. He is getting underway the first of next week. He is really sorry that he can't be here."

Kathryn looked across the room. "Why is there a smug look on your face, John Sullivan? Did you know that our children and grandchildren were coming for Thanksgiving?"

Jack wrapped an arm around her shoulder. "Did Dad know that we were coming? He orchestrated this entire gathering."

"What?"

"There is one thing that Daddy didn't orchestrate, and it's in the back of my car," Harper said. "It's an early Christmas surprise."

In a unique and satisfying way, inside a boat cooler wedged in the back of her SUV, Harper successfully transported the coast to the mountains. She hauled a bushel of oysters, all singles, iced and ready to be steamed, from Charleston.

The next day was Thanksgiving, and while the majority of Americans were carving turkey at their dining room tables, Kathryn's family was slurping oysters on the back porch.

"Granddaddy, look what I found." Caitlyn held up a tiny pearl on the end of her oyster knife.

"Well, well, well," John said. "That poor guy had a pernicious case of sand in his pants."

"Per — what?" Derrick asked.

"You know. Pernicious. Damaging, unhealthy or destructive." A talking dictionary, nine-year-old Trey defined the word.

"Like his father," Ginny said, "our son has a voracious appetite for words."

"Wow. I'm a year older, and I don't know that stuff," Derrick said.

Caitlyn diverted the topic of conversation back to her pearl. "Granddaddy, tell me about the guy with sand in his pants."

"Someone, grab an uncooked oyster from the cooler, and open it for me."

Jack deftly slid the tip of his oyster knife between the shells of the bivalve. With a strong twist of his wrist, he popped the hinge of the oyster and laid its opened shells in the middle of the table. Caitlyn squirmed into a prime spot on the bench next to her grandfather. Rachel and Samantha peered around his shoulder. The boys leaned across the plastic table cloth, oblivious to the fact that their sweatshirts were mopping up juice from the last batch of oysters.

"This goop of mucous is the mantle," John explained. "The oyster uses its mantle to build a shell. Sometimes a grain of sand wedges its way under the shell, and it irritates the oyster, kind of like when you get a piece of meat caught between your teeth."

"Yuck. It's like having spacers." With protruding buckteeth, Derrick was an authority on spacers and braces and any other hardware, which equipped his orthodontist's office.

"Precisely. An oyster tackles the irritation by laying down layers of pearl inside its shell."

"In concentric layers," Trey said.

John pointed at his grandson. "Bingo. Each concentric layer adds new growth."

Caitlyn was fascinated. "What are cultured pearls?"

"Cultured pearls are created by artificially imbedding sand underneath the mantle. Your grandmother loves cultured pearls, but I am fascinated by the uncultured ones, with all their flaws and imperfections."

"Your grandfather says the same thing about people," Kathryn said.

John slurped the oyster. "That I do."

Jack motioned for everyone to listen. "Now that Dad has offered his *pearls of wisdom*, I need you to clear the table for one last batch of oysters."

"Oh, no," Harper groaned, "We're not parading the family puns."

Ginny was droll. "Witticism with this group is like *casting pearls before swine*."

Laughter and applause erupted around the table, and everyone made room for the last of the oysters.

For five glorious days, their home was joyfully alive with the sounds of family. Shrill laughter and the whine of country music drifted downstairs from the girl's room. The whirr of a food processor in the kitchen prepared homemade salsa. College football, periodically interrupted by John arguing with the referee's call, resonated from the family room. Jasper barked incessantly at the squirrels scampering across the split-rail fence. Unashamed, somebody hollered for another roll of toilet paper from the hall closet.

Sound is a form of energy which radiates as waves in all directions. John and Kathryn unconsciously harnessed this energy, riding the crest of the wave through December's cancer treatments and the Christmas holidays, which otherwise would have been extremely lonely. If energy is not replenished, however, it inevitably becomes depleted. That's what happened to Kathryn on the twenty-sixth of December. Her memories from Thanksgiving ceased to sustain her, and her spirits began to sag.

Removing the last ornament from the tree and placing it on a layer of white tissue paper, she listened to the rain pelting the window pane.

Shivering, she pulled her sweater around her. The rain, moving in ahead of the cold front, made her joints ache.

Sadly, she glanced around the living room. Only one remnant of the holiday, the Christmas bracelet box, remained. She slipped the card from John on the bottom of the stack of envelopes and placed the stack in the solid cherry jewelry box... but not before reading his words one last time. Poetic and courageous, they refreshed her like a gentle spring rain.

Christmas 2007

My dearest Kathryn,

I thank God that life, for the most part, has been both predictable and kind to us. Unfortunately, cancer, like a jagged piece of sand, an irritant demanding our full attention, has worked its way into the mantle of our lives. In the midst of battle against a formidable foe, I am determined to let the iridescent beauty of our love shine like an uncultured pearl. Never have I been more in love with you.

Your loving husband,

John

Iridescent, the subtle reflection of a rainbow, the charm took her breath away as she held it up to the light. It was an uncultured pearl, set in silver.

She made a mental note: Tomorrow, after the rain stopped, she would venture to jewelry store and have the jeweler attach the charm to her bracelet.

Kathryn studied the magnificent pearl. Its colors seemed almost fluid, like the ripples of an eddy curving around the edges of a sand bar.

"A product of pain and suffering," she mused. "The oyster is left with a strand of pearls, and all that I am left with is another strand of gray hair."

Surprised by her own wit, she laughed.

Feeling lighthearted, she took a sip of coffee; then, she indulged her desire to reread John's card. This time she focused specifically on the last three lines, at first reading them silently and then repeating them aloud.

...In the midst of a battle against a formidable foe, I am determined to let the iridescent beauty of our love shine like uncultured pearl. Never have I been more in love with you.

Suddenly, the words quickened her heart, and she grasped their significance. John knew that he was dying, even then. Like the brilliance of autumn's foliage, he courageously chose to embrace life's splendor as his life ebbed away. And in his own special way, he gently urged her to do the same.

CHAPTER THIRTY-FOUR

WHILE EACH SEASON ALONG THE coast possesses its own unique beauty, Kathryn's favorite season was summer, the earlier in June, the better. On the second day of their vacation, shortly before sundown, Kathryn and John descended the beach house steps and crossed the sand dunes to the ocean. They strolled along an expansive beach, unveiled by the outgoing tide, and basked in the warm sand squishing between their toes.

A cacophony of sounds serenaded them on their walk. Sea oats, standing along the dunes like sentinels guarding against the ocean spray, rustled their golden heads in the evening breeze. Mosquitoes hummed; locusts fiddled; and cicadas drummed. A laughing gull squawked hilariously *hah-ha-ha-hah-hah* after stealing a small minnow out of the mouth of an unsuspecting pelican.

At first, they walked along the upper beach. Swash lines, made from sand and coquina clams entangled in seaweed, marked the height of the outgoing tide. John motioned for Kathryn to move closer to the water's edge when a cormorant circling overhead slicked back his wings and plummeted like a Kamikaze pilot into the ocean. The glossy black bird resurfaced moments later, tossed its catch into the air, and swallowed the unlucky fish, headfirst. Unimpressed, a handful of gray pelicans bobbed lazily, riding the waves up and down as the ocean swelled beneath them.

Having braved the scorching heat, a vast majority of beachcombers and surfers had turned in for the night. They were nursing nasty sunburns until tomorrow's jocularities once again beckoned them back to the beach. A lone man lingered in a lounge chair. Half-asleep, with one eye cracked open, he watched the tip of a fishing rod. Its line extended into the rough surf. A young couple with two small children grabbed one more hour of play before the day faded into night. Stretched upon the sand beside their oldest son, the father dug a moat around a sand castle. It was pitifully crafted but thoroughly enjoyed. His wife snapped pictures of their toddler, gleefully chasing sandpipers down the beach.

Kathryn pointed at the young couple and their children. "Who do they remind you of?"

Out of the corner of her eye, she saw him smile. It was the same smile that stole her heart and never returned it, not that she ever wanted it back anyway.

As the sun began its slow descent toward the horizon, the land began to cool. A strong offshore breeze developed. Kathryn laughed as the breeze flirted with her wardrobe and threatened to peek beneath the wrap covering her swimsuit. She kept one hand poised near the sunbonnet fluttering about her head. Piled on a shelf somewhere between cast nets and boiled peanuts, the straw bonnet was a prized possession, purchased earlier that morning from the corner hardware store. With the soft touch of his hand on her outer arm, John escorted her down the beach. Anyone watching would have thought that the two of them didn't have a care in the world.

"How do you think the children handled the news of our decision," he asked.

"They disagree with us."

"Why?"

"They want to keep the farm in the family."

"What about the decision to stop the chemotherapy?"

"They disagree with that decision, too."

"I know that it's come as a shock," he said, "but they'll adjust."

"When?" she demanded. "After you're dead and gone?"

"Kathryn, we've been through this over and over again. I want to enjoy the time that I have left."

With her big toe, she traced a heart in the sand. "But we want as much time with you as possible."

"Quantity time or quality time?" he asked.

"I don't know."

"Well, I know. I want quality time."

"Jack wanted to know how much time you have left."

"Did you tell him six months to a year?"

She nodded.

"May I change the subject?" he asked. "Did you check the crab traps this afternoon?"

"I did. One of the traps had three adult crabs already, including a stone crab. Surprisingly, the other trap was empty."

"I took the liberty to speak with the kids while you were on the dock with the grandchildren," he said. "I suggested celebrating Christmas at home this year."

"And?"

"They agreed. Harper suggested an old-fashioned Christmas, like we used to have when they were children. She mentioned gathering mistletoe and baking cookies. The boys offered to cut down a tree from the farm."

"That's a wonderful idea," she said. "Will Timothy be able to take leave at Christmas?"

"He thinks so."

"How tall does he want the tree? A million-billion miles high?"

"Or was it a million billion-billion miles high?"

They stood on the beach, roaring with laughter. Kathryn was reminded that John was still very much alive.

"This is what I'm going to miss," she said, contemplatively.

"What?"

"Moments like these, when it's just the two of us."

John drew her close, and they resumed their walk along the beach. Minutes passed before either of them spoke.

"Did you ever realize that, after Rose died, we never attended church as a family?" he asked.

She stiffened. "Do you mean on Christmas Eve? I thought that you wanted to attend the midnight service at All Souls by yourself."

"You could have gone with me."

"You never invited me."

He stopped walking and turned to face her. "Would you have gone if I had asked?"

"I don't know," she answered. "After Rose died, I didn't have much use for God."

He drew in a breath, preparing to venture into uncharted waters. "Have you ever thought about forgiving God?"

Kathryn's world momentarily stopped spinning. His words hung precariously in the salt air; then, they delivered a mighty punch.

She whirled around in the sand. "That's preposterous, and you know it. While I may not be as religious as you, John Sullivan, I certainly know that it's not my place to judge God."

"I didn't say to judge," he said softly. "I said to forgive."

"Don't be ridiculous."

"Haven't you ever gotten mad at God?" he asked.

"No."

"Not once?"

"I can't believe that we're having this discussion," she fumed.

John hit a raw nerve, and she was struggling to maintain control.

"When Rose died," he explained, "my heart was shattered into a million pieces, maybe even a million-billion or a million-billion-billion pieces."

She snatched the sunbonnet off her head and slammed it down on the sand. "And mine wasn't?"

"I didn't mean to imply that your heart wasn't broken." Sighing deeply, he searched the horizon for the right words to say. "One night you went to one of your meetings. It was PTO or garden club or the auction committee. I honestly don't remember--"

"There you go again complaining about my volunteer work."

"Will you let me finish?" he cried. "I was sitting in the rocking chair in Rose's room, and I got scared because I couldn't remember what it felt like to hold her. And I couldn't remember the cute, little look on her face whenever I walked through the door."

He paused to wipe his tears. "I became furious; you can't imagine how furious. I got on my knees, and I asked God why He allowed our daughter to die."

"Did He answer your question?"

John shook his head.

"That figures," she spat. "I could have spared you the trouble of getting on your knees."

"But He did say, 'I bear your pain.'"

Kathryn scoffed.

John persisted. "God's words were softer than a whisper, but they were aimed directly at my heart."

"I seriously doubt that the Creator of the universe is concerned about our pain." She scooped the new straw sunbonnet out of the sand and began marching down the beach as if to say, "This conversation is closed."

"What's the use?" he yelled into the wind. "Our daughter has been buried for almost thirty years, and we still haven't discussed it."

Ten paces separated the two of them when she whipped around with such fury that she nearly stumbled in the sand. She retraced her steps back to John.

"Twenty-seven years and four months, to be exact," she screamed, "and what is there to discuss? Our daughter is dead!"

Seething, Kathryn defaulted to her survival mode: Denying grief's crushing anguish by denying its sheer existence. She had become so masterful at shifting emotional gears in a moment's notice that her countenance, contorted in pain only moments ago, was now devoid of emotion. It was the mien that John dreaded the most.

For twenty-seven years and four months, John carried a flicker of hope that somehow he would be able to break the gridlock around his wife's heart. Unfortunately, the casualties from this evening's battle were too great. Like a flame snuffed out from a dying candle, his hope was extinguished. He slumped to the sand. The rocky groin, which held back his emotions, collapsed. Smashing his fist into the wet sand, he sobbed, "I can't do it anymore. I simply can't do it."

"What can't you do?" she demanded. Her tightly crossed arms crushed the new sunbonnet against her chest.

"I can't keep binding your wounds."

"I don't need your bandages, Dr. Sullivan," she retorted. "I'm fine."

"You are not fine. You are bleeding all over the place, and you're bleeding all over this family. I just want to know, who is going to clean up the blood when I'm gone?"

"I'll do it myself."

"Oh, I see," he said sarcastically. "The invincible Kathryn Sullivan will join another organization or spearhead another community project."

"That's not fair."

"It's the truth, Kathryn. We have buried a daughter and three parents, and you have yet to shed a single tear."

"Have you forgotten? Rose died a month after my father had his stroke. We buried him only six weeks after we buried her. When we lost your father, I had a farm to run. There were two mares to be fed, a cow to be milked, tomatoes to be picked, and watermelon to get to market the morning of his funeral. When did I ever have time for tears?"

"Would time have made a difference?" His voice could barely be heard over the wind.

She glanced down at the profile of the man whom she had loved for nearly fifty years. It was hard to believe that, less than five years ago, she chastised him for developing a middle-aged paunch. Now he was extremely thin and frail. Why were they wasting the precious time, which they had left, bludgeoning each other over their pain?

As the sun sizzled beneath the horizon, sending out red and orange streamers like fireworks in the evening sky, she lowered herself to the ground.

"I'm sorry," she said, "truly, I am."

She tenderly brushed a smattering of wet sand off of John's brow with her fingertips. A fresh stream of tears rolled down his cheeks, and as she reached up to wipe away his tears, the gridlock that encased her heart began to crack open. The crack was pencil-thin, but it was a crack, nonetheless. And for the first time in years, Kathryn began to cry.

CHAPTER THIRTY-FIVE

O NE WEEK LATER, JOHN AND Kathryn returned from their vacation, refreshed and determined to cherish the remaining time that John had left. Of her own volition, Kathryn stepped down from her volunteer work on the arts council and historical society; postponed her stint as president of the garden club; and reduced her hours at the county library to twice a month. They spent the lazy days of summer together as one, taking leisurely strolls in the country and delighting in green dragonflies skimming across the pond. They picked wild blueberries along the road and canned nearly two bushels of plump, red tomatoes.

John approached death in the same way that he approached life, with a unique blend of practicality and philosophy. On good mornings, he sipped freshly brewed coffee with Kathryn on the back deck, relishing summer's vivid colors. On bad days, he lounged on the family room couch and read a few pages of *The Hobbit* before drifting off to sleep.

While he napped, she ran errands and busied herself around the house. There were water hoses to be drained, ferns to be hauled into the garage, and compost to be mulched before the weather turned cold. As she covered the garden in fresh mulch, she wondered if her husband would be alive next spring when it was time to put the tomato plants in the ground.

He grew weaker as the days grew shorter. Their mornings drinking coffee on the back deck lessened while his naps on the couch increased. On some days, the cancer was merely a dark cloud hanging overhead, casting its ugly shadow. On other days, it was an advancing army, an enemy blatantly pillaging nutrients from his body and reducing him to nothing but skin and bones. Kathryn imagined herself launching an attack, violently screaming at an insidious enemy and pummeling it into the ground. Unfortunately, this offensive attack existed only in her imagination.

"I got the ham out of the freezer," she said. "Can you believe that it's Christmas Eve, and our children and grandchildren will be here in a few hours? They were lucky to get flights."

Weakly, John smiled. It had been a bad night, and he couldn't muster the strength to get out of bed.

The doorbell rang as she was tucking the afghan around his feet. "Don't sneak away," she jested. "I'll be right back."

Before leaving the bedroom, she kissed his forehead and caressed his cheek with her hand. She made her way down the hall, savoring the feel of his skin on her fingertips.

The doorbell rang again.

She peered through the glass etchings in the door. "Just a moment, Brian. I have to unlock the deadbolt."

"Is this a bad time?" he asked.

"I was in the bedroom with John. Please come in," she said, opening the door "Are you ready for Christmas?"

He stomped his feet on the welcome mat. "Unfortunately, no. I still have to finish writing tonight's sermon."

"Do you expect a big crowd?"

"I'm always hopeful." He followed her down the hall. "It looks like you are ready for the holidays. Your home and yard look beautiful, as usual."

"Icicle lights... fresh garland... benne seed cookies... the works. The children requested an old-fashioned Christmas, and I don't want to disappoint them."

"How are you holding up?"

"Okay, I guess. I'll be glad when the children get here this afternoon."

"Do you need us to go to the airport for you?"

"No. Harper will pick up the boys and their families on her drive up from Charleston. Thank you anyway."

"We are right next door if you need anything."

"I know. You and Sarah have done so much already."

"How is he doing?"

"Today's not a good day," she said sadly. "He'll be glad to see you, though. You always brighten his day."

Within a few minutes, Brian emerged from the bedroom.

"Are you leaving so soon?" she asked. "Can't you join us for lunch? I have soup simmering on the stove."

"I need to leave for the office in just a few minutes. I've got that sermon to finish." He kissed her on the cheek. "Remember to call if you need us."

She returned to the bedroom and found John lying against the pillow. In his hand was an envelope with *Christmas 2008* scrawled across the front. His other hand held a small gift box.

"What is this?" she stammered.

His attempt to smile was feeble. He lifted the envelope toward her. In a voice barely above a whisper, he said, "Brian helped."

She sat on the bed beside him and patted his hand.

"Please open . . . the two of us."

Kathryn grasped the significance of his words. This was their last Christmas together. It was a moment meant to be shared between the two of them.

Her hands trembled as she opened the oversized envelope, the kind that would have cost extra postage had it been mailed. The picture on the front of the card was a magnificent oil painting of a home that had been lavishly decorated for the holidays. It blurred through her tears.

John struggled to sit up so that he could speak. "Our home... all these years... thank you."

Kathryn reached out and gave his free hand a slight squeeze. "It has been my joy."

She opened the card and began to read the words which, in his weakened condition, were miraculously penned. She knew by the length of the text that the task had been tedious for him. It was a true labor of love.

She read the card aloud, slowly and deliberately.

Christmas, 2008

My dearest Kathryn,

While we are insignificant, God's love for us is not. It is deep and profound and mysterious. I believe that He laughs when we laugh, and He weeps when we suffer. In His unfathomable love, we find our significance.

To my precious wife, life with you has been wonderful. Like the waves upon the shore, my love for you is undying. I am and have always been eternally yours.

All my love,

John

As she read the message, John slipped quietly into a coma. Early Christmas morning, he walked into eternity.

Kathryn sat at the kitchen table, recalling that she never opened John's gift last Christmas. She reached into the cherry jewelry box and found the unopened present. It was still beautifully tied with the red satin ribbon.

During the days leading up to or following the funeral, someone must have placed the forgotten present at the bottom of her Christmas bracelet box. That person must have taken great care to slip the card in its proper sequence before placing the stack of envelopes in the jewelry box and draping her Christmas bracelet across the top.

With all the fortitude that she could muster to control her trembling hands, she untied the red satin ribbon and opened the box. The charm inside was a delicate silver cross.

The grandfather clock startled her. Was it four o'clock already? She had only an hour to get dressed before Brian, Sarah, and Abigail arrived with dinner. She wiped a tear from her cheek and stood up from the table. Placing last year's card at the bottom of the stack, she re-tied the envelopes and returned them to the Christmas bracelet box. On top of the stack of envelopes, she placed the silver cross.

"Maybe I'll revisit these memories tomorrow," she sighed.

CHAPTER THIRTY-SIX

KATHRYN WAS ANGRY WITH HERSELF. "After all that they've done for you, how can you even think about not going? The three of them are in the living room right now, hanging icicles on your tree. If out of sheer gratitude alone, you are going to their church service tonight. Whether you want to or not."

She ran a comb through her hair.

"What is it your granddaughters say? You need to get over yourself," she said with a spritz of hairspray, "You have no plans for Christmas, so you can mollycoddle yourself by staying in bed all day tomorrow."

Ouch. The voice of her conscience was cruel.

She blotted her lipstick and checked her reflection in the vanity mirror, reminding herself that it wasn't anyone's fault but her own, that her skirt was snug. No one forced her to indulge in a second spoonful of Sarah's lasagna and two benne seed wafers. Sighing in submission, she turned off the lights over her vanity mirror and grabbed her heels from the bedroom closet.

A portrait of sophistication in her black suit and pearls, Kathryn walked into the living room where Brian was waiting.

"Your chariot awaits you, my lady," he said playfully. "Sarah and Abigail are already in the car."

"Have I made you late?"

"If we leave now, we will be on time."

She noticed the Charlie Brown Christmas tree standing by the bay window in the living room. Magically transformed by twinkling lights and a vast array of ornaments and baubles, the tree cast a warm glow toward the center of the room. The fresh smell of pine, reminiscent of Christmas past, filled her with hope.

"Maybe Christmas will come this year, after all," she thought.

As soon as she buckled herself into the front seat of the car, Abigail began speaking. "Mrs. Sullivan, have you ever been to my church?"

"No, dear. This is my first time."

"Do you know what my church looks like?"

"I don't have a clue."

The only thing that she knew for certain was that Brian left a lucrative law practice in order to attend seminary. Two years ago, he purchased an old barn on the outskirts of Asheville. He gutted and refurbished its interior and began a fledgling, nondenominational church.

"I remember going to your church when Dr. John died," Abigail said. "There were paintings in the windows."

For the first time in a year, bits and pieces about John's funeral assembled in Kathryn's mind, like the pieces of a jigsaw puzzle. All Soul's Cathedral looked glorious that morning. Sunlight streaming through the stained glass windows reflected off the parquet floor and illuminated the altar. There weren't any red poinsettias, only white ones.

As the widow, she was seated with her children and grandchildren on chairs at the front of the church. The remainder of their family and friends were packed like sardines on wooden pews behind the row of chairs. Many of John's colleagues and countless others were forced to stand with their backs against the walls along the side aisles. From the moment that the pipe organ played "Amazing Grace" until the priest offered the last amen, the service was a tremendous tribute to John and his work within the community.

"Mama, my tights are scratchy," Abigail complained from the backseat.

"We'll fix them when we get to church."

"But, Mama--"

"Abigail, there's nothing that I can do about your tights right now."

"I can't wait. They itch so badly."

Brian looked in the rear-view mirror. "I would appreciate silence. I have to preach a sermon in less than thirty minutes."

Everything grew quiet in the backseat. Unfamiliar with this side of Asheville, Kathryn watched as they exited the four-lane highway and turned left on a newly paved road. After two more turns, Brian eased the car into a parking space marked *Pastor.*

Standing at the back of the church, waiting for Sarah and Abigail to return from the ladies' room, Kathryn removed her scarf and gloves and stuffed them into the side pocket of her wool coat. She noticed that the sanctuary in Brian's church was nothing like the sanctuary at All Souls Cathedral. Rows of metal folding chairs, ten across on each side, lined a center aisle. The floors were made of roughly hewn pine. The faint aroma of sawdust and wet hay lingered in the air. The altar, surrounded by a small rail, which someone painted white, was filled with red poinsettias. Suspended from the ceiling by huge bolts was a large, wooden cross.

Taking hold of Kathryn's hand, Abigail whispered, "Mrs. Sullivan, my tights aren't scratchy anymore."

"That's a relief."

"I asked Mama, and she said that you can sit by me."

"I would be honored."

Sarah beckoned for them to follow her down the center aisle to a row of open seats. Kathryn's attention was immediately drawn to the Advent wreath on the side of the altar. It surprised her that, instead of being purple, the candles were a lovely, soft shade of blue. Along the wall, a stringed guitar leaned in its stand. Next to the guitar was a beat-up kitchen stool, reminiscent of one that she had seen before in Sarah's laundry room.

Being as discreet as possible, she glanced at the people in Brian's flock. She nodded to Brenda, the owner of the local travel agency. Dressed in her winter-white pant suit and gold heels, Brenda didn't look a day over fifty. She also recognized Sally from the beauty shop, the city mayor and his family, and a young family who lived at the top of her street. She was pleasantly surprised to see so many familiar faces.

Growing warm, she removed her coat and draped it across her lap. She flipped to the program's insert and began reading the list of patrons who had donated poinsettias for the altar. Her heart quickened when she read that one of the poinsettias was offered by "Brian, Sarah and Abigail Hansen in the memory of John Sullivan."

"Please don't let me cry," she thought. "It's been an emotional day, and if I start crying now, the faucet may not stop dripping until morning."

A guitar chord in the key of C brought the entire congregation to its feet for the singing of "Joy to the World." Fearful that she would sing off key in the ear of the bearded gentleman to her right, she sang quietly under her breath. It shocked her that the young man playing the guitar was dressed in blue jeans, an Oxford button-down, and penny loafers. When the congregation had finished singing all four verses, he replaced the guitar in its stand and said the opening prayer.

After the reading of the Christmas story, Brian asked the congregation to be seated. He retrieved the stool from the side of the sanctuary and placed it in the center aisle, in front of the congregation. Wrapping the extra folds of cloth from his robe around his lanky frame, he seated himself on the stool, casually, as though he was about to share a cup of tea at a friend's kitchen table.

"My name is Pastor Brian Hansen," he began. "I would like to extend an extra special welcome to any visitors whom we have with us tonight. We pray that your worship here this evening will be blessed."

Someone in the congregation sneezed loudly, and Abigail giggled.

"May I have the children in the congregation join me for the sermon?"

Immediately, as if on cue, children of all shapes and sizes began moving out of their pews toward the center aisle. They appeared eager to hear Brian's message and quickly settled themselves in a semi-circle at his feet.

"What is the best thing about Christmas?"

"Santa!"

Kathryn chuckled. Why wasn't she surprised that Abigail was the first to answer?

"No school," an impish boy yelled. His freckles were as red as the suit that Santa wears.

"Patrick, I thought that you liked school."

To the delight of the adults, the boy emphatically wagged his head back and forth.

"What else?"

"Presents."

"Um, stockings."

A darling girl, dressed in a Scottish plaid skirt and white tights, raised her hand.

"Meredith, what is your favorite thing about Christmas?"

"I like snow."

"I like snow, too."

"Me, too," countless others shouted.

Brian calmed the children with his hand. "I have another question. Can you remember what you got for Christmas last year?"

"Santa brought me a necklace, but I lost it."

"My guitar string broke."

One boy was despondent. "I got a stupid sweater."

Thrilled for an audience, freckle-faced Patrick pointed to his temple, Winnie-the-Pooh style, as if to say, "Think, think, think."

A precious little girl, with cropped hair, stood on tiptoes beside the stool and patted Brian on the leg.

"Pastor Brian."

"Yes, Monica."

"I don't remember what Santa brought me."

"That's alright, Monica. I would venture to guess that many of our Christmas presents are lost or destroyed or even forgotten. I remember one Christmas, in particular. I was seven years old. I asked Santa for a bright blue, two-wheeled bike with a banana seat and hand brakes."

"A yellow seat?"

Brian laughed. "No. The seat was shaped like a banana. I told my mother on Christmas Eve that I wasn't going to sleep, not a single wink, until Santa came down our chimney. I lay in bed that night, not moving a muscle, quiet as a church mouse. I listened as hard as I could for the jingle of Santa's sleigh bells and the scratch of reindeer hooves on the roof."

A curly headed youngster inched closer to the stool. Any closer and the little boy would be sitting on top of Brian's foot. "Did Santa come to your house?"

"Not until I fell asleep."

Abigail interrupted him. "Santa won't come if you're awake."

He leaned forward. "Guess what I found parked in my bedroom the next morning?"

"A bike," the children shouted.

Brian was wistful. "You can't imagine how much I loved that bike."

"What happened to it?"

"Turn around and look."

The children whipped around to see one of the ushers carting an old, rusty bike from the back of the church. Its front wheel was mangled.

"I had a huge growth spurt that year," Brian explained. "After a few months, my legs had grown too long for the bike. I leaned it against a metal shed in our back yard, and it began to rust. That year, I made an important discovery."

The sanctuary was so quiet that one could hear a pin drop.

"I discovered that time weathers gifts, and new things become old."

Kathryn took a hard look at the Christmas bracelet and wondered if Brian was intentionally describing her life. Had her life become weathered and tattered, forgotten and old? Had she allowed John's death to reduce her world to series of memories and regrets, all delicately linked together on a chain?

She turned her attention back to Brian, just in time to hear him say, "There is only one gift that won't grow old or rust or tarnish. And that is God's love for us."

The man sneezed again, but this time Abigail didn't laugh.

"I have a question. How many of you like it when your grandparents come for a visit?"

The boy with the broken guitar string became excited. "My nana's coming tomorrow night."

"Mine, too," another exclaimed.

"Mrs. Sullivan is like my grandma, and she lives next door. She came with me tonight," Abigail announced.

Kathryn felt her cheeks grow hot.

"Let me ask each of you another question," Brian said. "If you have a choice, do you want your grandparents to send a card in the mail saying that they love you? Or do you want them to come to Asheville for a visit?"

As if on cue, the children shouted, "A visit!"

"Do any of you know what the Incarnation is?" he asked.

"My grandma drinks that," Patrick said. "She likes the chocolate, but not the strawberry."

The entire congregation erupted with laughter.

It took a moment or two for Brian to regain his composure. "And you wonder why I preach children's sermons."

Again, everyone laughed.

"Patrick, your grandmother drinks Carnation. The word that I said was *In-car-na-tion*. *Incarnation* means that God loves us so much that He visited the earth. Just like when your grandma and grandpa visit you. The Bible says that God came to earth as a baby to dwell among us."

Abigail spoke with authority. "You're talking about Baby Jesus."

"That's right. God came to earth as Baby Jesus, born to Mary and Joseph in the small town of Bethlehem. He was one hundred percent human and one hundred percent God, all at the same time. That is why we are gathered here tonight, to celebrate the arrival of Baby Jesus. Tomorrow morning when you are opening your presents, I want you to remember that Baby Jesus is the greatest gift of all. God Himself in a manger."

"What a remarkable Christmas sermon," Kathryn thought. Little did she suspect that the sermon was not yet finished.

CHAPTER THIRTY-SEVEN

B RIAN ADDRESSED THE ENTIRE CONGREGATION. "A friend of mine lost his battle against cancer last year. Before he died, I had the wonderful privilege of spending countless hours with him, talking about both life and death. It didn't surprise me when he told me that he would miss celebrating Christmas with his family the most. Christmas was a lavish affair at his house, heaped in tradition straight out of a *Southern Living* magazine. My years as a lawyer taught me not to assume the obvious, so I asked him, 'Why do you love Christmas so much?' My friend closed his eyes as if asleep. The cancer had spread to his brain, so it was not uncommon for him to drift off to sleep in the middle of a conversation. I stood up from the chair, preparing to leave, when he reached out for my hand and asked me to stay. He then proceeded to tell me a heartwarming story, one that I will never forget."

Kathryn felt her mouth get dry.

"As a physician, my friend had the opportunity to share in many adoption stories. There was one story, in particular, which affected him more than the rest. Years ago, a middle-aged couple traveled out-of-state in order to adopt a baby girl. The paperwork from the orphanage documented that the baby had some disabilities. The couple didn't realize the extent of the baby's disabilities, however, until they arrived at the orphanage and held her for themselves. The likelihood of this child living what you and I would call a normal life was slim to none.

"I asked my friend if the couple considered returning the child to the orphanage and canceling the adoption, and he shook his head. He explained that they loved this child long before they ever held her.

"Six months later, they sat in the judge's chambers waiting to sign the final adoption papers. The judge first counseled them, cautioning that it was going to require tremendous sacrifice on the part of the man, his wife, and their three biological children to raise a child with so many disabilities. Evidently, the judge asked them the same question that I asked my friend. Did they want to reconsider the adoption?

"The couple never wavered. They cried tears of joy and signed the legal papers for a child whom many of us wouldn't want. It is my understanding that the judge officiating over their case cried with them as well."

He stood up from the stool.

"Was this story simply the ramblings of a dying man? I don't think so. What then does this story have to do with Christmas?" His eyes scanned the sanctuary. "I believe that it has everything to do with Christmas. My friend loved adoption stories, and that is exactly what Christmas is. It's an adoption story. It is our adoption story."

Pausing, he looked at the congregation.

"More than two thousand years ago, our Heavenly Father, the King of the Universe, removed His crown and donned His traveling clothes. He arrived in Bethlehem as a precious newborn, God in a manger, fully human and completely divine, with the intention of signing a fistful of adoption papers. Adoption papers for Patrick and Meredith and Mrs. Nelson and Old Joe Simpson sitting on the back pew."

Monica was back on her feet, grabbing Brian's hand. "And me?"

He lifted the little girl into his arms. "And you too, Monica."

"God knows the extent of our disabilities and our brokenness. The Bible says that He delights in us with an unconditional love that honestly makes no sense to our world. He removed His royal crown and journeyed to the earth, because He loves us."

Brian gently lowered Monica to the floor.

"Don't get confused. Our adoption papers were signed, not in Bethlehem, but in His blood on Calvary. It was there that He offered us His Name. The Bible says that we did not receive the spirit of bondage again to fear, but we received the Spirit of adoption by whom we cry out, 'Abba, Father.' God calls all of us to be heirs in an eternal kingdom, sons and daughters, princes and princesses of the Heavenly King. The Book of Psalms says that he offers us crowns of tender mercies and loving kindness.

"The question for each of us gathered here tonight is this: Do we accept God's gift of unconditional love? Can we accept that, in spite of our brokenness, He delights in us and calls us by name? If so, it's time to lay down our pride and pick up our heavenly crowns. They are crowns that will never tarnish or be forgotten or grow old."

Brian's voice choked with emotion. "Now let us pray."

At the end of the service, Kathryn heard a parishioner speaking to Brian. "Did your friend ever say what happened to the young child in the adoption story?"

Slowly, a smile spread across his face. "He said that she developed into a beautiful rose."

Tears flowed silently and unashamedly down Kathryn's cheeks as she followed Sarah and Abigail to the car.

CHAPTER THIRTY-EIGHT

THE WIPERS ON BRIAN'S CAR swooshed back and forth like a metronome, wiping away a random snow shower on what meteorologists forecasted to be a brilliant, star-studded night. The subtle blending of Christmas carols over the radio with an occasional comment from Abigail, mostly about Rudolph, offered comfortable background noise. Brian and Sarah looked at the road ahead, neither of them speaking a word. Kathryn gazed out the passenger window, brushing away an occasional tear.

By the time the SUV climbed the treacherous driveway, the freak snow shower was gone. One or two isolated snowflakes fluttered in the headlights as the car rolled to a stop. Brian glanced in his rearview mirror. "Abigail, stay in the car with your mother, while I walk Mrs. Sullivan to the door. I'll be back in just a moment."

Without whining, the child obeyed.

Brian shook his head in amazement. "If Santa visited every night, we wouldn't need parenting books."

A thin layer of rock salt crunched beneath their feet as they trudged down the sidewalk and up the front porch steps. Slush from the melting snow seeped through Kathryn's stockings and chilled her.

"Thank you for a lovely evening," she said.

"Are you okay?"

"I'm fine. My mascara is smeared, isn't it?"

"Believe it or not, I wasn't asking about your appearance."

"Young man," she mocked, "have you not realized that to a Southern lady everything is about appearances?"

"If everything is about appearances, God would have chosen a different venue for His debut. I doubt that a manger on the outskirts of Bethlehem would have sufficed."

"That's a great closing argument. The question is, 'Why didn't I ever think to tell my mother that?'"

His voice became soft and tender. "Kathryn, I'm worried about your heart."

"My heart is in better shape right now than my mascara." She fished around at the bottom of her purse. "Now where did I put my house keys?"

"You still haven't answered my question. Are you okay?"

"Here are my keys," she announced. "Trust me; I'm fine. The only thing wrong with my heart is that life has chipped it away, piece by piece."

"Have you considered that God is carving His reflection in you?" he suggested. "Tonight from the pulpit, I wasn't talking only about your daughter. I was talking about all of us, including you."

Wordlessly, she watched him unlock the front door for her.

"Kathryn, God loves you. He knows your brokenness and your pain, and that is precisely why He signed an adoption paper at Calvary for you, too. Believe it or not, in His reflection, you *are* a beautiful rose."

"I'm more like a thorn in His side." She stomped slush from her feet and stepped into the foyer.

"Sin was the only thorn in Christ's side. And it wasn't a thorn; it was a spear."

"Brrrrr. Let me close the door before this Arctic blast gets in," she said hastily. "Merry Christmas, Brian, and thank you again." With the word *merry* hanging in the air like an icicle waiting to drop, she closed the front door.

It had been an emotionally exhausting day, and she desperately craved the silence and solace of her home. She slipped off her heels and hung her coat in the hall closet, acutely aware of a symphony playing in her mind. Brian's words, *a beautiful rose*, repeated themselves in her brain like quarter notes rapidly ascending and descending a musical staff. She was relieved when a light emanating from upstairs demanded her attention. Somewhere between the bottom and top steps, Brian's words played their last measure.

She reached for the light switch in the guest bedroom but stopped short. Turning out the light wasn't the only thing that she and Abigail had forgotten. Scattered across the bed were the pieces of the Nativity set and wads of used tissue paper.

She lingered a moment, as she did every Christmas season, to appreciate the workmanship involved in each piece. She admired her father-in-law's attention to detail in the perkiness of the donkey's ears and the curious tilt of the lamb's head. A piece of hay sticking out of the mouth of the one-eared cow never failed to make her laugh. She marveled at the wonder, carved into the face of her favorite shepherd, the one who was leaning with both hands against his staff. The incredible sadness filling Mary's eyes haunted her, reminding her of the day that this magnificent work of art came to reside in their home.

It had been a dreadful morning, little more than a week after Rose's funeral. The children were at school, and John was at the office. Suffocating in the dreadful silence of an empty house, uninterested in reading the morning newspaper and unwilling to write another thank-you note, she was relieved to hear John's father knock at the mud-room door. Tucked under his arm was a sizeable cardboard box.

"William, what a pleasant surprise," she said. "Come in."

"I should have called first."

"Don't be silly. You know that you're always welcome."

Bending, he set the cardboard box on the floor. "I was saving this for Rose's sixteenth birthday. It's the Nativity set that I carved for John's mother."

Overcome by a tidal wave of emotion, Kathryn squeezed his hand. "Thank you. Rose would have loved it."

He grabbed a handkerchief from his back pocket and wiped his nose. "Well, I had better get going."

"Do you have time for a cup of coffee?" she asked. "I just brewed a fresh pot."

"I don't want to intrude."

"Please stay. This morning, I could use the company."

He stuffed the handkerchief into his pocket and followed her to the kitchen.

She poured the coffee. "How did you do it?"

"Do what?"

"How did you survive after John's mother died? How did you make yourself wake up and get out of bed in the morning?"

"I didn't have a choice. The boys kept me going. When my wife died, they needed both a mother and a father." He sipped the hot coffee. "Somehow, I'm not sure how, I plowed through the muck."

"Plowed through the muck?"

His eyes clouded with pain. "Yep. I plowed through the muck."

By mid-morning, she had dismissed his words as a strange remark and nothing more.

Unwilling to cave into human nature's proclivity for procrastination and equally unwilling to leave a mess until morning, especially Christmas morning, Kathryn shook away the memories. She lifted the one-eared cow off the bed and rewrapped it in a piece of tissue paper. Next, she selected the lamb.

For the first time in nearly twenty-nine years, she reconsidered her father-in-law's words. *Plowed through the muck.*

"Is this a rudimentary and unsophisticated way of describing the journey through grief?" she wondered.

Despite the late hour, it suddenly seemed a pity not to set up the Nativity on the mahogany sideboard. She returned the pieces to their original box and carted the entire set, including the stable, to the dining room. She arranged the Holy Family in the center of the stable, setting Mary to the right of the manger and Joseph to the left. Except for one tiny lamb nestled at Joseph's feet, she placed the cattle and sheep outside the stable with the two shepherds. She positioned an angel to peer over Mary's shoulder while situating the other two angels among the shepherds. She knew from her Episcopalian roots that the Wise Men were still a long way off, so she moved them to the side of the crèche.

As she laid Baby Jesus in the manger, a phrase from Brian's sermon popped into her mind: *God in a manger, fully human and completely divine.* The thought made her shiver. She had always envisioned Christmas as the sweet story of Baby Jesus, a precious little newborn lying meekly in a manger. She was shaken by the vision of God journeying to earth, cloaked as a human, and carrying her adoption papers in His hand.

The mental picture became staggering. Forgetting to switch off the downstairs lights, Kathryn dragged her exhausted self to the master bedroom. She slipped into her nightgown, slid between the cool sheets, and drifted off to sleep--without even brushing her teeth.

CHAPTER THIRTY-NINE

SLEEP CAME FITFULLY FOR KATHRYN. Images and dreams, some comforting, others troubling, tumbled one right after another. She dreamed that she was standing at a wooden gate on the southern side of a magnificent field of daisies. The centers of the daisies were brilliant as the sun; their petals were pure white. A high split-rail fence, the kind that would enclose a horse pasture, surrounded the field. She saw Rose, dressed in a long white gown with her hair tied back by a large satin bow, running barefooted through the flowers toward a man. Despite his pressed khaki pants and a button-down shirt, the man was without shoes. Kathryn strained to see the features of his face.

As the distance between Rose and the man gradually closed, his features came into full view. It was John, looking healthy and robust, not a day over thirty. Rose bounded into her daddy's arms. Elated, he twirled her around and around among the daisies; she squealed with laughter as he turned faster and faster.

Kathryn noticed a man and woman walking through a pasture gate located at the northern end of the field. Striding confidently toward the center of the field, appearing as young as the day Kathryn first met him, walked John's father. From her pictures, Kathryn recognized that the woman walking at William's side was John's mother. Joining hands, the foursome crossed the field of daisies and passed through the eastern gate. They disappeared from sight, totally unaware that Kathryn was hysterically screaming their names.

Anguished, she tugged the gate open and dashed into the field of daisies. Brambles instantly began growing up between the flowers until she found herself stumbling in a nasty briar patch. Thorns grabbed at her, tearing holes in her clothes and ripping her flesh. She hopelessly swatted an irksome swarm of gnats buzzing around her face.

Thinning, the briar patch eventually became navigable.

She bent to catch her breath and to wipe away a trail of blood running down her calf. In front of her, at the edge of a forest, was an open casket, adult sized, carved from a freshly hewn pine. As she smoothed her hair and straightened her clothes, she walked over to the casket and peered inside.

Willy Bear, Timothy's long lost teddy bear, was seated at the far end of the coffin. His fur was still nappy and the color of green tea, and the arm that once dangled by threads was now gone. Having lost his other eye, Willy Bear was sightless.

"He really is a pitiful looking bear," she thought.

"Whose worth is measured in God's love." It was her mother's voice.

Frantically, Kathryn looked around for any sight of her mother, but to no avail. Instead, to her absolute delight, she sighted a pair of pileated woodpeckers before they disappeared among the trees.

The late-afternoon shadows fell, and the forest green faded into a monotonous shade of gray. It started snowing heavily. The surrounding landscape became cloaked in white.

Snowflakes landing in the warm casket melted quickly, and within a matter of minutes, the pine box and Willy Bear were soaked.

As daylight was snuffed out, the coffin receded into nightfall. Kathryn became terrified. Unable to move, she stared straight ahead into the darkness, gazing neither to her left nor to her right. Minutes later, or it could have been hours for all she knew, the shadows separated like a thin veil. A wooden manger, illuminated by a faint light located somewhere above her head, emerged where the coffin had been sitting. As soon as her eyes adjusted to the light of a lantern hanging from a set of rafters, she realized that she was standing inside a rickety, old stable. A one-eared cow stood in the far corner, leisurely munching hay.

"I know this story," she thought. "It's the Christmas story." She glanced into the manger expecting to find an infant wrapped in swaddling clothes. Instead of a baby, the wooden slats of the feeding trough were bare. That is, except for a royal crown.

A voice whispered to her. "You, too, can be a princess."

Kathryn awakened with a start as the grandfather clock chimed three. She lay in the stillness of her room like a child awakening from a nightmare, trying to assimilate her dream into reality. Grabbing her robe from the end of the bed and sliding her feet into a pair of slippers, she padded her way down the hall and into the dining room. She rested her elbows on the sideboard and cradled her head in her hands. Then, gathering her courage, she peered at the crèche. It was only a dream. Or was it?

She stared at the Baby Jesus lying in the manger, and her lips began to move. Halting at first, a mere trickle, her words gained momentum and rushed headlong, cascading one on top of another. Kathryn was arguing with God.

"After all that I have done, how could you ever think of offering me a crown?" she contended. "I signed those adoption papers for Rose. When the judge asked me, I looked at him, straight in the eye, and solemnly promised that I would love her and protect her and give her the best possible care that I could give her. But, I abandoned her when she had the sniffles. What made me think that my father's nursing staff was incompetent without my supervision? What was I thinking?"

"And Rose isn't the only one I failed," she ranted. "What about the time I knowingly walked out on John's father and our son, leaving them stranded with a field of fresh watermelons to pick? For what? A vacation at the beach? A loggerhead turtle? It is my fault that Timothy still shoulders the burden of his grandfather's death."

There it was, out in the open. The agonizing guilt, which simmered almost thirty years, bubbled up like gas emitted from a dying salt marsh. Undetected, like a vicious cancer, her torment had spread. Kathryn was emotionally and spiritually dying.

"You can't possibly love me." She laid her head against the polished surface of the mahogany sideboard and sobbed uncontrollably.

An inaudible voice answered her.

"It is not about who you are; it is about Who I AM."

AWESTRUCK, KATHRYN SANK TO THE floor. As she leaned her head against the sideboard in the pre-Christmas dawn, a massive weight lifted from her chest. She drew in a deep, cleansing breath and exhaled slowly. Joy spread through her heart like wildfire. Beneath the flame's embers flowed an incredible and incomprehensible peace. For the first time ever, Kathryn embraced the God who loved her.

Unencumbered, she felt as fresh and pristine as newly fallen snow. Her heart soared. Sleep was the furthest thing from her mind as she brewed a fresh pot of coffee. She settled into a kitchen chair, anxiously awaiting the first rays of morning.

CHAPTER FORTY

CHRISTMAS DAWNED GLORIOUSLY. A FAINT hint of orange creeping across the horizon served as a quiet prelude. It was followed by a kaleidoscope of colors, magnificent banners harmoniously bursting across the morning sky, announcing the birth of a new day.

Kathryn stood at the kitchen window, peacefully watching the birds at the feeder. She contemplated the hike down the drive for the morning newspaper. A blue jay, parading its brilliant blue plumage like a pompadour, jeered from his perch in a nearby oak tree at a squirrel scampering among the branches.

The phone rang and startled her.

"Hello?"

"Merry Christmas, Mom. Are you awake?"

"Timothy, what a wonderful surprise. I've been up for hours. Where are you?"

"Here in Kodiak. I had the duty yesterday, but I am off now until after the New Year. How's the weather there?"

"We had our first snowfall the other night. It's in the twenties. How's yours?"

"Much colder. A ton of snow."

"How are Susan and William?"

"You can ask them yourself. I'm going to put them on the speaker phone."

"Merry Christmas, Kathryn."

"Susan, it's so good to hear your voice." She had a special fondness for Timothy's wife.

"Nana, can you hear me?"

"Merry Christmas, William. I can hear you, fine."

"Guess what?"

"What?"

"I lost another tooth."

"You did?"

"Guess what else?"

"What?"

"We're coming to visit."

"You are? When?"

Timothy interrupted his son. "Well, that's what we wanted to talk to you about. I've been telling William and Susan about growing up in Asheville. I found a family Christmas photo taken at Grandpa's farm. It was Rose's first Christmas, and you had her bundled in your lap."

Kathryn laughed. "And you had Willy Bear on your head."

"Mom, do you still remember Willy Bear?"

"You mean the naked teddy bear with a missing eye and one arm dangling by threads? How could I forget him?"

"I loved that bear."

"My curiosity is killing me. Tell me about your visit."

"The short of it is that I have leave-time that I need to take, and I want William and Susan to experience Christmas in Asheville before you sell the farm. I found a cheap air fare. We are arriving tomorrow night. It will be late, so we'll rent a car."

Susan was quick to apologize. "We're sorry for the short notice. You know how impulsive Tim can be."

"It's perfect. I'm just surprised," Kathryn said. "William, are you still there."

"Yes, ma'am."

"Have you ever made a gingerbread house?'

"No ma'am.'

"Would you like to learn?"

"Yes ma'am."

"Mom, please don't do anything special," Timothy said. "We just want to spend time with you."

"What could be better than building a gingerbread house with my grandson?"

"Guess what, Nana?"

"What, dear?'

"I'm going to have a baby sister."

"You are? When?"

"The middle of June," Susan said. "We had given up the hope of ever conceiving again, but then this miracle happened."

"If it's okay with you, Mom," Timothy interjected, "we would like to call her Rose."

Kathryn was dumbfounded.

"Mom? Are you there?"

"I'm sorry," she said. "It's wonderful news. I'm just a bit overwhelmed; that's all."

By the time the phone call ended, her mind was whirling with excitement. She was planning her grocery list, when a gentle knock at the front door interrupted her thoughts. Through the etched glass, she recognized Abigail's bright pink snowsuit.

She unlocked the deadbolt and opened the door. "Merry Christmas. What brings the whole family out so early in the morning?"

"Merry Christmas," Sarah said. "I made another batch of cinnamon rolls, and they are fresh from the oven. Would you like to come over for a cup of coffee?"

Brian handed Kathryn her newspaper.

Abigail was jumping up and down. "Santa brought me a new sled. Do you want to come outside? You can watch me slide down the hill."

"It all sounds wonderful. First, let me change my clothes."

Brian lingered on the porch, while Abigail and Sarah descended the icy steps.

"Your mascara looks better this morning," he teased.

"I really was a mess last night, wasn't I?"

"Are you okay?"

"I'm better than I've been in a long time. I have so much to tell you that I don't know where to begin." Her spirit soared. "Timothy called this morning. He and his family are coming for a visit. They will be here tomorrow night. Susan is expecting their second child, a daughter, and they are naming her Rose. I am going to be a grandmother again."

She wanted to share more, but something held her back.

"Daddy, hurry. Come watch me," Abigail hollered from the hillside.

Brian grinned. "You'll join us?"

"I have a few things to do first, but then I'll be out," she answered. "Who knows, I might even try my hand at sled riding again. A woman in her seventies isn't too old to start a new hobby, is she?"

"No, never."

Smiling, Kathryn closed the door and made her way toward her bedroom. She sat down at the antique secretary and pulled out the bottom drawer. Sifting through an assortment of greeting cards, she selected a beautiful Christmas card with the words *Emmanuel, God with Us* scripted in gold lettering across the front. She reflected upon the events of the past twenty-four hours, and then she began to write.

Christmas 2009

My dearest John,

A beautiful card and a new charm awaited me every Christmas morning, thanks to your love of tradition. This year, however, it is my turn to write to you.

A special Guest graced our home last night. It was God, and He spoke to my heart just like you said He would. I reference Brian's sermon, which I might add was both moving and powerful, when I say that God came to deliver my adoption papers.

So I am now a child of God, the daughter of the King. Abigail was right when she said that I could be a princess. If I only believe.

I do believe, John, I really do.

I have more good news. Timothy called, and they are going to have a baby. A daughter. They are naming her Rose. Isn't that wonderful? All of the other children and grandchildren are doing fine. I will call them today and wish them a Merry Christmas. But first, I am going sled riding with Abigail. You are ever-present in my heart, and I will love you forever.

Your adoring wife,

KATHRYN

EPILOGUE

Christmas 2010

HAVING DEBATED FOR TWO DAYS between her elegant gray wool suit and the stylish new black pant suit, Kathryn decided to slip both outfits into the hanging garment bag before fastening the bag closed. The decision basically came down to the shoes. Her black pumps, which were already packed in a side pocket of the open suitcase lying on her bed, could easily be worn with both suits; hence, there was no reason not to pack both outfits.

She was traveling cross country this Christmas. Elated by the thought of having ten glorious days in the Rockies with her three children and seven grandchildren, she eagerly accepted Jack and Ginny's gracious invitation to spend the Christmas holidays at their home in Colorado. It seemed unfathomable to her that the last time their entire family was gathered under one roof had been for John's funeral.

She picked up her cosmetic bag and tucked it into a narrow gap in the center of the suitcase, between a stack of thick winter sweaters and her lined snow boots. She lifted a white christening gown from the bed. Crinoline with pale pink smocking through the bodice, the gown was a special gift for her six-month-old granddaughter, Rose. She folded the gown between white tissue paper and carefully laid it on top of the opened suitcase. Then she zipped the suitcase closed. There was a time when she smocked all of her children's clothes, but not anymore.

Her seventy-five-year-old eyes didn't tolerate the fine details involved in smocking, and the arthritis in her hands had definitely worsened in the two years since John's death.

Kathryn still missed John desperately; she always would. Throughout the past year, however, she embraced a new life, a new normal. She rekindled her interest in English gardens; her volunteer work at the library; and most importantly, her relationship with God.

Before catching a ride to the airport with Brian, she had one last thing to do. She sat at the antique secretary in her bedroom and pulled out the bottom drawer. Sifting through an assortment of greeting cards, she selected a simple Christmas card. It was white with silver snowflakes on the front. She began to write.

Christmas 2010

My dearest Abigail,

Not long after the turn of the twentieth century, a gentle and loving man named William Sullivan gave his wife a charm bracelet. Every year at Christmas, his two sons and he surprised her with a new charm. The tradition continued after she died when one of his sons, Dr. John, fell in love and married me. My Christmas bracelet became as traditional in our home as benne seed cookies and gingerbread houses.

Traditions are meant to be treasured. Therefore, I am passing this tradition on to you. I am beholden to you, dear friend, for introducing me to my identity as an heir of our Glorious King.

I love you dearly,

Kathryn

With two strokes of the pen, she underlined *our Glorious King*. Satisfied, Kathryn slipped the card back into the envelope and wrote Abigail's name on the front. She opened the narrow jewelry box for one last glance. Inside was a silver bracelet with a single charm attached. The charm, a silver crown, made her smile.

About the Author

SHERRY IDENTIFIES WITH WOMEN OF all ages. Active in ministry, she lead women's Bible studies, co-chairs a community James 1:27 Team, and organizes the town's Senior Citizens for Roscoe Reading Program. Her wildlife photography is presently being used in healing services at their church. She and her husband, Sammy, reside in Moncks Corner, South Carolina. They are blessed with three wonderful sons, a beautiful daughter-in-law, two terrific mothers, and an English setter named Finley.

CPSIA information can be obtained
at www.ICGtesting.com
Printed in the USA
FSHW021703300419
57709FS